KT-474-287

We hope you enjoy this book. Please return or renew it by the due date.

You can renew it at www.norfolk.gov.uk/libraries or by using our free library app.

Otherwise you can phone 0344 800 8020 - please have your library card and PIN ready.

You can sign up for email reminders too.

WITHDRAWN

Discover more at millsandboon.co.uk.

HIS INHERITED DUCHESS

Bronwyn Scott

MILLS & BOON

First published in Great Britain 2023
by Mills & Boon, an imprint of HarperCollins*Publishers* Ltd,
1 London Bridge Street, London, SE1 9GF

www.harpercollins.co.uk

HarperCollins*Publishers*
1st Floor, Watermarque Building,
Ringsend Road, Dublin 4, Ireland

His Inherited Duchess © 2023 Nikki Poppen

ISBN: 978-0-263-30495-4

01/23

MIX
Paper | Supporting
responsible forestry
FSC™ C007454

This book is produced from independently certified FSC™ paper
to ensure responsible forest management.
For more information visit: www.harpercollins.co.uk/green.

Printed and Bound in Spain using 100% Renewable Electricity
at CPI Black Print, Barcelona

For the super-cool members of the
creative writing community of practice at my college.

I love hanging out with you—Sam, Jenny, Vernon et al.

Chapter One

~~~~~~~~~~❦~~~~~~~~~~

Logan James Montfort Maddox, Fifth Viscount Hailsham, was the epitome of his age. Society's most sought after contradiction; the *Responsible* Rake, the titled gentleman who lived lavishly and flagrantly in the moment as if he hadn't a care beyond the day while privately shouldering the enormous concern of his family's well-being for the present and securing it for generations into the future. He was a man for whom the concepts of dissipation and dependability lived cheek by jowl with one another.

To the untutored debutante straight from the schoolroom it made him an enigma, layers of handsome masculinity wrapped in an intriguing mystery. To their mamas, however, it made him something much more: eligible; marriageable. Preferably sooner rather than later now that he came with the extra caveat of possibly being the next Duke of Darlington. Such an enticing combination of wealth, lineage and dedication to family didn't come on the Marriage Mart often. When it did, people were bound to pay attention, to the man *and* his circumstances, because when something was too good to be true, it quite often was. Best one knew before one married into it.

Such considerations were the precise reasons he and his mother, the viscountess, were tucked into the well-sprung but utilitarian Maddox family travelling coach, hurtling over the weather-rutted roads of late winter toward Darlington Hall in Surrey with all haste possible. Logan, having ignored the initial summons two weeks ago, had now received word in no uncertain terms that such disregard for his situation was growing less possible to maintain as was his fate. Every day that passed seemed to indicate he would indeed be the duke.

'I haven't been to Darlington Hall since the old duke was alive and you were small. You must have been four.' His mother tried for a smile. It came out small and tremulous. No one had smiled for weeks. The news had stunned them all with its suddenness coming swiftly on the heels of Christmas, its repercussions continuing to shock and shape them in the unfolding weeks. 'Do you remember nothing of that visit? You and your cousin, Adolphus, played soldiers in the nursery.' He did remember that visit, although he wisely said nothing. It wasn't polite to speak ill of the dead. Adolphus had been a bully and when he'd not got his way he'd punched him.

His mother's smile, not strong to begin with, faltered. 'And now...' Her voice trailed off, the rest unspoken. Now Adolphus was dead along with his father, Logan's father and Logan's brother, Griffin. The male limbs of the family tree pruned down to Logan and his younger brother, Rahnald, a prospect that had once been so improbable to consider that Logan had never dwelled on the idea.

It was that improbability that had been a source of significant anxiety of late. The old duke had died of natural causes a few years ago as had Logan's father, who had died when Logan had been fifteen, preceded by his own son Griffin's death when Logan had been thirteen. But now Adolphus was dead. What the cause of *his* death was had not been imparted to Logan, but whatever it was, it was not natural. There were, in fact, few natural causes that would fell a healthy thirty-six-year-old, which was why there *would* be speculation.

The one silver lining in all of this, Logan supposed, was that speculation would run its course during the imposed social isolation of winter with most families tucked up in their country manors before Society returned to Town in the spring. Other things would run their courses, or not, much sooner, in the next few days, if the solicitor could be believed. Soon, they would know if he'd be the duke, and the solicitor felt he should be on hand when the determination was made. There was only one person who stood between him and the dukedom now: Adolphus's widow. Olivia Maddox, née DeLacey, a woman Logan had met once at her London wedding to his cousin five years ago. He did not know her well and barely recalled her except that she'd been quite young, a debutante fresh from the schoolroom with an ancient name who'd snared a ducal heir within weeks of being out.

'You are most likely the duke already.' His mother's sea-glass eyes met his, serious with intention. 'It is unlikely that she's with child after so many years of nothing, and even if she was, what are the chances the child would be male?'

'One out of two, actually,' Logan replied drily, his tone sharper than he meant it to be. Adolphus had done his duty in wedding and bedding, but he'd failed to leave behind an heir of his body. Hence Logan hurtling to Surrey *with* his mother. She was the widowed half of a mostly happy marriage, and a mother to two living sons, although she'd conceived seven children. She knew about loss, not just the loss of a husband, but the loss of children, of possibility and what might have been.

His mother would know what to say when Her Grace of Darlington officially discovered she was not with child, that all chance of Adolphus leaving a direct heir was gone, that she would now, as a result, be dispossessed of her home and security. Logan did not envy the duchess. His mother's words would put a touch of soft femininity on what he viewed as nothing short of a barbaric, insensitive ordeal the solicitors and the law were putting the widowed duchess through at a time when so much else was on her mind: grief and the uncertainty of what life held for her without the umbrella of her husband's protection. He could not spare the young widow that ordeal, but he could allow his mother to soften it. She was good with emotions; he was not.

'I do not know what I wish for, Mother,' Logan confessed as the wide, sandstone facade of Darlington Hall came into view, its gothic spires soaring into the grey winter sky. 'That she is with child and that it is a son, perhaps for her own comfort and for mine. A child means my life does not have to change, nor does hers. I never expected to be duke and she never expected to not be the Duchess of Darlington. She can continue as duchess here at the estate until her son is old enough to marry and manage on his own.' Logan gave a wry smile. The duchess wasn't the only one who could go on as usual. As for himself, he could continue his rather immersive pastime of managing his carriage racing syndicate and running the Hailsham holdings. 'On the other hand, perhaps it would be best, if there's not to be a son, to rip the bandage off the wound immediately and get on with it.' He could not imagine the agony for anyone involved of waiting another nine months if the duchess was indeed expecting.

'Well, either way, we're about to find out. Here we are.' His mother offered a smile of encouragement as the carriage came to a halt. 'For better or for worse.'

'I'm glad you're here, Lord Hailsham. I trust your journey was not too onerous?' The solicitor took his seat behind the desk in the estate office of Darlington Hall. There was a certain relish to the man's movements that said he was enjoying the temporary appropriation of the last duke's desk. Pompous little prick, Logan thought uncharitably, but what else was to be expected of a man so dedicated to the letter of the law that he thought nothing of commanding a viscount, a peer of the realm, to wait upon *him* at immediate convenience while demanding a grieving widow keep him informed of the intimate details of her body. All so that paperwork could be satisfied.

'You will be wanting to go over the inheritance, of course.' The solicitor tapped a sheaf of papers on the desk's surface, aligning the edges in an annoying show of fastidiousness.

'No, actually,' Logan said in part to be contrary and in part because the solicitor's dry callousness toward the situation offended him. A man had died, by God. A *young* man in the prime of his life, and that death had disrupted multiple lives. A moment of humanity would not be amiss before getting down to the business of inheriting a dukedom. 'My cousin is dead and while your notes were quite thorough in what that entails going forward, there has been no mention of how he died.' Logan speared him with a strong stare meant to intimidate. He did not want this petty little man being the gatekeeper of *his* family's private business.

The man cleared his throat nervously. The stare had done the trick. 'I did not think the details appropriate for a letter, my lord.' No, but the poor duchess's condition had been fair fodder for one.

'Well? Now I am here, so those details can be imparted.' Logan offered a cold smile and sat back in his chair to indicate he was settling in for the duration. He was regretting leaving these particular details alone for so long. Ledgers could keep, but somebody somewhere knew how his cousin had died, and if they spread the story first Logan would lose his ability to control tonnish gossip come spring.

The solicitor favoured him with a single

word. 'Pistols.' He leafed through his stack of papers and pushed one forward. 'This is the coroner's report, the one used for the death certificate.'

Logan scanned the sheet, his eyes landing on the reason for death. 'Misadventure?' He grimaced. The word connoted a variety of unpleasant implications. Misadventure suggested an accident but was often used as a genteel lie to cover up death by suicide or perhaps by duelling or other unsavoury and dangerous activities that lived on the illicit edges of tonnish life. Dear heavens, the gossips would have a heyday once they linked pistols with misadventure.

'You will have to do better than that, I'm afraid,' Logan warned. 'My cousin was a crack shot.' As were all the Maddox males. Shooting was in their blood. 'No one would believe he accidentally shot himself most fatally. The wound was where?' Logan scanned the sheet again and quirked a brow in challenge. 'His inner thigh? Very difficult to shoot oneself there, I think.'

'As you say, my lord. I am sure the coroner would be able to satisfy any of your questions on that account far better than myself.'

Logan let the silence stretch between them in the hopes the solicitor would be more forthcoming. When he was not, Logan pressed on. 'Where did it happen?' Perhaps there would be a clue to his cousin's death in the location.

'An estate called the Grange, outside of London near Hampstead Heath. I understand he was hosting a gentleman's weekend.'

'Do we know who was there?' That seemed odd, a gentlemen's weekend coming so quickly on the end of Christmas, when people were still with their families. It was an awkward and unlikely time to be away.

The solicitor looked put out by the question. 'I am not privy to that sort of information, my lord. Ledgers, accounts, holdings, investments, *that* is what I know.'

Ah, so the pompous man hadn't been in Adolphus's social confidence, only financial. Logan rose, leaving the man no choice but to rise with him. 'Thank you for your time. I'll look over the books and let you know if I have any questions. Until then, please make free of the comforts of the inn in the village. We'll expect you tomorrow afternoon for the reading of the will.' He could not make a dismissal any clearer. It was an eviction, really. If the solicitor couldn't shed any further light on his cousin's death, he had little more usefulness. But perhaps the duchess could. Knowledge was the key to preparation, and he *would* need to be prepared. People *would* talk when a young man died under curious circumstances. There *would* be rumours. But he'd wait until the rumours came to him. If he was too proactive in combatting them, people would assume there was something to hide, and he'd risk giving those rumours credence by addressing them prematurely. For now, he preferred to take the high road, and let sleeping dogs lie.

She'd lied about everything: what her marriage had really been like; what her husband had been like. She'd even lied about the possibility of a child. She'd needed time. And now time had run out. The month was up in all ways.

Olivia backed away from the curtains and the hall window overlooking the driveway. She was the duchess no more except for the courtesy of a title that no longer meant anything. Now that the heir and her courses were here, arriving within hours of each other, neither of them a surprise, both of them inevitable, she was Olivia DeLacey once again for all intents.

Her stomach cramped as she made her way down the hall to her chambers. All she wanted was a lie-down. She did not want to send her maid to that pompous solicitor with the news he'd been craving since his arrival—that there was no heir, that he could hand the dukedom and her over to Adolphus's male successor. What she wanted instead was to send her maid for a hot water bottle. *Her* chambers. *Her* maid. Those pronouns were a temporary courtesy, on loan to her as were the items they attached to. The maid would stay with the estate, as would her jewellery, as would the art and book collections she'd spent the past years curating in her short tenure as duchess. All her efforts weren't truly hers. Her efforts belonged to the Darlington Dukedom. She resented that.

Olivia opened the door to her rooms and slipped inside with a grateful sigh. She'd made it to her chambers without any interference. Sanctuary at last. Perhaps the heir would be with the solicitor long enough for her to have that lie-down before she was summoned. If she was lucky, she might escape notice until supper. Her maid came out of the dressing room and took one look at her face. 'Oh, Your Grace, they've come, haven't they? I'm so sorry. Shall I fetch you some warm milk and a hot water bottle?'

She would miss Mary when she was gone from here. She might not grieve her husband's passing but she did grieve the loss of all this. She'd liked being the duchess; she had purpose and agency, the ability to affect change, and Adolphus, who did not care for those things, had given her free rein in his long absences. It was an arrangement that had come to suit them both.

'Yes, thank you.' Olivia lay down on the bed, weary of it all. The past month had been agonising with the funeral, the paperwork, the questioning, the prying, the planning and the uncertainty of what came next for her, all of it demanding her attention against an emotional backdrop of grief, disbelief and relief that Adolphus was gone, an interesting and contradictory palette of feelings she'd barely begun to sort through.

'And the solicitor, Your Grace? Shall I tell him?'

Olivia gave a nod. There was no sense in perpetuating the lie further. She'd had her month's reprieve; it was time to move on, ready or not.

She closed her eyes as the door shut behind Mary. Who would she be if she was not the active duchess of Darlington? She was far too young to truly be a dowager, but the viscount would marry and have his own duchess. The estate and the new duke had no use for her now. She *should* celebrate that. She was at liberty to redefine herself, perhaps discover herself for the first time since she'd turned eighteen or maybe ever.

Being a duchess and a wife had been thrust on her before she'd experienced the world. She'd been married within weeks of her debut for her name, old and as distinguished as the Conqueror himself. Before she'd been the duchess, she'd been the living embodiment of all the DeLacey lineage stood for, a line of greatness designed to cloak the shortcomings that lay behind the Darlington wealth so that none would guess the secrets Adolphus kept.

It was a trade she'd been naively happy to make five years ago. 'I will keep your family from want. Your sisters will have matches worthy of their name,' Adolphus had promised. 'And in return, I ask only that you keep my secrets.' Her family had needed that promise. Her sisters needed their own debuts; her father needed funds for the estate. There'd been nothing left to sell but her and the DeLacey name. When the chance had come, she'd done her part, which had not been all that difficult when approached by a handsome ducal heir.

In her naivete, she'd not been concerned when Adolphus had asked for her promise. What could such a dashing man have to hide? She thought perhaps it might be an illegitimate child. She could live with that if her family might be safe. She laughed now at the innocence of that girl who could imagine nothing worse, who hadn't believed that a handsome visage might harbour a multitude of sins.

Mary returned with a tray. 'Thank you.' Olivia gratefully took the hot water bottle and placed it on her belly, the heat immediately soothing. 'Did you tell the solicitor?'

'No, I could not, Your Grace.'

'Could not? I know it's difficult, Mary, to discuss such personal things with *that* man, but he must be told so things can be settled.' Olivia sighed. She, too, found the idea of reporting to the solicitor humiliating even though the law required it. How ironic that for the estate to be settled, its duchess, the woman who had been its caretaker, must be unsettled.

Mary shook her head. 'No, Your Grace. It's not that. I couldn't tell him because he's not here. Lord Hailsham, the heir, has sent him packing to the inn in the village. I could not tell him because he was not here to be told.' There was a gleam of satisfaction in Mary's usually calm gaze.

Olivia sat up against her pillows. 'You saw the viscount, then?' She ought to have referred to him as His Grace. He was more than a viscount now. He was Darlington.

'I did see him, just for a moment in the hall. He's brought his mother. Mrs Aldrich and Moresby are seeing them settled.' Mary paused before adding, 'He sends a message, Your Grace. He would like your company at supper if you felt up to it.'

She *would* feel up to it. She must. 'Let me rest, Mary. Wake me in time to dress for supper and let the viscount know I'd be pleased to join him.' If she hid away now, she would send the signal that she was weak and unimportant. That would not do. The viscount would have questions about the estate, about Adolphus. If she was not on hand to provide answers, he would go to others. She did not want that. She needed to control the information. Her family's financial security depended on it.

Keep my secrets, the ghost of Adolphus whispered. It was what he'd asked of her the night he'd proposed and the last words he'd written to her, left with a ledger that had arrived by post, wrapped in brown paper the day before he died. It was full of names of fictional characters from literature, and while those names meant nothing to her, it obviously had meant something to him or he would not have sent it into her keeping. He also would not have sent it if he had not felt the ledger was in danger.

He'd thought there was a chance he would die.

It prompted several questions about just what had happened at the men's weekend. Whatever that ledger represented, people had felt they could not put their own names to it. That never boded well. It also prompted other fears, more personal ones: What had she unwittingly got herself into when she'd made her reckless promise? Before the journal had arrived, the secrets she had thought she was keeping had been more of a private nature, something just between the two of them, between a husband and a wife. But then the journal had arrived, full of names, indicating that there was a secret that went beyond their bedroom door, a secret she'd never known about. Reading the names had made the idea of secret-keeping a reality, and along with it had come the reality that she'd been complicit in something she'd had no idea about all along.

She would keep Adolphus's secrets. She had no choice in the matter. She would keep them because they were her secrets, too, and had been since the moment she'd married him. Her family's continued security depended on her word, and Adolphus was reaching past the grave to make sure she kept it.

Chapter Two

Actions, like reputations, often preceded a person, shaping impressions before one even met. Olivia wondered, as she descended the stairs for supper, if that was why the viscount had done it; dismissed the solicitor to spare her the ordeal of reporting to him. Had he wanted to lead with a favourable impression? But to what end? He held the title and the power that went with it. He did not need her favour, so why curry it? No one did anything without motive or meaning. Once she'd realised that, she'd seen the world through a whole new lens; a more honest lens if also a more jaded one. She would be cautious tonight, on the alert for what it was he thought his favour had bought him.

Olivia paused before entering the drawing room and smoothed her black skirts. She'd dressed carefully tonight in an off-the-shoulder gown of black taffeta devoid of trim for now, of course, jet beads being off-limits for at least six months, but the cut was in the latest fashion. About her neck was a cameo strung on a black satin ribbon and matching combs in her hair. Mourning required her to wear black; it did not require her to look like a dowd. She reached the drawing room and straightened her shoulders, prepared to take a man's measure, well aware that he would be doing the same.

Hailsham stood at the fireplace, preprandial drink in hand and turned out in formal, dark eveningwear. Mourning was so much more forgiving and flexible for men than it was for women. A man might wear black for mourning and still be in the first stare of fashion for evening attire while a woman was usually discouraged from black except out of the necessity of mourning. A woman in black was a woman relegated to the dustbin of life, of no use to anyone, and a subject of pity by everyone. No one would pity Hailsham if they could see him, so urbane and polished as he conversed with an older woman Olivia guessed was Hailsham's mother.

Hailsham spotted her immediately and came

forward. 'My Lady Darlington, it is good to see you. I want to offer my condolences in person although you already have them in writing. I am sorry for your loss.' He'd written immediately upon receiving word, a precise, polite letter expressing all the correct sentiments for the occasion.

'And I for yours,' Olivia replied. 'It is your loss as well, since he was your cousin.' Did Hailsham feel a sense of loss or only a sense of all he'd gained? A dukedom from a cousin he never spent time with from what Olivia could tell. Perhaps they'd met in Town during the Season, but Hailsham had never come to the hall during her marriage. She'd not seen him, in fact, since her wedding day. Whatever she knew of Adolphus's presumptive heir had come through the Society pages of days-old newspapers. Which meant she knew two things: he was a man about London *and* he was a profligate rake.

Looking at him now, she could see the Maddox traits: the dark hair, the green eyes, the long, straight, strong nose. He shared those traits with Adolphus while still managing to look like himself, an individual entirely unique from his cousin. There would be no mistaking the two for one another. Adolphus had been thicker in build where Hailsham sported a lean, athletic grace. Where Adolphus had been ruggedly attractive, Hailsham was urbane, easily carrying off his reputation as a rake about Town. She could see that about him. Women would find his sophistication attractive; the Society pages had not misreported that. Where Adolphus's features had been given to a jowliness that had grown over the years, Hailsham's features were precise and chiselled. Adolphus had been a good-looking sportsman in his early thirties, but he'd not aged well.

'May I offer you a drink? Sherry perhaps?' Hailsham moved to the decanters and poured her a small glass. 'Allow me to make introductions.' He gestured to the woman on the settee before the fire. 'May I present my mother, Viscountess Hailsham. Mother, Her Grace of Darlington.' Olivia schooled herself not to cringe at the address. It felt almost fraudulent to hear it applied to her. She wasn't the duchess anymore, not really, and yet if she wasn't the Duchess of Darlington, who was she? She'd been the duchess her entire adult life, except for the month she'd been a debutante.

She'd come to understand over the past

month that the title was something she both despised and desired, just as it was something she would both keep and give up, something she wanted to lay down and yet something she did not want to surrender. The duchess had security; Olivia DeLacey did not. The duchess could protect her family; Olivia DeLacey could not. The duchess knew who she was and her role; Olivia DeLacey had yet to discover herself.

The petite woman on the settee rose and extended both her hands to take Olivia's. 'I am truly sorry for your loss, my dear.' Her words carried the sincere warmth Hailsham's had lacked, and they carried a confidence that all would indeed be well. They were the first *real* words Olivia had heard in a month. 'Rest assured we'll see everything put to rights. Hailsham is not one to shirk responsibility.'

'Yet, the viscount waited weeks before arriving,' Olivia put in somewhat sharply. The viscountess's last words made her wary despite the comfort of the former. Was that how the viscount saw her? Another responsibility to be managed and filed away? That would not do. She could not control the direction of his thoughts and attentions if she was a passive player. She needed his attentions focused on the estate management, the accounts, the thousand daily details of running the dukedom that could swallow a person whole if they allowed it. She'd allowed it. It had been a convenient distraction from the realities of her marriage. Now she needed Hailsham to do the same so that he simply could not give closer attention to other aspects of his inheritance.

'You must excuse my belated arrival.' Hailsham made her a short bow with exacting politeness, his sharp green gaze holding hers in study. 'I had arrangements to make in case my absence from my own estates was prolonged, and I wanted to give you time before descending on you.' She heard the unspoken message for her: he'd wanted to make sure she wasn't carrying Adolphus's heir. He'd not wanted to prematurely assume the dukedom. It was further proof that she was right to be wary about this cousin of her late husband's. He was a planner, a strategist, who thought several moves ahead and considered the consequences of actions. 'Besides, the will could not be read with any authority until now at any rate, so it seemed best to wait.' To wait until he'd seen her maid in the hall with a hot water bottle and warm milk, which provided a man who knew women well all the implied confirmation he'd needed to know that the dukedom was his.

The viscount straightened, his eyes still on her, studying, watching, assessing. 'Speaking of authority, I hope you don't mind that I dismissed the solicitor to the inn. I found him superfluous at this point in the process. He'll come tomorrow afternoon to read the will and remain a few days at the inn if there are any new arrangements to make, but other than that, he no longer needs to be underfoot here. I felt he'd imposed long enough.'

Olivia found a gracious smile. 'I do not mind at all, my lord.' Although she *did* mind on precious principle. He knew this was not something she'd argue with him. How shrewd he'd been to break the loss of her own authority to her gently. He'd dismissed the solicitor, perhaps as a favour to her, an action she did not oppose, and yet his power to make that decision was a reminder that she was no longer in charge here. That mantle was being inexorably shifted from her slim shoulders to his much broader ones.

'I am glad it pleases you.' He inclined his

head at her approval and Olivia imagined she saw a quick flicker of compassion flare in them. Perhaps it was what she wanted to see, needed to see. Perhaps she'd been hunting for a spark of compassion from anyone ever since the news had come that Adolphus had died. When she'd told her father, his first concern had been for the security of the family. What would happen to the annuities Darlington paid him? Her sisters had been no better; their own concern about their upcoming Seasons had overridden their concern for her. She'd been alone this past month in all ways. Now here was this viscount with broad shoulders, ready to take the burdens, and it was so tempting to let him.

Not all burdens, though. You promised to keep my secrets. You will lose so much if you break that promise.

The words whispered and the temptation passed. The new duke was not her friend, could not be her friend. Her own independence relied on remaining free of entanglements with men.

Moresby announced supper and Hailsham promptly offered an arm to her and to his mother. Perhaps it spoke well of him to think so highly of his mother as to value her input during this transition time, or perhaps there were other more strategic reasons for having brought her along. Perhaps the viscountess was here to act as a confidante in order to report to her son all the things Olivia would not tell him herself; or perhaps she was here to hurry along Olivia's departure from Darlington? If his mother was here to handle the woman's role at the house, Olivia would be *de trop*. It prompted the question: How long *did* she have here before the viscount would expect her to leave? The question lent an air of the condemned eating a last meal as they went into the dining room. How many more meals did she have here?

Moresby pushed open the doors leading into the formal dining room of Darlington Hall as if he was entertaining the queen herself, revealing the long, walnut-panelled room in all its glory despite there only being three guests to dine. Of course, Olivia reminded herself, the staff would be eager to make a good impression on the new duke; already they were transferring their loyalties and priorities.

No effort had been spared in the short time available between the viscount's arrival and supper. Between them, Moresby and Mrs Aldrich had seen the dining room turned out in elegance. The table was set with the Darlington china, designed especially by Josiah Wedgwood in 1790 for Adolphus's great-grandmother. A flight of crystal goblets stood like sentinels at each place, and the filigreed silverware gleamed with polish atop pristine white Irish linen. Two eight-armed candelabras ablaze with long white wax candles stood in the centre of the table at one end, bracketing the crystal vase of creamy roses plucked from the hothouses that kept Darlington in the luxury of flowers year-round. Even without her explicit direction, the staff had outdone themselves.

Lady Hailsham smiled approvingly as they sat. 'The house is a credit to you, Your Grace, as are the staff.' She smiled kindly. 'They are loyal to you.' As she was to them. They had quietly seen her through this first month of isolation. The realisation lent a new perspective to this supper. Certainly, there was no denying it was meant to impress and welcome the new duke for whom they'd be working, but she saw it now also as a farewell, a tribute. This was for her as much as it was for the viscount, and she was touched by the gesture.

Moresby stood behind the viscount's seat at the head of the table, overseeing the serving of the hare soup. When the soup had been placed in front of them, Olivia nodded toward the butler. 'Lord Hailsham, might I allow Moresby to pour the wine? His selections are always perfection. If you please, Moresby, tell us about the wine you've chosen. I always find it instructive.' Moresby would not have deigned to share the information on his own. She would do this for him, offer him the chance to step into the spotlight with the new duke.

Moresby cleared his throat and stepped forward. 'For tonight I have decanted a Pinot Noir from Vosne.' He poured for the viscount and set the glass before him. 'You will note the earthy tones and the light tannins.'

'It is an excellent choice,' Hailsham approved after taking a swallow. It was a given that a good butler had a superior knowledge of wines but Olivia wanted Hailsham to understand what a gem he'd inherited in Moresby. The Darlington wine cellars had earned their reputation because of him. Adolphus may have loved his wines but she and Moresby had been the ones to order them, to keep the best vintages on hand. Adolphus could never be bothered with stocking cellars, only drinking from them as if they were bottomless wells that would never run dry.

'Darlington has wine holdings in France,' Olivia began after the wine was poured. This was exactly where she wanted the conversation to go—to the estate and its holdings. It was an ideal topic for small talk and for directing the viscount's attention to where she wanted it. 'In fact, everything served tonight is a product of the estate. Our gamekeeper, Mr Phelps, is responsible for the hare and for the partridge that will be served later.' Olivia smiled over the rim of her wineglass. There was nothing she didn't know about the estate. She could keep up this line of conversation all night. By the time she was done, Viscount Hailsham would be so immersed in the details of running Darlington he'd forget to enquire about the nature of his cousin's death.

Her Grace of Darlington was exceedingly well informed about the estate, an estimation that Logan ratcheted up to *remarkably* well versed by the time the larded partridge with bread sauce on the side and glazed carrots arrived and then elevated once more to *suspiciously proficient* by the time the apple tartlets were served at the meal's end. Logan sipped at the excellent wine, ate locally curated after locally curated dish and listened to Her Grace.

It was easy to watch her with her long, elegant fingers gesturing or lifting her wineglass as she spoke, her gold hair burnished by candlelight, piled atop her head, exposing the slender length of her neck, her blue eyes serious and intent. Even dressed in black, she was a beauty of classical proportions. Yes, indeed, it was easy to watch her; so easy, in fact, one might forget to *listen* to her, to truly hear what she said and what she didn't. Logan forced himself to do both, to not be distracted by appearances, no matter how lovely. Appearances, after all, could be deceiving. He'd learned that the hard way as a young man and the lesson had stuck.

He only needed the soup course to recognise that his cousin's duchess was an asset to the estate, and far more capable than she'd appeared at their wedding five years prior. Of course, she was five years older. She'd been a pretty but young eighteen-year-old on her wedding day, still a girl in all respects. There was little evidence of that girl tonight. But by the time the tartlets arrived there was evidence of something else; another game was afoot, perhaps. He'd offered questions about Darlington to be polite, to show his interest in the conversation, but she'd *wanted* to discuss the estate. He had the distinct impression that this was precisely the conversation she wanted to have.

He found that rather interesting and alarming. It occurred to him that she might be auditioning for the role of being *his* duchess, now that the position was no longer hers. That was rather bold of her considering her husband was barely cold and the will had yet to be read. It was also rather desperate given that she didn't know him at all. He might be any sort of man. Or perhaps she didn't care what type of man he was as long it allowed her to maintain her status? Such a conclusion spoke of avarice, more than desperation. Although avarice did not fit the larger picture. She and Adolphus were supposed to have been a love match, their marriage the product of a whirlwind romance. So perhaps desperation then, after all, assuming he was right about the audition.

Logan took a long swallow from his wineglass, watching her expression as she explained how the estate was noted regionally for the cheese served alongside the apple tartlet. Was she hoping he would see the expedience in such a choice? She knew the estate; she could help him take on his role. She could maintain her position while he could avoid the Marriage Mart and the time-consuming prospect of finding his own duchess; why not inherit a duchess along with the property and the title, especially if one must marry anyway? She was not far wrong. The responsibility of being the viscount and now being the duke required he marry. It was one more service he would have to perform for the title. It would be nothing more than that—just another transaction in the business of running the estate and the family.

He didn't have the emotions for it to be anything more. Losing Griffin and then his father had stripped those emotions clean away. Marriage for him would be a thoroughly considered business contract. If she thought she could entice him into a quick, quiet marriage, she would be disappointed. Finding the right woman to be his duchess, to run the estate, to raise his children, was not a matter to be rushed into blindly. It demanded careful research even when time was of the essence.

He exchanged a look with his mother, wondering if she'd picked up on the duchess's gambit. He would like to speak with the duchess frankly and he felt privacy was required. His mother gave a short nod and rose as the dessert dishes were cleared away. She stifled a yawn, perhaps not feigned; it had been a long day. 'I do not wish to be rude, but I am wondering if it would be all right to excuse myself. Travel by coach has a way of exhausting me, I fear. All that jolting around.'

The duchess rose as well. 'I can go up with you,' she offered. But that did not suit Logan's needs.

'I'm sure Mother can find her way or a servant can assist if needed. I would enjoy talking some more, Your Grace, if you are up to it? I don't believe we've discussed the apple orchards yet from which this delicious tartlet must have been made.' Logan smiled and gestured for her to retake her seat. She would not escape him so easily.

He was aware of the duchess's eyes on him, her blue gaze narrowing in scrutiny as she sat. She waited until his mother had gone to level her accusation. 'I think you are mocking me, my lord. Do you really wish to hear about our orchards?'

He met her gaze with a steady stare of his own, his own dry wit at the ready. 'Why do you doubt my interest? Do you think I have heard enough about the estate already?' He levelled his own accusation. 'You've got your way all evening, Your Grace, with a rather excessive amount of discussion about the estate. Now we'll discuss *my* topics of interest, starting with, what are your plans once things are settled here?'

Her blue eyes flared. 'Are you that desirous of getting rid of me? Shall I pack my bags and be gone tomorrow?'

He'd not meant to put her on the defensive. 'If I know what your plans are, perhaps I can help you facilitate them.' Surely, she'd given those plans some thought in the intervening month? Or perhaps not. He had no idea about the current state of his cousin's marriage. Had the early romance of their pairing been sustained? If so, perhaps she'd truly thought there would be the chance of an heir, that she might not need to leave? It occurred to him rather belatedly that today she was mourning the loss of more than a husband—the loss of the possibility of a child, and also the loss of hopes that she might maintain the life she'd had. 'I am in no hurry to see you go. It's clear there is much you can help me with. I'd be a fool not to take advantage of your wealth of knowledge,' he assured her. 'I appreciate that you're in an awkward position. It's never easy for the woman when these things happen. But let me assure you, you are my responsibility now and I will see you safe. I assume provision has been made for you? That there is a dower property?' What financial support she had would be made clear tomorrow when the will was read.

'There is a dower house on the northern edge of the property,' she offered noncommittally. Really, she was not helping him here. He might not be known for his emotions but he was no cad. He would not toss her out or cut her off. She was part of the family now and as such, she was his responsibility as the head of that family.

'We could ride out tomorrow morning and see it, if you like. We can discuss whatever repairs or remodelling it needs in order to suit you. The dukedom will pay for it, of course. I am sure my cousin would want you kept in comfort. My mother can assist you in selecting anything you'd like to take with you. You do not need to leave all your usual comforts behind.'

'That is very generous,' she said but her tone was cold. Somehow, his generosity had gone amiss. Had he not just offered her the world? She rose, putting an end to the conversation.

Logan put a hand on her arm to stall her. 'I understand this is a difficult time for you. There is much that is out of your control. I am sorry for that. I saw my mother go through such a time when my own father died. I did not intend my questions or my offer to offend you. I meant only to reassure you that you are safe.' Safe from having to sell herself to the next duke to ensure her security; safe from wondering what happened next; safe to remake her life if she desired it; to travel, to remarry a man of her choosing, to have a family, to return to Society when mourning had been observed. But that message seemed lost on her.

She waited for him to remove his hand. 'None of us are ever safe, my lord. Only a fool would believe otherwise.'

Chapter Three

He thought she was a responsibility to be borne, another chore to add to his list! Olivia was still fuming the next morning over his rather nonchalant classification of her as they rode out to the dower house. Although the classification did not surprise her. Men, it seemed, had two extremes when it came to dealing with the women in their lives. Women were either chores to be managed—married off to other men to become their responsibility—or if that wasn't possible, to be tucked away, disregarded and forgotten until one needed something from them like a dowry for a new roof or an heir for the succession. Adolphus had been of the latter camp. He'd needed her body. After it became clear that need would go unsatisfied, he'd tucked her away. His cousin, however, appeared to be of the former persuasion. To him, women were responsibilities to resolve.

Olivia slid Hailsham a sideways look, studying him as they rode through the muck. He had a good seat. Straight back, firm but quiet hands on the reins as he guided his mount through the mire left behind by last night's rain. Good form was as apparently important to him riding through the mud as it was in the drawing room. He'd been quite eager to see the chore of settling her managed last night. He'd offered her renovations and the option to take certain items with her when she moved. The offer had kept her up most of the night wondering what motivated his generosity. Perhaps he already had a duchess in mind?

The dower house came into view; an ivy-covered brick manse known simply to those on the estate as North House for its location on the property. The place showed poorly today, its overrun state not enhanced by the grey February skies. She watched the viscount for any sign of disappointment. The more work the house needed, the longer her departure from Darlington Hall would be delayed, but the viscount showed no reaction. He showed very few reactions, she was coming to realise. He was neutrally polite and entirely rational at all times, always in command of his manners and the situation. What he thought or felt was hidden behind all that politeness. Hiding emotions seemed to be a Maddox family trait. The viscount was like his cousin in that regard. A shiver of caution moved down her spine. In what other ways was the viscount like his cousin? Did the similarities end there or did he, too, possess her husband's penchant for secrets?

In the drive they halted their horses. The viscount came to help her dismount, hands firm and competent at her waist, lingering not a moment more than necessary to complete the task. He took a long look at the outside of the manse. 'In the spring, the gardeners will have this set to rights in no time.'

'I do not think inside will be much better,' Olivia cautioned as he produced a key for the front door. 'My husband's mother did not live here long and no one has been here since.' He ushered her through the door, a grim set to his aristocratic mouth as if the neglect of the manse displeased him.

There was much to be displeased about. The house smelled musty, and it looked musty, too.

In the front parlour, Holland covers shrouded the furniture, cobwebs clung to the ceiling, dust coating whatever surface it could find. Grime on the windows made it difficult to peer out. But with clean windows, Olivia could see the possibility of the room. The front parlour would get a lovely morning light. In her mind's eye she arranged the room: a vase of flowers on the table, her favourite figurines on the mantel, some books on the shelves, a cosy blanket of soft, creamy lambswool draped over the settee. Such additions would give the room a feminine personality. Perhaps she would read in here or write letters. There would be room for her small escritoire by the window.

'You may assign staff to cleaning as soon as you'd like.' While she'd been designing the room the viscount was already making lists of tasks, already deciding what she could do. Part of her rebelled at the idea of him *giving* her permission to have staff come clean. Did he ever stop to listen to himself? How he gave commands and granted boons, ordering everything and everyone to his liking? Had anyone ever told him no? Had anyone ever disagreed with him and gotten away with it?

You will have to get used to it, the voice of

reason in her head reminded her. *You are no longer in charge here. Your title means nothing, not to him.*

They moved into the dining room and then the kitchen, the viscount continuing to make pronouncements as if she couldn't see what needed doing or hadn't been running a household far larger for years now. They climbed the oak stairs to the upper chambers, taking in the four bedrooms and returned downstairs to the front parlour. The viscount stood in the room's centre, surveying it with a critical eye one more time. 'Seeing this house reminds me you've spent most of your marriage in and out of mourning,' he said solemnly. 'First, my uncle barely a year after you'd wed my cousin, my aunt the following year, then my cousin two years later. It can hardly be how any young bride wishes to spend the early years of her marriage.'

It was on the tip of her tongue to ask exactly how he thought a bride spent her early years but she held back. Such a remark invited too many questions. Nor could she answer those questions truthfully without revealing too much. He would be encouraged to dig deeper into his cousin's marriage and exhume things she'd rather leave unearthed. To expose Adolphus was to expose herself. She had sisters to protect. Scandal was the last thing she needed. But any scandal that touched her also touched the dukedom. She doubted the viscount would stand for that for his own sake. 'I am not the first person to be plunged into a cycle of mourning. If I was, mourning would not be the thriving industry it is in Britain.'

'It has been argued that mourning is both universal in its rituals and unique in its grief,' the viscount ceded, his eyes intent on her now instead of the room. That gaze made her wary; it saw too much. 'I am truly sorry for your loss, Your Grace. Not just the loss of your husband, but all that goes with it. I was fifteen when my father died. I saw what my mother went through, what I went through, as we all navigated the transition of the viscountcy. It was a difficult time just as this is a difficult time for you, transitioning into widowhood at such a young age.' He offered her a small, polite smile. 'I don't imagine you will stay a widow for long, though. Once mourning is passed, I will do all I can in assisting you with a match if that is your wish.'

'I do *not* wish it,' she said sternly. The remark shocked her back to reality. For a moment he'd almost been human. He'd almost moved past the urbane politeness he demonstrated so well. That piece about losing his father had been touching. But no, it, too, had been couched in terms of the law, the inheritance and the transition of power when one scrutinised it. She might have missed that if it hadn't been for the last bit. 'I find it unseemly to talk of remarriage at this point.' She hoped her response would chastise him for his insensitivity. Who spoke to a widow about remarriage with her husband gone only a month?

A viscount who is eager to dispatch his duty, manage his responsibilities.

'Ah, forgive me my impertinence. It *was* a love match, then?' To some small credit, the question was asked with gentle solicitation. Too bad that gentleness was not mirrored in his eyes. Those were as sharp as cut emeralds. It didn't matter; the question neatly caught her either way. Did she lie about the match? Would he believe the lie that it was a whirlwind romance? Why shouldn't he believe it? All of London did.

'You were at our wedding.' She moved about the room to escape his gaze, fingering draperies and peeping beneath Holland covers to take stock.

'Yes, the romance of the Season. Love at first sight, the gossip pages reported.' He gave a dry chuckle. 'How fortuitous for my cousin that his declaration to marry just two weeks prior led to love at first sight so soon.'

She glanced over her shoulder at him, assessing. 'I suppose you don't believe in love at first sight?' It was time to put him on the defensive.

Again, the worldly chuckle. 'Do *you*, Your Grace?' So much for putting him on the defensive.

'I was swept off my feet,' she admitted freely, meeting his gaze with a direct stare of her own. After all, it was true. 'It's not every day a debutante is pursued by a charming ducal heir. Usually it's the other way around, or so I am told.' She'd been dreading the machinations of the Marriage Mart but to her pleasant surprise, she'd not had to worry about snaring a man's attention at all. Adolphus had been right there, waiting for her. It had seemed too good to be true. He had been charming. He had charm in spades when he chose. However, he did not always choose to be except when it suited him, something she'd soon learned *after* the wedding.

'Did it last? In my experience, love at first sight translates to nothing more than infatuation. A marriage needs something substantial if it's to thrive.'

'What is that *something substantial*, in your opinion?' She definitely needed to move the conversation into other territory than the state of her marriage.

He seemed to give it some thought. 'Partnership, a sharing of responsibility as well as a shared vision for the future. Marriage is work. It's laying the foundations for a lifetime and beyond.'

'Your version sounds rather sterile,' she goaded him then regretted the use of that word. Her own marriage had been literally sterile. She'd rather not call attention to that.

'My version of marriage is practical. My descendants are counting on me. Perhaps if more great families thought that way, the peerage would be in better shape, less debt ridden. Too many people think only of now and not of later.'

'I find such wisdom ironic coming from a man who is reputed to run through women at an alarming rate, or perhaps you expect to keep a mistress for pleasure and a duchess for business? Do you have someone in mind already?' A man like him probably had a list and kept dossiers.

'If you are trying to needle me, Your Grace, you will find I don't prick so easily.' He gave her a smug smile. 'I know what Society says about me and I know what I am. When it comes to affairs I am absolutely a rake. I do not dispute it. I've sought out my share of physical pleasure with women who are willing to engage in such liaisons. But when it comes to the viscounty and now the dukedom, I am absolutely serious about my duty. Now that Adolphus is dead and the succession hangs by a thread, I shall marry within the year. The Crown will appreciate the need for it. However, I will not let that haste rush my choice. I will be diligent in finding a woman who will also be serious about her duty.' He pulled out a gold pocket watch and checked the time. 'Now that's settled, we should head back. The solicitor will be at the house to read the will.'

There were no surprises in the will; at least the duchess's face did not register any. Logan spent more of his time watching her than listening to the solicitor drone on with self-importance as he read through the pages of Adolphus's will. The estate was his, all the entailed lands were his, which included two smaller estates, one in Hertfordshire near Wales and the other up north. There was a special, rather large, monetary bequest left for his cousin's valet, which Logan found mildly peculiar, but all else was as it should be. He would start going over the books tomorrow to ascertain any outstanding debt and the state of the Darlington coffers. He debated whether or not he should ask the duchess to join him in that effort.

The only real surprise since he'd arrived was her. He'd been prepared for a teary-eyed girl entirely at sea with the loss of her husband, and a house at sixes and sevens. What he'd found instead was a smoothly run home even in a time of mourning and the chaos of succession, the duchess competently at the helm. This woman was a warrior even in the midst of whatever grief she might be grappling with. There'd not been one tear from her.

He did find that stoicism at odds with the idea that her marriage had been a love match, a concept he'd tried to vet at the dower house this morning. Society told the tale of a whirlwind romance between them. She had not denied that. Perhaps that part was true. But had it lasted? She'd not answered that question. She'd deflected it to a more philosophical discussion of what made a good marriage. Had marriage to his cousin been all she'd hoped? Probably not given the amount of mourning that had occurred in their five years together. She'd not come up to Town during that time, or Logan would have been more familiar with her. Town was where he occasionally saw Adolphus for a drink at the club. He was too busy with his estate to idle away time at Darlington. His younger brother, Rahnald, saw more of Adolphus than he did, in truth. Rahnald had nothing better to do than move from house party to house party in the off-season, and from reckless debacle to debacle during the Season. Perhaps he should give Rahnald an estate to look after; that would keep him out of trouble.

'As for my wife, Olivia Maddox, the Duchess of Darlington, I leave…' The words brought Logan back to the reading. He saw the duchess stiffen and sit up straighter, if that was possible, and his attentions reverted back to the reading although his gaze remained fixed on her face. 'The right to live in the dower house known as North House for the remainder of her life, and the pension established for her upon our marriage of one thousand pounds per annum. I also leave an annual allowance for each of her three sisters until they marry or reach the age of twenty-three. These funds are to be used to support their debuts and dowries in order to make suitable matches. To her father, the Earl of Aylesmere, I leave a sum of fifteen thousand pounds to be drawn from in annual drafts. These sums shall remain intact until their natural expiration dates as stated above, or they shall expire should the current duchess remarry before said time. At which point, I would expect her future husband would assume those obligations.'

Now, *there* were some surprises, Logan thought. His cousin had been extraordinarily generous with his wife's family. He'd not have thought Adolphus would care quite so much about three girls or his father-in-law. Did he imagine it or did the duchess's shoulders slump just the slightest with relief upon hearing the words? What did she think of her own settlement? Perhaps that was not a surprise given it was based on her marriage contracts. Still, those settlements were not nearly as generous as those given to her family. One would think a man madly in love with his wife would leave her more than he left her sisters. A thousand pounds a year was nothing to scoff at for country living, but a woman of her status could not maintain a London residence and a wardrobe for the Season on that.

Her allowance would effectively keep her in the country, a prisoner in the dower house. Unless she remarried, at which point she would forfeit her gains and, depending on how soon she remarried, the comforts afforded her family as well unless the new husband was of a mind to take them on. These conditions did not sound like the conditions of a loving husband. Why did his cousin want his widow immured in the countryside? Darlington was well-to-do enough that Adolphus could have bestowed any kind of lifestyle on his widow that he chose. That he'd chosen to bestow this one spoke more of punishment than reward.

Logan thought again about her dodge of his question at the dower house. Had that infatuation lasted? Had it been brought to its knees by the lack of a child? Adolphus was not a patient man. He liked things done *now*. Perhaps he'd imagined a wedding followed by a babe in the cradle within the year? Perhaps there had been miscarriages? Dashed hopes could be as damaging as no hope. There were four little white crosses in the Hailsham family graveyard that attested to that. Two brothers and a sister Logan had never known. Was Adolphus punishing her from beyond the grave, or was he trying to control her from there?

He wants her to remain in the country. He wants her to remain unwed. Why would he want that?

The thoughts chased about in his head, another option forming. Was this the act of a jealous husband who felt that if he could not have his wife, no one else could? Jealousy, he supposed, was another, less functional, type of love. 'Is there nothing else?' Logan put in when the solicitor laid down the last of the papers. Was there no personal letter for the duchess? A man in love might leave his beloved a final epistle, some written confession of feeling that would live beyond him. His father had left his mother a letter she treasured to this very day and their marriage had not begun as a love match, although it had become one over the years, further proof that love was complicated. Too complicated for Logan's preferences.

'There is one more thing,' the solicitor said smugly. 'There is this.' He pushed forward a lumpy envelope. 'For you, Your Grace.' He nodded to the duchess. Her brow knit for a fraction of a moment. She'd not been expecting this, Logan thought.

Her slender fingers opened the envelope and withdrew a sheet of paper wrapped about a key. From the movement of her eyes, there wasn't much written on the paper. She lifted her gaze to meet his. 'It is for a vault at Coutts.' She handed him the sheet of paper. 'The bank has been instructed only to allow me to use the key and to access the vault contents. Whatever the vault contains I am given jurisdiction over.' She summarised the brief contents of the letter even as he read.

Well, that was certainly playing it a bit mysterious on his cousin's part. A special key, a vault with limited access for the duchess's eyes only. 'Do you have any idea what it might be?' Logan asked, handing the paper back to her.

She shook her head. 'No idea at all.' But that was a lie. Not knowing didn't align with a love-match marriage. If they'd been in love, surely Adolphus would have told her about the vault? People in love told each other everything. It was nauseating, really. Yet, this key was clearly a surprise. Her face had gone pale, her fortitude finally wavering. Whatever lay behind the vault door was a chink in her armour, and *that* piqued his interest. Things were not as they appeared at Darlington Hall. The duchess bore watching.

Chapter Four

❦

Safe behind the doors of her chambers, away from watchful eyes, Olivia took out the ledger of names from its hiding spot and laid the key beside it as if seeing them side by side would prompt a hitherto unlooked-for insight. But the sight of them only prompted fear—fear of what she'd committed to, fear of what she was now and had been complicit with after having haphazardly given her word. Seeing the ledger and the key were like seeing those fears personified, brought to life. Of course, she might be letting her imagination get the better of her. Were the ledger and the key even connected? At this point it was naive to assume they weren't.

Connected or not, she had no idea what they meant, but it seemed to bode no good; a ledger full of aliases and a key only she was allowed to use. If there was nothing to hide, why would it matter who opened the vault? She very much feared what she might find inside. And yet, she was in no hurry to race to London and open that vault. It would only raise more questions not only for her but for the viscount as well. She could not open that vault until or if she was ready to tell him about the journal or until there was a time when she might do it without his knowledge, perhaps later when she was moved into the dower house and had a life of her own. For now, though, her life was inextricably linked with his.

That was apparently a trend with her—having her life, her fate, her choices, inextricably linked with a man's. First, her father, then Adolphus with those secrets she'd promised to keep, secrets she didn't even understand. And now her life was attached to the viscount. Oh, how she was regretting the promise she'd made Adolphus despite the aid it offered her family. That promise had been given blindly in the excitement of the moment by a girl overcome by the delights of her first London Season; the glitter, the gowns and the attentions of fine gentlemen. She'd been overwhelmed, too, by the burden her father laid on her to marry well and secure the family's finances. So much had been riding on her and then Adolphus had appeared.

Olivia rocked back on her heels. Those days had been like a dream; waltzes at midnight, drives in the afternoon, outings to museums, picnics at Richmond watching the carriages race, all with the gallant Adolphus at her side, the Season's most eligible bachelor. That had been heady enough, but then there'd been the gifts he'd lavished on her: the chocolate bonbons drizzled with pale pink icing, the strawberries dipped in chocolate that he fed her on the picnic blanket when no one was looking, the book of Shakespearean sonnets he'd given her because he knew she liked them, even though he'd openly confessed he didn't care for poetry himself. At the time, she'd taken the gift as a sign of his thoughtfulness. How considerate it was to take an interest in her interests not because he already shared them but because they were simply hers. She'd been so very wrong. They hadn't been gifts; they'd been bribes. She knew that now. She just didn't know for what.

Olivia opened the ledger and stared blankly

once more at the pages. She could discern nothing about them that offered any inkling to what the names represented or what the accounts had been kept for, but she could see the moment that had changed her life like it was yesterday—the night he'd proposed; the night he'd extracted his promise.

Come walk in the garden with me. The Ardmoors are said to have a beautiful fountain imported from Italy.

Adolphus was already steering her toward the French doors that opened across the far side of the ballroom into the outdoors. They both knew she wouldn't refuse. People nodded with knowing smiles as they passed. They'd become the Diamond and the Duke since the Season had opened and Adolphus had made her the singular focus on his attentions. She'd only known him a month, it was barely June, but she was sure he would ask her tonight. He'd called on her father this afternoon. She'd been atremble with anticipation ever since.

At the fountain Adolphus bent on one knee and reached for her hand, the moonlight limning his face, his eyes intent on her as he professed his affections and made his promises; promises to provide for her and for her fam-

ily if she consented to be his wife. 'All I ask of you in return is to keep my secrets.' His eyes twinkled, his smile enchanting as he said it.

She laughed, the cup of her happiness spilling over. 'Of course I will.'

He lifted her hand to his lips, kissing her gloved knuckles. 'A man must be able to trust his wife's loyalty. I will hold you to that.'

But all she was interested in being held to at that moment was his body.

Foolish girl. Olivia sighed. Had he gone home and laughed at how cheaply that promise had been bought? For bonbons and books, trifles, really, in exchange for what he asked. She'd promised to protect something sight unseen, something of unknown magnitude. Some would say it was unfair of him when he knew what he was asking for and she did not. Sometimes she wondered if knowing would have made a difference to her. Probably not. She'd still needed what he had to offer. She'd still imagined herself in love with him, that he loved her, that the courtship was real, that it was an indicator of what their life together would be like.

She'd never been so wrong about someone before or since. The fairy tale had not lasted long, not past the wedding night, in fact. The romance of the courtship and the wedding had disappeared with the guests. Once they were alone, Adolphus's charm had been absent. In hindsight, she understood it was because there was no one else watching, no one to perform for, no one to write about it in the papers the next day. Adolphus needed adulation like a fish needed water. But originally, the untried debutante she'd been had attributed the lack of intimate chemistry between them to her own inexperience.

She'd thought it would grow as they grew, as they learned one another. At first, he hadn't seemed to mind the clumsy sex but when one month, then two, and three and four months passed and there was no child, the distance between them grew. Again, she'd made excuses for it and for him, chalking the difficulties up to the loss of his father and the extra responsibilities he had to bear as the new duke. By the second year of their marriage, he was gone for extended periods of time, travelling to the other estates he'd said. It had made sense at the time given his inheritance. But now she wondered what else he'd been doing and why? Had those absences been truly all about the estates when he couldn't be bothered to manage Darlington? When, by that time, Darlington had become her responsibility? She'd not thought to question it.

By then she'd been all too happy to see him go. When he was gone, she needn't be faced with constant reminders of her failure to conceive and she needn't endure his lacklustre attentions in the bedroom. No one liked to be reminded their spouse no longer desired them. Looking back, that may have been a tactical error on her part. She'd been so caught up in her own miseries she'd not paid attention to other things going on around her.

Olivia pushed the ledger back between her mattresses and put the key about her neck. She should have spent more time wondering about those secrets, should have asked more questions, should *not* have ignored their existence because they weren't staring her in the face. Now she was tethered to the weight of their great unknown. This afternoon had been proof of that. Her family was provided for and would be as long as she kept her part of the bargain. But what bargain was she keeping? What was she protecting? It bothered her that she didn't know. She doubted it was anything good. Good things didn't need to be hidden. If she kept hiding it, she was complicit with whatever it was. It bothered her that she might be hiding a great ill; that her silence had been bought.

Yet, she was bothered as well as to what breaking that silence might mean for her family, of all they would lose. She might be more mature than the starry-eyed girl who'd said yes to the proposal, but she still didn't have a choice. Olivia fingered the key at her neck. She might not have a choice, but she could figure out what she was hiding. There would be power in that knowledge if she could acquire it, and she could use a little power, especially when the viscount started asking questions.

The viscount did not start with his questions at dinner, much to her surprise and perhaps even disappointment. She'd been braced for an interrogation. The expression on his face at the reading of the will said quite plainly he'd caught the contradictions represented by the settlements. He *had* questions. But perhaps he had better manners than to pepper her with personal questions in front of his mother. In addition, there was other news for them to discuss. His younger brother, Rahnald, had written saying he was coming for a visit.

The announcement was met with differing responses, she noted, from mother and son. The viscount's mother was clearly thrilled that her oft-absent youngest son was paying a visit. The viscount, though, met the news with cynicism. 'He'll probably want money or he's hiding from some new scrape he's got himself into,' he cautioned his mother. To which she said only, 'You were young once, too, Logan. I remember the time when *I* had to bail you out of that gambling hell you were so keen on frequenting because you couldn't pay your bill.'

'We later discovered that the roulette wheel was rigged, so it wasn't as if I'd lost on purpose,' Logan corrected. 'And for the record, it was the first and last time I gambled beyond my means.' It was quite fascinating to watch the viscount and his mother argue politely, each intent on making their points. She did not think she'd ever argued with her father. Then again, perhaps fathers and daughters were different than mothers and sons. What an interesting dynamic that must be, and how difficult to be both the mother and matriarch of the family while one's son held all the publicly recognised power regardless of the difference in ages.

The countess smiled. 'Which proves my point beautifully. People can learn their lessons. People can change. You did. Rahnald will, too. It's been some time since he's been in a scrape.' A quiet battle of wills ensued after that, putting off the viscount's opportunity to question her until after his mother had retired.

'Shall we retreat to the library this evening for a sherry?' he suggested. 'We have not had time to talk since the solicitor left.' No, they hadn't. She'd departed the estate office as soon as she could decently exit, claiming a widow's prerogative for privacy. Now he was making her accountable for that absence. Was the library a strategic decision on his part? Had he guessed it was her favourite room in the house? The place where she might feel most relaxed? Was he counting on her being more likely to let down her guard because of that? He may have overplayed his hand there. If anything, it made her more wary.

Tension gathered between her shoulder blades as she walked with him to the library, aware of his hand guiding politely at the small of her back, as if she needed an escort in her own home.

It's not yours anymore. It's his.

But she rather thought any space he was in quickly became his. He carried a proprietary authority about him naturally, as if he'd been born with it. She thought she might very well feel this way whether he'd been the heir or not, though. She sensed it was something he couldn't help. Adolphus hadn't had that subtle air about him. He exerted his authority instead by simply taking up space with the mere largeness of him. One could not overlook Adolphus in any room, and if there was ever a question of it, Adolphus had mastered the sprawl in which his arms and legs deliberately took up as much space as possible.

'Your Grace.' The viscount held the door for her and ushered her inside.

'You needn't call me that.' Olivia took a seat in a high-backed chair set near the fire.

'It's your title.' He paused at the console to pour their drinks. Brandy for him and sherry for her. 'Would you prefer I call you *my lady*?' He crossed the room with his long-legged stride.

'No. I am not your lady any more than you

are my lord.' Her eyes clashed with his as he handed her the small sherry glass. This was her best line of defence against his probing, she'd decided; to convince him he need not concern himself with her private matters.

'You are my cousin by marriage, and I *am* technically *your lord*.' He settled himself in the chair opposite her.

'You needn't be. I am a grown woman with her own residence and her own funds. I am of no blood relation to you and the relational connection I once had to your family has been severed now. When I move to the dower house, you will probably not see me more than once or twice a year. I will be independent of your household here at the hall.' It was a hurtful realisation after years of dedicating herself to the welfare of Darlington but a life in isolation was a necessary step in keeping her word and protecting her family.

'I hope that will not be the case.' His gaze held hers and she felt as if she was being subtly stalked, his green eyes reminiscent of a prowling tiger. 'I admit to being mystified about why you'd seek such solitude when it seems your husband has enforced a significant amount of solitude on you already.' It was said with nonchalance as he casually fingered the stem of his brandy glass with the same absent attention he'd ushered her down the hall, but she was aware this was the question he'd waited all evening to ask. It had come not as a blunt interrogation as she'd expected but in disguise as conversation, riding the coattails of a polite invitation. No wonder he was such a successful rake in London. Everything he did carried an air of seduction to it, drawing someone in before carefully springing the trap.

'It was what was agreed upon. At the time it seemed adequate.' She sipped her sherry, answering obliquely. 'One never expects their husband to die so soon.'

She was prevaricating, being vague on purpose. He made her nervous. He could see the tension in her shoulders. She was holding herself with the same rigidity she'd held herself this afternoon with the solicitor, as if she must be alert, ready to protect something. He might have understood such a reaction if she had a young heir to protect from an avaricious uncle but she had nothing to protect. The law had already decided that. There was nothing to be on guard against. There was nothing left to take from her. Her widow's portion was surprisingly small.

But her family's wasn't.

Did she think those funds were in any danger from him? From the reading today, the only danger posed to those funds came from her. 'Do you miss him?' Logan asked directly.

'What sort of question is that?' Her blue eyes flared with indignation.

Logan swirled his brandy, watching the amber catch the firelight. 'One I cannot puzzle out for myself. You did not answer my question this morning at the dower house and now you're dodging it again even when asked a different way.'

Her chin went up a fraction. 'Perhaps I refuse to answer on the grounds that the state of my marriage is none of your business. My marriage is over and my marriage is private. It does not affect your inheritance.'

'You are part of that inheritance whether you wish it or not. Therefore, you are my responsibility, as I believe I've mentioned before,' he repeated patiently. She did not like that. Her eyes narrowed and Logan braced for battle. He'd never met a woman quite like her, so fiercely stubborn. He was usually successful in winning a woman over with little effort, but he was making no inroads with her. Instead, every day seemed to entrench her against him even further, which was interesting because entrenchment traditionally came with demands and opposing positions but not with her. She demanded nothing of him, didn't complain about her circumstances. She wanted only to be left alone and that smelled suspicious to him.

'Have you ever considered, Lord Hailsham, that a woman might not want to be a responsibility? That perhaps all she wishes is to be free? Able to control her own life?'

She had a very expressive face. He'd spent a considerable amount of time watching that face in the past two days: at the supper table, at the dower house, with the solicitor. She tried to school her features, but she was seldom completely successful. Her eyes always gave her away, a small flicker here, a flash there. She was someone who felt things to the depth of her soul. She was quick to argue with him, something only his best friend, Carrick, ever did with him these days. No one argued with a viscount; even fewer would dare to argue with a duke. Except for her, it seemed. She was quite willing to argue and that would be refreshing under other circumstances. But under these circumstances, argument was an impediment to unearthing the truth.

'But you're not free,' Logan pointed out. 'Living in the dower house does not make you free. In fact, I would suggest that the conditions read today make you something of an isolated captive on Darlington land. You cannot afford to go to London, to meet people, to start a new life. And even if you managed to do that on your budget, a marriage would cut your family's financial support from Darlington. Your husband didn't want you to leave here. Was he jealous? Was it truly the love match London believed?' They were back to that again. He'd asked her about it once before when he'd first arrived.

He stood now, pacing the length of the fireplace like a barrister laying out his case. 'That's what I can't figure out. If it was a love match, why didn't he tell you about the key and why didn't he settle more on the wife he adored? But if it wasn't a love match, why would he seek to keep you here? Perhaps for revenge of some sort? But then, why support a family he had no real emotional investment in? Which—

ever way I turn the pieces, they don't fit.' He gave her a moment to digest that. He wanted her to know that he'd noticed the inconsistencies and he'd been thinking about them. 'I was surprised today about those conditions but you weren't.'

She gave an elegant shrug. 'Many of them were previously agreed to with my knowledge,' she explained without explaining anything useful at all. She might have known about them previously but that did not account for their oddity.

Logan nodded. 'I understand that. What I *don't* understand is why your father needs to be propped up by the dukedom? Why is he unable to provide for his daughters' debuts and dowries? He's an earl, a peer of the realm. He gained much when you married into the Maddox family. What more does he still need that requires you to forego a life of your own?' That particular provision had sat poorly with him. What sort of grown man relied on his daughter to support him?

Olivia looked down at her hands. The question had made her uncomfortable and Logan felt a moment's guilt. He didn't know the man; perhaps there was something he'd overlooked?

'Is your father ill? Does his health make it impossible for him to run the estate as it needs? If that is the case, I can assign a trustworthy steward to take over.'

She looked up, eyes flashing. 'No, that is not the case. My father is perfectly well. He is just unlucky with his investments, and the estate has borne the brunt of that over the years,' she snapped.

It should have been a warning to Logan, but he was hot on the scent of a problem to solve. 'Surely, once those losses are settled, though, he can begin to rebuild his fortune. I can recommend someone to look at accounts. Someone who could discreetly put up some artwork for auction or jewels.'

'It's a rather chronic condition with my father,' she said sharply. 'Without regular funds, the estate will cease to function and fall further into disrepair.'

'It sounds to me like it's a case of funds disappearing down a bottomless pit. I should like to take the situation in hand and see what can be done about it,' Logan persisted.

Her answer was sharp and quick. 'I already have. Those funds are not misappropriated, I assure you. They are spent solely on the estate and keeping the family fed and clothed.' She offered a smile, perhaps to take the bite off the edge of her comments. Ah, so she was running her family home from afar, keeping her father on a checked rein, at least. No wonder she'd not been keen to discuss it. What a burden that must be for her. He could fix that; take at least one thing from her plate.

'I do apologise for intruding,' Logan replied. 'Should you ever want a hand with it, I am more than happy to lend one.' He tapped the base of his neck. 'As for the key, that was another surprise today. Any thoughts about the vault?' Not that she'd care to share them, but he could at least ask.

Her hand went to her own neck, gripping the chain the key was strung on. 'I know nothing about the key.' She was quick to rejoin; too quick. She knew something she just didn't want to tell him.

'Would you like to go to Coutts? We could leave the day after tomorrow?' he offered. If she knew nothing, her curiosity might be eating her alive. If she did know something, this would force her to cut to the chase. He'd prefer to have everything out in the open.

'There is much to be done here. I am in no

hurry.' She declined his offer. 'We have tenants to meet and your brother is scheduled to visit. I doubt the vault holds anything exciting beyond a few pieces of jewellery.' She should have stopped with the scheduling conflicts. Those he would have believed as viable reasons not to hare over to London. He didn't believe the last. It was not so much that she wasn't curious about the vault's contents, he thought, as she was afraid to face them.

'Very well. Let me know when you'd like to go.' Logan dismissed the key. No one was getting into the vault. Whatever was in there was safe and it would keep. He'd let her have her way for now. After all, it was arguably more important what the key stood for, what it was connected to, than the actual items in the vault. 'We could puzzle out the key together, here, if you were willing.' It would require her to open up about the state of her marriage. 'However, it may necessitate answering questions that might be difficult. In fact, I am sure they *are* difficult or you wouldn't have deflected my questions both times I asked.'

'A woman does not discuss her marriage with another man. Your questions are unseemly.' She scolded, actually scolded him.

How delightfully refreshing that was. He could not recall the last time a woman had thought to scold him for bold behaviour. Usually, such boldness was seen as an invitation to foreplay. But he was not ready to give up.

'Perhaps she does discuss such things when that man is a relative with her best interests at heart and her husband is no longer here to see to those interests.' Logan swallowed the last of his brandy. 'The decision is quite obviously yours, though. Tomorrow I am looking over the books and I am expecting a visit from the coroner to discuss the cause of my cousin's death. You are welcome to participate in both.' He'd been hoping for a reaction, some clue that either event made her as nervous as he did. But she merely rose and set aside her glass.

'Then I must get some sleep. It will be a busy day. Thank you for including me.' She was all stiff propriety as she took her leave and Logan couldn't help puncturing that commendable reserve with a parting salvo.

'Good night… Olivia.' More boldness, and more foreplay in its own way. He was determined to push this relationship forward, determined to win her trust and mine her secrets.

He could not help her otherwise and he was absolutely convinced she needed help.

He watched her graceful body pause at the door for a moment before exiting but she did not turn as he'd thought she would, some parting shot on her lips. She'd let him have the last word, quite literally. He wondered how many times she'd let his cousin have the last word. Always? Seldom? Never? Had she argued with Adolphus the way she argued with him? With her eyes, with her pointed conversation? With a stubbornness that never backed down? He'd known women who were firecrackers with a short fuse that went off spectacularly and then fizzled out, unable to sustain such crackle. Olivia was not a firecracker, but no less fiery for it. Olivia was a slow burn, an ember with its blue hot flame at its core, lying in wait but she would singe a man just as surely as the spark that leapt from the fire. Had she singed his cousin?

Logan helped himself to another glass of brandy, his conscience pricking at him to be honest. What *was* the source of his interest in her marriage to his cousin? Was it *all* because he felt she was his responsibility as the new duke or would he have wanted to know regardless? He sat back down and stared into the flames, brandy at his elbow. She was an intriguing woman, not only because of her beauty but also because of the mystery in her eyes, eyes that invited a man to come and solve her if they dared as if she were a riddle to rival the Sphinx.

And yes, he did feel obliged to solve that riddle for myriad reasons: his responsibilities to the dukedom required it; she was under his protection whether she wanted to be or not. But also, in his experience people who protested too much were quite often the people hiding something, who needed the most help and who were in the most trouble. But before he could help her, he needed her to trust him.

Chapter Five

⤜⧽∿⧼⤛

She did *not* trust him. No matter how…*competent* the viscount looked, fresh from his morning toilette dressed in a sombre dark grey morning coat and blindingly white linen beneath the dove grey silk waistcoat, a black band about his upper arm out of deference for his cousin, as he sat across from her at the estate desk the next morning. He not only looked good, he also smelled good; winter cloves mixed with citrus and bergamot. When something looked—or smelled—too good to be true, it most definitely was. Olivia had learned that the hard way and it was not an experience she was keen to repeat. Her father and her husband had both failed her spectacularly. Or perhaps, it was also that she didn't trust herself when it came to men. She'd put her faith in her father and her husband thinking they would take care of her, that they would have her interests at heart. Instead, she'd acquired the lesson that she was the only one who was looking out for her interests.

Now there was another man imposing himself into her life: the Viscount Hailsham—she really ought to start thinking of him as His Grace—and he was offering to take care of her. The very thing she'd originally sought from her marriage. Only now she didn't want it. What she wanted was to take care of herself. His wasn't so much an offer as it was a bargain. To let him carry her burdens meant she had to trust him with them. She'd have to tell him about the reality of her marriage, and about the cryptic ledger. She'd have to betray her promise to Adolphus. Keeping secrets meant not sharing them, not even with a man's cousin. Sharing those secrets jeopardised her sisters' security. It was simply too risky to consider especially with a stranger. Cousin or not, that was what Logan was—a stranger, a person who was unknown to her up until a few days ago.

And yet, the temptation still whispered: *what if this time it could be different?*

What if she was a better judge of character these days? What if he could help her with the ledger? What if it could be done in a way that didn't break the requirements of the will? Would he even allow the solicitor to make such a decision against her? Then she could at last be free of Adolphus's ghost.

That's exactly what Hailsham wants you to think, the voice of caution rallied against the temptation. *Why else do you think he invited you to go over the books with him? He is seducing you with the one thing that matters to you: the estate. He is pretending to make you a partner in this transition because it helps him get what he wants.*

If he was pretending to be interested in her opinions, he was doing a very good job. He asked questions of her and sought out information, weighing her responses carefully with a nod of his dark head and jotting notes. It was flattering to be shown such respect; perhaps because of that, it was difficult to believe it wasn't real, that he wasn't in earnest. The more hurtful the lie, the harder it was to accept, just like the truth of her marriage. She'd spent the first year in denial. She'd thought if she worked hard enough, pleased Adolphus enough, that it would indeed *be* enough to win his affections in truth. By the time she'd figured out there was nothing she could do, she was already running the estate.

'These ledgers are in fine condition,' Hailsham said at last, leaning back in his chair. 'I am impressed by several things, in fact. Mainly, I am impressed by you. I take it you had no estate management experience before you wed my cousin, and yet in a short period of time you've grasped its mechanics with nothing short of excellence, and you're running your father's estate as well.' He closed the last ledger and fixed her with a stare. 'I am also left with the question, what did my cousin do with himself if you had the estate well in hand?' He paused, drumming his fingers on the desktop. 'There isn't a single entry made by him in these ledgers. It makes me wonder if he was even here. But that's preposterous, isn't it? If this was a love match, why wouldn't he be where his beloved is? And why would he allow her to do his work?' He offered her a half smile smug with victory. 'You forget, madame, that I know my cousin. He was a prideful man. He'd never allow a woman to do his work for him, at least not when others might find out about it.'

'Your cousin, about whom you claim to know so much, preferred his estate up north. For the hunting.' Of course, it wasn't just for the hunting. It was to put as much distance between them as possible once the marriage had gone sour. She wondered now if it hadn't also been something related to the mysterious journal. She couldn't help but be a bit smug about dropping that piece of information. What else did he think he knew about his cousin? It would probably shock him, and while there would be some delight in perpetrating that shock, there would be implications to her that would outstrip the short-term pleasure of surprising him. She doubted many people *could* surprise him.

'Your Grace.' Moresby cleared his throat in the doorway and she turned her head before realising Moresby did mean her. 'The coroner is here. I've put him in the blue salon and asked Mrs Aldrich to prepare some refreshment.'

Hailsham rose and tugged at his jacket. 'Thank you, Moresby. Please let him know we will join him directly.' Once Moresby had gone, he turned to her. 'Do you still wish to join me? It may be a rather graphic, perhaps disturbing, discussion.'

She nodded. 'I think I must know.' It might offer insight into the secrets she so blindly protected, and it certainly kept her on an even pitch with Hailsham. She couldn't risk him knowing something she did not.

'Very well,' he said, accepting her decision. 'Might I ask, though, did you see him, I mean afterwards when they brought the body back?'

'No, I did not.' At the time it had seemed unnecessary. Adolphus had been dead for three days. The corpse had been examined in Hampstead Heath and then transported home to Surrey and examined once more by the man they'd meet today, a Dr Green. She was regretting that decision now, as gruesome as the option might have been. But she'd been stunned and in the first throes of complicated disbelief. 'I've seen the report, however,' she offered as they made their way to the blue salon. 'An accidental self-inflicted shot to the thigh. There wasn't much more detail.' She paused. 'It was very straightforward. I think the visit today might disappoint you. There's nothing more to add except to hear from the coroner what he's already committed to paper.'

'Perhaps, but I have questions,' Hailsham replied. 'In my experience nothing is ever simple, and nothing or anyone is ever quite what they seem.' His gaze said she was included in that assessment.

She slid him an enquiring look. 'Do you apply that rule to yourself as well?' She did. The viscount might have a certain reputation in Town, but she wondered if he preferred it that way in order to make it easier to hide what he really was: a man who was sharp, and dangerous, just like a knife.

Moresby had done well in selecting the blue salon for this meeting, Logan noted. Its appointments, from the thick, floor-length blue velvet portières with their gold-fringed trim to the Turner nautical paintings tastefully dominating the walls, were large and imposing, chosen to be a reminder that whoever called here was being received by a duke. The room was doing its job a little too well in regard to Dr Green. The man looked nervous to Logan's eye as they entered the room and he rose to greet them. Was it the room that provoked such a response or the nature of the visit?

Logan gestured for the man to take his chair

as a tea tray was delivered, stocked, thankfully, with more hardy, masculine fair than petits fours and small slices of cake. 'Thank you for meeting with us,' Logan said, taking a teacup from Olivia as she gracefully poured out. 'I have seen your report, but naturally, I have questions.' Better to cut straight to it. He hoped he might get more direct answers from Dr Green than he got from Olivia. Of course, he had his answers anyway. One could learn as much from what went unsaid as from what was said. The books this morning had told their own story.

'What questions might those be?' Dr Green set down his plate of sandwiches and rubbed his hands on his thighs. Sweaty palms? Logan hoped so. Things were growing more curious by the moment at Darlington. The duchess had been in charge here, his cousin an absent landlord who treated his wife apparently as a land steward, a love match that had been a short-lived facade and an otherwise healthy cousin dead under vague circumstances.

'My cousin's fatal wound was in his thigh,' Logan began, 'quite high up, from the report. The report seems to conclude that he must have shot himself while cleaning his weapon.

But the original report was from the coroner in Hampstead Heath. Did you concur after your examination?'

'The wound was clearly in the thigh, Your Grace. There's no disputing that,' Dr Green answered. 'It pierced the femoral artery. He would not have lived long enough to be saved.' Dr Green glanced at Olivia. 'My pardon, there are no delicate words.'

'No pardon is required, Doctor.' Olivia inclined her head but her face was pale and her plate untouched.

Logan reached for the poker beside the fireplace and laid it across his lap. 'I fear I must require you to be even more indelicate, Dr Green. I am sure your assessment of the wound is correct, but the cause brings me questions. Misadventure? A cleaning accident?' He gestured to the poker laid across his thighs. 'If I am cleaning my gun or loading my gun, the barrel is pointed outwards, over my thigh, like this, not *into* my thigh. If I were to misfire, I would perhaps shoot myself in the hand, perhaps my foot, or hit an object in the room.'

'What are you suggesting, Your Grace?'

'That a shot to the thigh is not usually accidental. One must wish to do himself deliberate damage.' Logan moved his gaze slowly between Olivia and Dr Green, gauging their reactions. 'Could it have been that he took his own life?' Now he was the one being indelicate. But this reference was less delicate than the other option; that if he had not taken his own life, someone had taken it from him. That implied murder. It also implied there was indeed someone out there who knew exactly what had happened at the men's weekend. That someone had been there, had been someone his cousin had likely known. Or perhaps if there had been another shooter, it had been an accident? Had they meant to kill or merely to wound and the bullet had gone astray? Logan stilled the racing of his mind, forcing himself to focus on the doctor and the duchess.

'I could not say,' Dr Green prevaricated. 'I understand your questions, Your Grace, but I saw only the body. Perhaps the coroner in Hampstead Heath might have better answers?' He was trying to deflect responsibility, Logan saw that, but there was truth in what he said as well.

'Do you know if the bullet was still embedded in his thigh?' Logan asked. 'And if so, was it removed?'

'I do not know.' Dr Green rose with a sad shake of his head, recognising the limits of his assistance. 'I do apologise I cannot be of more help.'

Logan debated whether or not to let him go. He was cognizant that the doctor had not responded to his first claim; that a shot to the thigh such as the one recorded in his report was not a logical outcome of the scene described. Did he want to press Dr Green on it? Perhaps later. Perhaps his best option now would be to press Olivia for more details. He saw Dr Green to the salon door and thanked him for coming before turning him over to Moresby to be escorted out.

'You suspect something,' Olivia challenged before he even returned to his seat.

'I think any reasonable critical thinker might suspect something,' he said offhandedly. 'Were you not thinking the same thing?' He took his seat and picked up the poker again, laying it across his lap in demonstration. 'It was not an accident. There is simply no way.' He knew it in his gut. He didn't need to match a bullet to his cousin's gun to know it wasn't an accident. But he did need to find that bullet, if possible, to determine if it was a suicide or something worse.

He studied her pale face, watching for the slightest reaction. 'Was my cousin depressed? Was there some burden he carried that would cause him to seek such an end?' Even as he said it, he found the question unbelievable. He'd seen the books. The accounts were flush. His cousin, thanks to his wife's efforts, did not have money problems. His cousin had assets. Three estates and a ducal seat that contained carefully curated collections of books and artwork, a capable wife who kept it all running so that he might hunt to his heart's content up north instead of doing his duty in begetting an heir.

'Not that I'm aware of.' She was taking a leaf from Dr Green's book of vague answers. But unlike Dr Green, Logan was unwilling to let her get away with it.

'Because there was nothing to be depressed about? Or because you simply don't know?' He paused, a thought coming to him. 'When *was* the last time you saw your husband?'

'What are you insinuating?' She met his stare with a blue-eyed glare. Her defences were up. Dare he hope he'd scored a direct hit?

'I am insinuating nothing. I am merely asking a question. When did you last see him?' Suddenly, it seemed as if everything hinged on that answer. What sort of marriage did they have? Had his cousin been regularly absent? Why would his cousin have made that choice when the lovely Olivia waited here for him? The room fell silent, the only sound the quiet whickering of the flames in the fireplace as if even the room held its breath waiting for her answer.

'In November.' It came out as a whispered confession. Did she think he would judge her? Logan was careful to school his features, to give nothing away as his mind pieced together the implications of that revelation: she'd lied about the possibility of a child. Where there was one lie, there were usually others. Which, on a whole, didn't surprise him. Her reluctance to answer any of his questions when they grew personal suggested she was hiding something. People lied all the time. Just ask his brother, Rahnald. Everything Rahnald said was part truth, part lie. The trick was in separating the two and knowing which was which.

'I see,' was all he said. He *did* see. People lied to protect themselves because the truth was too awful. What awful truth was she hiding? Who or what was she protecting? The lie had bought her time. Perhaps she'd needed that time to accustom herself to all the changes that went with being widowed. Perhaps she'd needed time to plan her future. Maybe, if he'd been in her situation, he would have done the same. No, he would not judge her. A woman alone had to use all the resources available to her. But he *was* disappointed.

He could not change the laws of entailment. He could not change the fact that she was being dispossessed of the life she'd married for. But he had made every effort to be courteous about it. He'd offered to help her, to take responsibility for her well-being, to assure her that she was not being cast out. In return, he had hoped to be taken into her confidence. He was not used to women being wary about him. The women he knew appreciated a man who took charge. This was something of a first for him.

'He came to Darlington between grouse season concluding and Parliament opening. He left here and went to London, where he spent Christmas.' It was the first piece of unsolicited information she'd shared with him. Logan fitted that piece into place as well, careful to sift through what it told him: that she'd spent Christmas alone, while her husband had spent it in London, likely among friends, ignoring his wife although Surrey was an easy coach ride away. A half day at most would have seen him at her side. 'Permit me to be bold, but it appears you spent a lot of time apart for a couple so newly married and in possession of a cradle in desperate need of filling.'

Today, instead of scolding, she met his question head-on, her gaze hard. 'Your cousin had decided by then that no amount of time together was going to correct that.' Logan wondered who Adolphus blamed for that. Himself or his wife—a duchess perfect in every way except one perhaps?

'That must have been a blow for him,' Logan said carefully. He reached for a sandwich from the tray. Had such a realisation led to depression on his cousin's part? 'How did my cousin seem in November? Was he moody or down? Did he appear troubled?'

'No. He seemed quite himself.' Although Logan noted she didn't elaborate on what that meant. She leaned forward and selected a sandwich for herself and changed the subject. 'You intimated to Dr Green that it might have been a suicide. I doubt it. Adolphus loved himself above all else, Lord Hailsham. I cannot imagine any circumstance where he would deliberately make an end of himself. He loved himself too much. As hard as it might be to believe, his death was an accident. Even the best marksmen have them. There's no other explanation.'

Logan caught her gaze and held it. 'Yes, there is. If he would not have shot himself on purpose, and if the likelihood of accidentally misfiring into one's upper thigh is improbable, then we must consider the possibility that he was shot by someone else. After all, he wasn't alone. He spent the weekend surrounded by others.'

To her credit, Olivia didn't flinch at his bald conjecture. 'You think he was shot by someone on accident or on purpose?' He could see her mind working behind her eyes.

'I don't know. But either way, if that were the case, someone knows who did it. Perhaps even several someones know. There might be witnesses, people on hand when the gun went off, if it were an accident. I would very much like to know who was at that men's weekend.' It did seem odd to Logan that after four weeks since the event, that no rumour had surfaced about Adolphus's death. Rumours were useful in that they could be traced to a source. But no one was talking. Anyone who'd been in Hampstead Heath at the house was keeping quiet.

He wasn't sure how he felt about that. On the one hand, he was relieved not to have to answer gossip. On the other, it wasn't like the ton to overlook such a delicious story to sink their teeth into, especially in winter when truly good scandals were thin on the ground. Then again, what good was a scandal if there was no one to tell? Perhaps people were just waiting until spring.

'You think someone shot my husband,' Olivia said quietly.

'I think it's *possible*,' Logan clarified, watching her intently.

'Then you must also think murder is possible.'

'Possible but not probable. Murder is a large leap and the logic is not clear there. One would assume a house party is attended by friends. But friends don't shoot friends. The motive for murder is elusive there. There's also the fact that one does not go around shooting dukes.' He waited a moment before adding, 'Unless you know something I do not?'

Her hand froze halfway to the tea tray. 'Why ever would you think that?' Because, Logan thought, I'd bet my favourite horse you're hiding something and you've already lied to me once.

Chapter Six

She had to hide the journal somewhere better, somewhere safer. Just in case. Just in case Hailsham's conjectures this afternoon had any teeth to them. Just in case there was a connection between those conjectures to the journal that had arrived right before Adolphus died. It was possible, *if* his death hadn't been a self-inflicted accident, or an accident at all. Whatever that answer was, it had always been clear Adolphus had not wanted the journal found, which meant two things in her opinion: that the journal had the power to be dangerous, and things that weren't meant to be found were quite often hunted. If the journal was associated with Adolphus's death, someone might come looking.

Admittedly, it was a lot of *mights* and *ifs*

at this point. Perhaps it was merely paranoia that had her stealing through her own house in her nightdress and a robe with a basket over her arm, the ledger hidden at the bottom, covered with linens. She'd waited until the house had settled; the servants abed, Lady Hailsham retired to her chambers and the viscount sequestered in the office writing letters. One of which, no doubt, was to the coroner in Hampstead Heath.

Her destination was the wine cellar, the one place in a big house a lady usually had little familiarity. The wine cellar was typically the domain of one's husband and butler. No one would anticipate she would choose to hide something there, and her hope was, if anyone came looking, they would not look there. Even if they did, she thought their chances of success were small. The cellar was cavernous and dark, filled with nooks. They would not find it on the first try and the cellar was not accessible without a key. Guests did not naturally roam there.

The cellar might be the perfect destination but never had it seemed so far away as it did tonight. She just wanted to reach the cellar without encountering anyone and it suddenly seemed to her that there were so many chances of that occurring; a maid up late on a midnight task offering to take the basket, or Moresby doing one last check of the house offering to accompany her to the cellar. Even worse, she feared running into Viscount Hailsham and his sharp eyes, and sharper mind, particularly since this afternoon's discussion after the coroner left. He'd courteously not pursued any questions regarding the quality of her marriage after she'd revealed Adolphus had not been here since November. Nor had he called out her previous claim for time to see if a child may be imminent when that had clearly never been a possibility. But he didn't have to. He *knew* she'd lied and that had raised his suspicions of the situation and of her.

She approached the study door, stealthily on tiptoe, careful to walk around a floorboard that creaked. All she had to do was get past here and the wine cellar was hers. The door had been left ajar and light spilled through. She could see him sitting at the desk, coat off, shirtsleeves rolled up, dark head bent as he wrote, absorbed in his work. She was, quite honestly, intrigued and slightly intimidated by the viscount. Not intimidated physically by him, as one might have been intimidated by Adolphus based on his sheer size, but Hailsham wore his power in other ways and exercised it in other ways, too. He had a canny way of asking questions one ended up answering even when one chose not to. She'd given far more away today by what she'd not said than through her words. Which raised the question: Why not tell him what he wanted to know? He was going to guess at most of it anyway, or drag it from her piece by piece. What would happen if she made an ally of him? If she took the support he had offered on two occasions now? What purpose did it serve her to make an enemy of the viscount?

It had occurred to her as she'd debated the ledger in her rooms this evening that whatever hurt the dukedom also had the power to hurt Hailsham. If so, wouldn't he be as willing as she to keep the secrets Adolphus had bequeathed to her, whatever they were? Keeping those secrets would be vital to protecting himself, his dukedom. Or would Hailsham feel ethically compelled to address them and let the pieces fall where they may even at the expense to her and her family? That last was what worried her the most. Hailsham would be tenacious in ferreting those secrets out and uncovering their truths, which had the potential to be disastrous to her. She would not be able to stop him, nor was there any guarantee he would make decisions that protected them both. What happened if he chose to protect himself but not her? Her family?

She risked more than her own livelihood on that gamble. She risked her sisters' futures. Her silence bought them a chance to be well settled in life.

At the potential price of your conscience, came the whispered reminder. *He would ferret out the truth; you should do the same. You should know what you're hiding. You can no longer pretend it's of no significance. What harms might you be allowing to continue all so that your family is safe?*

She might have been able to ignore such prompts in the past when the secrets had existed to her in less tangible ways. But the defence was no longer as acceptable to her. The secrets had become real things, but she still felt she was better off figuring them out alone.

So instead of walking into the study and plopping the ledger on his desk, she chose instead to slip past the door, carefully shielding the light of her candle, and continued on to the wine cellar. She could always change her mind and show him the ledger later when she was more certain of the situation and more importantly, when she was more certain of him. Trusting men had got her into this mess. It seemed unlikely that trusting a man would get her out of it.

A fleeting flash of white caught the corner of Logan's eye as he looked up from his letter writing. He'd had the distinct feeling of being watched, but the house was abed. His gaze drifted toward the door. Was someone in the hallway? If they were, he didn't think they were there now. He stood and, taking up a lamp, went to investigate.

There was no one, but someone *had* been there. He'd smelled the scent of wax and smoke, and something else. He inhaled again and closed his eyes, letting the scent wash over him. Lavender and vanilla, a warm, inviting scent that spoke of an inviting feminine softness. A pure scent, a simple scent. *She'd* been there; Olivia, with her secrets, with her fierceness. She was anything but the simplicity of her scent. Without second thought, he turned and followed her trail.

In the past two days, she'd taken up a considerable amount of his thoughts. Even tonight, as he'd written to the coroner in Hampstead Heath with his questions, she'd been on his mind. Any further probing he did in regard to his cousin's death affected her, too. She would be connected to whatever was brought to light. Asking questions required that the state of her marriage be exposed and that was something she was loath to share on her own. Protectiveness rose, even as he realised he was the person she needed protection from. *He* was the one doing the probing, the one forcing a look into her marriage. It had been tempting to not write the letter at all, to spare her. But his own sense of rightness would not allow it. Personal discomfort was sometimes a price to pay for seeing justice done.

Her trail led him to the wine cellar, an odd destination this time of night. The door had been left slightly ajar and he went inside, carefully taking the steps that led downward. 'Olivia? Are you in here?' He called out to avoid startling her. No doubt, she was not expecting company. One did not make midnight visits to the wine cellar with the expectation of being joined. Which had him second-guessing his decision to call out. If she was doing something illicit, he wouldn't catch her at it now.

Why would she be doing something illicit? Because she's lied to you once already. Yes, but that was for good reason. She wouldn't be the first woman to lie about the possibility of an heir.

His mind argued with itself as he perused the aisles of casks and bottles, his gaze seeking another flash of white in the darkness.

Perhaps she's just come down for a drink to settle her nerves. There are decanters above stairs for that. One doesn't need a whole cellar.

'Lord Hailsham, what are you doing down here?'

He found her at the end of a row of reds, in a white nightdress, a china-blue Norwich shawl wrapped about her shoulders, a thick blond braid glinting over one of those shoulders. 'I think the better question is what are you doing here? It's after midnight. Hardly an ideal time to visit the cellars.'

'And yet, here we both are.' She gave a laugh and moved toward him, then past him, leading him away from where she'd been. 'I thought

I'd come make sure we had enough of that red on hand you were so fond of the other night. You'll want to show it off to your brother when he arrives.'

If he wanted to continue the conversation, he had to follow her. 'That's very kind of you, although it hardly warrants a late-night trip. I don't need such elaborate attentions. Moresby could have seen to it in the morning,' he pointed out politely.

'I couldn't sleep and by morning I might have forgotten. I am sorry to have disturbed you, though. It was not my intention.'

Oh, he was sure it wasn't. That was probably the truest thing she'd said in the past two days. She wasn't dressed for company. Whatever she'd been doing down here, she'd meant to do it alone. He noticed the basket on her arm. 'Allow me to take that. it looks heavy.' For a moment he thought she might not relinquish the basket. It the dimness of the cellar, it was hard to read her face. He could have mistaken it for a trick of the light. The basket *was* heavy when she handed it over to him. 'What's in here?'

'Bottles. The red I told you I was fetching.' She gave a smug laugh. Despite their circumstances, he was coming to like matching wits with her, especially if the conversation was innocuous. A draught in the cellar brought her scent close to him, sweet femininity, a reminder that there was never anything innocuous about talking to an attractive woman after midnight dressed in a nightgown. At this rate she wouldn't be the only one who wouldn't be able to sleep tonight. One way or another, thoughts of her would keep him up. Olivia DeLacey Maddox was a woman who tempted without even trying.

'Shall we try some?' He gestured to a small round table and two tall stools pushed up against a brick wall. Likely, this was where Moresby and Adolphus stood while sampling the wares. 'Neither of us seems intent on sleeping at the moment and wine can sometimes help with that.' He set the basket and his lamp on the table and pulled out one of the bottles. 'Tell me about the pinot.' He rooted about for two goblets, finding them on a shelf nearby and opened the bottle.

'It's a favourite of the Duke of Cowden, so I merely followed his lead and bought in. I haven't been sorry.'

'*You* did?' Logan quirked an eyebrow as he

poured. After the ledgers today, he shouldn't be surprised she had a hand in it.

'Well, with Moresby's help.' She took the glass and out of habit put her nose to it.

'I did not think Adolphus was friends with Cowden or with his sons.' Logan respected the older man, although he couldn't see Adolphus befriending him. Cowden headed up the Prometheus Club, a highly influential investment circle. He had three sons but they were all younger than Logan. Two of them were on Grand Tour at present, if he recalled correctly. They seemed unlikely comrades for his cousin.

Olivia smiled over the rim of her goblet, perhaps thinking the same thing. 'No, Adolphus was not friends with Cowden. I read a snippet about his wine in the *Times*. That was all.'

'It was a well-done investment, then,' he complimented. Here was one more thing to be impressed with. She'd not only kept the books for Darlington and run the estate, she'd run the cellars as well. He noted she'd not yet taken a sip of the wine. He raised his glass. 'To following hunches.' Or at least to following an intriguing woman into a dark cellar after midnight.

Chapter Seven

~~~~~~~~~~~~~~~~~~~~~~~~~~~~~~

She should not be down here with him. This was a scandal in the making. She should also have said no to the invitation to drink with him. She pulled her shawl closer about her, conscious that she was wearing nothing more than a cotton nightgown and he was in shirt-sleeves. Silence stretched between them. Was he waiting for her to say something first? What did he expect her to say? 'Do you want to talk about this afternoon?' he prompted. 'I imagine it was somewhat unnerving. I apologise for that.'

Her gaze remained intent on the stem of her wineglass. 'Apologise for verbalising your opinion? That an accident seems unlikely?' She looked up then. 'I wonder how many people have been thinking it but not saying it?

As you mentioned this afternoon, if there was another party involved, someone out there knows.' The prospect of that was the reason she'd been desperate to hide the ledger.

'It isn't so much the talk of blood and guts that is unnerving as the idea that someone may have shot him and it was likely someone he knew, accident or not.' She stifled a shudder at the last thought, the *or not*. Surely, that was just her imagination running away with itself. She watched his fingers caress the stem of his wineglass, a different sort of shiver running the length of her spine now. How delicious it would be to be touched like that; to be stroked with contemplation, with deliberation. How many women had watched him do the same and wished to be his wineglass?

'Do you know who his friends were? Who might have been there?' he asked in an idle tone, soft in the darkness. It might have been a seduction instead of an interrogation. But she did not miss the fact that despite the wine and the late hour he was still probing.

She shook her head. 'No. I wonder if it matters, though. Can we not let it lie? Other than for our edification do we have to know?' If no one came looking for the ledger, if no one else talked, perhaps it could all be swept under the proverbial rug. 'After all, knowing can't bring him back. It can't change anything.'

'Would you want him back?' Green eyes glittered catlike in the dark.

'I would never wish anyone dead.' She met him levelly.

'That's not what I was suggesting,' he said gravely, pouring each of them another glass, his voice a low husk. 'Was my cousin a good husband to you? I ask because I see evidence that he was not despite the story spun in the ton.' He was making confession easy for her by leading with his own conclusions so that anything she might say would not be a shock. 'You were alone for Christmas, you ran the family seat. There is every indicator that the two of you lived apart. You were never in London for the Season, but he was there.' It was another way of addressing the question he'd raised earlier and she'd shut down about the lack of an heir, about the lack of any marital life between them.

She gave another of her elegant shrugs. 'What is there to say, then? You've got it worked out. You hardly need me to tell you.'

The wine in her glass was going down easier with each swallow.

'I want to know why,' he said with quiet steel. 'Why did the romance go sour or—' he eyed her carefully '—was there ever any to begin with?' He leaned over the small table. 'Because if I was married to a woman like you, I would not leave her alone for a moment.'

Dear heavens, this man could sell a line. All he was missing was a little hand-kissing to go with it. 'I did not peg you for a romantic, Lord Hailsham.'

He gave a harsh laugh. 'I'm not. It's only that my cousin thought he was.'

'A marriage needs more than romance to thrive. Your cousin was not prepared for that. For better or for worse were just words to him. He'd never experienced the worst of anything.' It was what she liked to think. She took a sip of wine, wetting her lips. 'There was so much tragedy in such a short space. There was no heir. Then his father died and he had to take on the responsibilities of Darlington while still being a new husband. His mother stepped in to lend some direction and assistance. But then his mother died and there was truly no one left to steer him.'

'Except you,' Hailsham interjected.

'He was not interested in my directions. We'd had two years of no success in the heir department. He'd decided by then I was of no use to him.' Although that second year had not been full of attempts. He'd started living away from Darlington by then. She'd been relieved to see him go. 'He blamed me, of course. It is always the woman's fault in these cases. It wasn't hard to believe. No one looking at Adolphus would ever think he could possibly have issues with his virility.' She could still hear the cruel things he'd yell in a rage once it became clear another month had come and again there would be no child. Useless, worthless, he'd called her. All this from the man who'd waltzed her senseless and brought her roses. She'd felt betrayed.

'And what do you think?' Logan's question was asked quietly in the dark intimacy of the cellar. 'It isn't always down to the woman, you know.'

'I do not know. I tried herbs and all sorts of remedies but to no avail for him or for me.' The dark and the wine was making her careless or perhaps it was the interest in Logan's green eyes, riveted on her, on her every word and her desire to keep him riveted. How wondrous it felt to be listened to.

'For him, too?' He offered her a smile. 'That sounds intriguing.'

'They were meant to help with his potency, his ability to stay…um, aroused.' What an indelicate word that was.

'You mean he could not maintain an erection?' Hailsham clarified, making it sound so matter-of-fact, making it sound normal instead of sordid to be discussing such things. She was grateful to him. Of course, a seasoned rake would know just what to say, would understand such things.

'Yes, exactly.' She couldn't help but smile in relief. 'Perhaps if I'd been more skilled, knew more tricks…' She was thinking out loud now, reliving the disappointment of those years. 'He said it was because I couldn't hold his attentions.' That was a polite way of putting it. 'For a while I believed it, too. That I was worthless, that it was my fault there was no child. I threw myself into estate management to prove to him I was not worthless, at least. But he was not impressed with those skills. They only served to remind him of his own inadequacies.' He could not sire a child; he could not run an estate. But he could shoot a buck dead at over forty yards with a bow and could shoot the centre out of a target at seventy-five. He immersed himself in his successes, hunting, shooting, riding. He defined himself as an outdoorsman. 'As long as he had plenty of money to spend on horses, guns and hunting parties, he was quite content to forget he had a wife.' And she'd been quite content to forget she had a husband. Each other were only reminders of their failures.

'I am sorry for that,' Hailsham said softly. 'As you noted, marriage can be so much more. Even if it is not a romantic venture, it can be a pleasant, shared venture in which two people build something mutually together—a home, a family, a legacy.'

'I do not know if he ever loved me, if he ever wanted those things *with* me or just for himself.' Olivia held her glass out for Logan to fill. 'I think he must have for a little while, at least. Otherwise, I can't imagine why he would have married me at all. He was a duke's heir, and he was young. He could have married anyone. Why choose a girl with nothing but an old prestigious name? I had no money, no dowry. Nothing that added value to marrying me.' Never had she voiced such a thought out loud until now. But he had secrets to hide, perhaps one of them the reality of his own virility. A naive girl would not know better, would believe what she was told, would be the scapegoat for his failings.

'I will have to think on that,' Hailsham sighed. 'I am sorry, though, that my cousin treated you poorly. You did not deserve that.'

She drained her wineglass. 'You've known me for two days. Are you sure?' Perhaps she did deserve it. She'd sold herself and her conscience on the auction block of her family's security. Perhaps such consequences were the prices to pay. Perhaps this was exactly what she deserved.

He gave her a half smile, looking disarming in the lamplight. 'Strangely enough, I am. I can well imagine my cousin's rage over not getting something he wanted.' His smile widened and she felt herself relax further in his company. He leaned forward, eyes suggesting he was about to impart a confidence of his own. 'I visited here once as a child. Adolphus and I argued over some toys in the nursery, and he punched me until he got his way even though I was only four and he was six.'

'That's terrible!' she exclaimed, but she believed it. Adolphus had hit her once, toward the end, after a particularly disappointing night, as if he could force her to become pregnant by dint of his physical strength, as if not conceiving was something she was choosing to do simply to thwart him.

Hailsham nodded his head solemnly. 'It *was* terrible. It set the tone for our relationship for the rest of our lives. I steered clear of him after that. Even as adults, I didn't seek him out in London for any extended contact. We met once a year to discuss the estate since I was heir. Neither of us thought I'd actually inherit. We'd have a drink or two but that was all.'

Because I am not like him, was the unspoken message. *I am the very opposite. I am rational, responsible. I am not a romantic.*

She didn't suppose he was. Perhaps he was a hedonist, though. With his love of the tactile, the way he touched wineglasses, the way he touched *her*, said he was no innocent to the pursuit of pleasure. He simply didn't attach emotion to it. Sex would be for physical pleasure, for procreation, an act, nothing more. It would not be an emotional expression of feeling. Perhaps he had the right of it. Perhaps she'd hoped for too much there. Adolphus's betrayal would have hurt less if she had.

He tipped up the bottle and offered her the last splash. 'Shall I open another?'

'No, it's late. I should go up.' Her thoughts had wandered too far already. Who knew what confessions she'd be making halfway through a second bottle. She hopped off the tall stool, wobbling a little on her feet. He was there to steady her.

'This was nice, just the two of us talking.' His hand dropped to her back as he guided her up the steps. Did he know how lovely the warmth of his touch felt? How long she'd been without any touch at all let alone touch that wasn't…forceful? That wasn't designed to exert authority over her? She wouldn't think of that now. Adolphus was gone. There would be no more of that. Tonight had been nice indeed. Hailsham was an attentive listener. Women would find that attractive. Too many men didn't listen, really listen. She had the sense he understood far more than what was said.

His voice was low at her ear as he held the door for her leading out into the hall. 'I do want for us to be friends, Olivia. Perhaps we might start with you calling me Logan? I admit to feeling 'between' titles, not quite Hailsham nor Darlington at the moment. Logan seems the best option. Would you do me that favour, just when we're together, perhaps, if that makes you more comfortable?'

She ought not agree to it. But what harm could it do? Surely, no more harm than drinking wine in the dark with him, she dressed only in her nightgown. There'd be no one to hear just as tonight there'd been no one to see.

'I would ask one more favour, if I could?' He halted before the study door. 'Tomorrow I will go out and meet the tenants. I would like you to come, perhaps ease the way for me and for them with introductions.'

'I'd be happy to,' she agreed, feeling a little light-headed as she made her way up the stairs to her chambers. Tonight had been a truce of sorts, she thought sleepily. They had not sparred. They'd talked, and all because she'd been willing to open her gates, just a bit. It had felt good to share with someone things she'd not dared to share with anyone else. In truth, it felt good to have someone to share with at all. There'd been no one at Darlington whom she could have shared with. She certainly could not have shared any of this with

Adolphus's mother. She would not have believed her. She would have put the blame back on her. That woman never could conceive of anything wrong with her son. Perhaps the best thing about tonight was that she didn't feel quite so alone.

Then why do you hold back? Why didn't you tell him about the ledger? the voice in her head prompted just as she drifted off to sleep.

She jolted awake. The journal! The basket! The basket was still down there sitting on the table, the journal tucked beneath the linen towels at the bottom. There'd been no time to hide it before he'd found her. She'd only had time to pile a few bottles on top to make her lie believable.

What a cool liar she'd become. She didn't want to lie, especially not to Logan. He was not a man who tolerated dishonesty. He would feel betrayed and while he might not be given to the uncontrollable, unchanneled rage of Adolphus, he would be given to cold, calculated revenge, something far worse. But it wasn't only the fear of revenge that made her not want to lie to him. It was the man himself. She didn't want to lie to *him*.

Be careful, her inner self warned. *He's a*

rake, a seducer, he knows how to charm. You heard his line tonight; I would never leave you alone. Because he wants something from you. He wants to shake loose everything you know. Perhaps even now he suspects you're holding back. Tonight you did not satisfy his appetite for information; you only whetted it. If the marriage was troubled, what else might lie beneath the surface?

He was already probing those depths with his question about why Adolphus had married her. She recalled his remark this afternoon, *Unless there's something more you know?*

Logan had not missed the mark. She *did* know more than she'd shared. She knew about the ledger. She knew that Adolphus had sent it to her before the trip to Hampstead Heath. She knew that only real concern over the ledger being discovered in his possession would prompt him to send it to her, a woman he'd chosen to ignore for four years. He'd wanted to get that ledger as far from himself as possible and so he had by sending it to the person he associated with the least. Adolphus had been hiding something he didn't want found. She yawned, sleep and wine catching up with her again, as she thought drowsily; *maybe I will tell him about the ledger, once I am more certain of him, once I can trust him. It would be good to have an ally, especially if there was trouble.* Even if the trouble was all in her head, it would still be good to have an ally if he had green eyes and warm hands that touched like sin itself.

She was tired, so tired of being alone. She'd been alone, not just for the month since Adolphus's death, but long before that. For years. She needed to be careful here. She was more vulnerable than she'd thought if a few glasses of wine in the dark was enough to start eroding the barricades she'd placed around her heart. She'd vowed not to be swept off her feet again, when the time came; not to be overwhelmed by the excitement of a heady courtship. She'd prepared for a barrage. She'd not prepared for a siege—a slow, steady erosion of her defences.

A siege would definitely be the viscount's strategy of choice—a deliberate, methodical dismantling of her resistance. Not because he wanted to bed her, necessarily, but because he wanted to know what she knew. He wanted access to the depths of her.

She'd already given up ground there, persuaded by his offers of partnership; helping with the books, accompanying him to visit the tenants. He'd so easily found what appealed to her, what was important to her, and capitalised on it. He'd married that with little intimacies: his hand at her back, the request she use his Christian name, stealthily conflating business with pleasure. And now here she was, lying in bed thinking about him and giving him what he wanted—her secrets, even though she didn't even know them herself. Logan Maddox drew her like a magnet, a very dangerous magnet. She should not find him even remotely attractive for any reason, yet she did.

Chapter Eight

He should absolutely not be attracted to his cousin's widow. But Logan had been attracted to women long enough to know the signs: cataloguing the little details of her, knowing her scent, her gestures, watching her face, acquiring an awareness of when she was near, wanting her near, wanting to know her, to mine her until he knew her inside and out.

Those signs were definitely in evidence, he thought, as they jogged along in the gig on their way down to the village to meet his tenants. Last night had been heady down in the cellar, not all of it owing to the wine. Watching her in the lamplight, how the light caressed her face, caught the gold in her braid where it lay over a breast, had been intoxicating. Talking with her had been even more so. What a woman she was when she let down her guard long enough to let someone in, and what a bastard his cousin had been. He had no reason to doubt that what she'd shared was true. The spoiled child Adolphus had been had grown into a spoiled man. His blood had boiled at the thought of Adolphus laying a hand on her.

It was still boiling when they'd parted. He'd stayed up, his mind too roused for sleep as it parsed through what her carefully worded sentences had left out: his cousin had not shown her a lover's reverence. He had rutted on her, nothing more, sex being simply a tool for procreation, another attempt at proving his all-important manhood. It was always about Adolphus, the bloody fool, and the woman beside him on the bench seat had borne the price of that self-centredness.

Even in the morning light, without the enchantment of midnight and wine, that one thought raised the hackles of Logan's need to protect those around him. He'd been there for his mother when his father had passed; he'd done his best to stand in as that father for Rahnald who was five years younger than he. He'd not done a good job there, perhaps coddling his brother, being too quick to rescue him, only to see in hindsight that what Rahnald needed in those formative years was to learn how to solve his own problems.

He slid Olivia a look as he drove. She was quiet this morning, dressed in a black carriage ensemble, the cuffs and collar of her coat trimmed in soft black rabbit fur to keep out the winter cold. She had a muff to match in which her hands were deeply buried. She managed to somehow look both demurely appropriate to the occasion of mourning while also appearing fashionable. Her gold-blond hair was tucked beneath a simple drawn bonnet of black velvet with a matching satin ribbon, the brim of the hat wide enough to keep him from seeing her face. She looked lovely but he much preferred her dressed in white as she'd been last night in her nightgown. He preferred her hair down in a braid instead of hidden away.

'Did you sleep well last night?' he asked as the village came into view, mostly to redirect his thoughts. It wouldn't do to meet his tenants with thoughts of their duchess on his mind.

'Yes, did you? Sometimes it can be difficult to sleep when one is in a new place.' She was very circumspect this morning. He wondered if it was because she regretted or was embarrassed over what she'd shared last night. He hoped not. He'd enjoyed their frank talk. And regret meant she did not yet trust him, and if there was any embarrassment to be had, it should be on his cousin's behalf, not hers.

'Tell me again about the villagers. Remind me of their names and the shops they run,' he said, more to put her at ease, to show her that nothing had changed between them because of last night, than of his need. He'd been over the rolls and had committed the names to memory after they'd been over it the first time.

You pity her. It's not heartstrings that are being plucked, he told himself. *It's that she's in an unenviable position after having come from an even more unenviable position. You want to protect her, that's all. Protection is one thing; love is another. Don't confuse the two.*

'And Mr Beane runs the bakery. Well, it's more like he bakes and his wife runs the bakery.' She cocked her head, allowing him a glimpse of her face from beneath the brim of her bonnet. 'Have you heard a word I've said?' It was the first smile she'd given him since they'd left the house.

'Yes, Mrs Beane runs the bakery,' he laughed, turning the gig onto High Street. He let his gaze take in the neatly kept storefronts with their brick facades and white bow windows. The street itself was paved with cobblestones. A well-fed man with a wide white apron about his girth stepped outside a shop to wipe a smudge from a windowpane. 'The village looks prosperous,' Logan commented to Olivia as he gave the man a nod. One could tell a lot about one's tenants based on how they kept their homes and businesses. People who were content had pride in their premises. There was plenty pride of ownership on display here. It was encouraging. Shopkeepers couldn't prosper without prosperous farmers who had money to spend in the shops.

The man waved back, recognition registering on his face when he saw Olivia. 'That's Mr Henson, the butcher.' Olivia leaned close to him. He caught a whiff of her lavender and vanilla soap. 'He's a terrible gossip. I bet he's sending an errand boy out the back door right now to spread the word the new duke is in town. We won't have a moment's privacy.'

'I hadn't expected we would,' he chuckled. 'The point of today is to meet them, after all.' Logan found a place to park the gig and motioned to a couple boys to come watch the horse. 'A penny for each of you, if you do a good job,' he told them. 'I'll be a while. Do you think you can handle that?' He patted the horse's neck and came around to help Olivia down to find she'd already got down on her own. 'You couldn't wait a few more seconds?' he teased her. 'What will people think of my manners?'

He offered her his arm and stepped out into the street. The villagers were on their best behaviour, allowing them to make an orderly progress, stopping at each store, chatting with the shopkeepers and meeting their families. Olivia made the introductions at each shop, joining the discussion briefly before slipping away to join the shopkeeper's wife and children. Logan found it took all of his attention to focus on the shopkeeper's conversation when his eyes wanted to wander to the stove where Olivia held court. What was she talking about? Children? Babies? Items of interest in the latest shipment?

The people liked her; that was clear to Logan. Faces lit up when she came through the shop doors. She seemed to know something specific and personal about each of them. At one shop she enquired about a teething child.

At another she asked after the shopkeeper's newly married daughter who'd recently moved away with her husband. *That* had brought out a letter the shopkeeper's wife proudly shared.

At times Logan found himself reaching for patience. He wasn't particularly interested in newlyweds and grandchildren he hadn't even met. But Olivia had patience in spades. She greeted each story with genuine interest, asking questions, offering suggestions or commiseration as needed. 'You are a saint,' he murmured at her ear as they left the dry goods store. 'I didn't think Mrs Simmons would ever stop about the grandchildren. When I heard there were six of them, and realised she meant to go through each of them in turn, I began to panic. It reminded me of my grandfather whenever he would say, 'Let me give you a little history on that. It all began with the Romans...' Then you knew you'd be there for a while.'

Olivia rewarded him with a laugh. 'Everyone has a story and they *need* to tell it. Telling requires listeners.' She gave him a little smile. 'I'm more than happy to listen. Everyone wants to be heard.' His mother would approve of such a sentiment. He approved of the sentiment; he just wasn't very good at it. Although he had been last night. Last night it had been easy to listen to her. She, too, whether she realised it or not, needed to tell her story. He was putting that story together piece by piece.

'As I said, you're a saint. Everyone wants to be heard, but not everyone wants to listen.'

She laughed. 'Nonetheless, you're doing very well for your first time. I think they like you.'

He chuckled at the compliment. 'I think they like you and are willing to tolerate me.'. But he did appreciate her words. It mattered to him that she thought he was doing well. He was acutely aware that she was handing over her work—the relationships she had cultivated—to him. He would be the caretaker of her efforts. The realisation sobered him. He wanted to ask her how she was holding up. He wanted to say, 'I know today must be difficult.' But he held back.

She will not want your pity.

They saved the inn for last: the White Stag, at the top of High Street. By the time they reached it, the townsfolk had gathered for a spontaneous party of sorts. Planks had been laid across barrels outside the inn to make impromptu tables, and full casks of ale were being tapped. 'To welcome you, my lord,' the innkeeper, a large, florid man by the name of Trask, greeted them as they approached. 'I hope you don't think it unseemly.' His gaze darted in Olivia's direction. 'We don't mean any disrespect to the former duke.'

Logan clapped the man on the shoulder in reassurance. 'None taken. My cousin is dead and it's a tragedy to be sure. There's been too much tragedy at Darlington of late. But that's no reason for us not to get to know one another over a pint of ale and that's all this is, just common courtesy between neighbours.'

The man beamed, relieved. 'That's how I saw it, my lord. Thank you.'

'That was very diplomatic. Nicely done,' Olivia complimented as a tankard was thrust into his hand. 'I think that's my cue to leave.'

It was the last exchange they had for the next two hours. As often happens with such events, the men and women gradually drifted into two groups. The women gathered together, admiring babies and swapping household receipts along with the village gossip while the men gathered around the kegs to discuss local politics and crops. It was not unlike visits he paid at his own estates, and he was quite used to the camaraderie of village men. But he found he missed having Olivia at his side. It had felt good to be with her. They'd been a team today, working together, and he dared to hope, building on the foundations they'd laid last night over wine.

He glanced in her direction where she sat with the women, someone's baby on her lap. She looked…happy. Content. A natural with the child. She should have children of her own. She should have a husband who valued her, a family of her own to love. The absence of a child had pained her; he'd heard it in her voice last night, not just the disappointment in not providing an heir, but the disappointment in not having a child to love.

She jiggled the baby and smiled at something the young mother said, listening intently. She looked over and he caught her eye. He raised his tankard in a subtle salute.

Everyone needs to tell their story.

That included her, although Logan suspected she didn't tell her story to many. He'd learned some of it but there was more to tell, more that she was hiding.

Olivia glanced away, her cheeks flushing from Logan's salute. It wasn't the salute so much that had her blushing; it was that he'd been watching her, making her the focus of his attentions. Logan… His Grace…had been a revelation today. He'd been commanding but not off-putting. The shopkeepers had warmed to him. She'd feared they wouldn't. They'd not cared for Adolphus, and Logan was another Maddox and an outsider to boot. But Logan had asked good questions and offered thoughtful input. Of course, he had experience. He did manage his own estates. But that didn't always work in one's favour. Whatever concerns she'd had about him valuing the Hailsham lands over Darlington's were effectively banked today. Logan Maddox might be a rake, but he was also a serious businessman when it came to land.

'His Grace is young and handsome,' one of the women said slyly. 'Is he planning to wed soon?'

'He has not shared his plans with me,' Olivia answered diplomatically. 'I am sure he'll wait until an appropriate amount of mourning for his cousin has passed before he pursues a wife.' But the thought of Logan married conjured provocative questions in her mind. What sort of wife would he take? What sort of woman would become the next duchess of Darlington? She pushed the thought away, refusing to let it hang a cloud over an otherwise enjoyable day. They'd been partners today. It was the kind of day she'd foolishly dreamed of when she'd first married Adolphus: the two of them in the village, meeting with villagers, discussing the town.

A dangerous seed took root in her mind. How different life would have been if she'd married Logan Maddox, if she'd met him first. Or even if she'd married a man like him, a man who took his responsibilities seriously, who wanted a partnership with his wife, who didn't run at the first sign of difficulty. That was a perilous fantasy and a path she could not let herself walk down. She would only disappoint herself. She was here to help Logan transition into his role as duke; she was here to see her family secure; she was here to see Adolphus's secrets safe. There was no room in those tasks for girlish daydreams. She was a widow now. Girlhood for her was long gone as were any hopes for a family of her own. She would be thirty-three when her youngest sister turned twenty-three. What man would want such an aged wife? Not a man who was looking to start a family.

She passed the baby back to its mother when Logan came to collect her, bowing to the ladies and saying it was time to return home. This time she let Logan help her into the gig as the villagers waved them off. Logan was in good spirits on the drive back, talking through all he'd learned that day. The baker was hoping to invest in a new oven that would allow him to bake more bread, and the butcher was hoping his nephew would come apprentice with him in the spring.

'I want to make sure the innkeeper is paid for his largesse today. I'll need to make a note to have him reimbursed. Perhaps he'd like to be repaid in part with some of our wine? What do you think?'

Our wine.

What do you think?

Such heady phrases to her ears. She would enjoy it while it lasted. It wouldn't always be *our wine*; it would eventually be his. She was about to answer when she saw his face change; his jaw tightened as they pulled into the drive at Darlington House. Through a window, she saw a maid lighting a lamp. 'What is it?'

'We have company.' He grimaced, nodding toward the horse being led away by a groom. 'It looks like my brother has arrived.'

Ah, the brother who had been a source of tension between Logan and his mother. 'I'll have Mrs Aldrich prepare a room, and tell Moresby to set an extra plate,' she soothed. 'It's no trouble.'

He cocked an eyebrow. 'My brother is always trouble.'

Chapter Nine

The trouble with Rahnald was that he was always charming, and dinner was no exception. Logan spent most of the meal with a forced smile on his face watching Rahnald tease his mother and flirt—yes, *flirt*—with Olivia as he told story after story from London, where he'd spent Christmas, flitting from party to party and making the most of his dark, troubadour-esque good looks. With those long, wild curls, all Rahnald was missing was a doublet and some hose, Logan thought uncharitably as Rahnald won a smile and a laugh from Olivia. He didn't like the idea of Rahnald stealing a smile from her, he thought rather possessively. Olivia was *his* responsibility. He was the one who'd drunk wine with her in the cellar, who had seen her in her nightgown, her hair in a braid.

It occurred to Logan as Rahnald shared yet another story from London that his brother might have by chance, seen Adolphus. There weren't so many folks in London that time of year; it *was* possible. It would be worth asking when they alone with the port. Logan added it to the growing list of questions he meant to pepper his brother with, among them: What are you doing here? What do you want? How long are you staying? Because Rahnald always wanted something: money, a favour, help getting out of a scrape, somewhere to lie low while a scandal blew over or a jealous husband cooled off.

'Rahnald, we are a family in mourning,' Logan reminded him after a particularly rowdy story. 'Perhaps such topics are not seemly.' His mother made a pout with her eyes, telling him without words he was being a spoilsport on purpose. Dammit, he hated that. He was thirty-five and his mother could still manage her sons with a single look.

Rahnald merely smiled and tossed his curls. 'Perhaps it is the perfect time for such stories because of that. We all need something to lift our spirits.' He leaned forward as if to tell the table a secret. 'If I were king, I would abolish the mourning traditions. They are ridiculous, entombing whole families for years on end.' He leaned back and tossed down the rest of his wine. 'Life is too short to wear black, I say.' He fixed his sea-green eyes on Olivia. 'You, Your Grace, should be in colours. If I were your dressmaker, I'd clothe you in ultramarine, that colour so favoured by Titian in his painting, Bacchus and Ariadne.' Logan stifled a groan. The way Rahnald was looking at her didn't suggest clothing but it's opposite. Not dressing but undressing.

Rahnald poured himself more wine and leaned in again, his eyes fixed on Olivia across from him. 'I had the good fortune to view the oil painting in a private collection when I was in Italy on my Grand Tour a few years back, courtesy of my dear brother.' Rahnald offered him a nod supposedly of gratitude as if gratitude had anything to do with it. They both knew why that Grand Tour had come about. It had nothing to do with Rahnald's desire to improve his education and everything to do with a pretty daughter of one of their tenant farmers. 'Splendid work, Titian. Such a master of colour.' Great. Rahnald had used the Grand Tour to improve his flirting repertoire. All that classical education wasted on seduction.

Rahnald took a swallow of his wine, his brow furrowing in dramatic contemplation. Logan rolled his eyes. Dear heavens, did he practise that look of impromptu consideration in the mirror to get it just right? More importantly, did Olivia see it as such or did she think it was real? Surely, she was smarter than that? 'Do you know the story of Bacchus and Ariadne, Your Grace?' A smile best reserved for private moments and *not* dinner tables curved on Rahnald's mouth. 'She's been abandoned by her lover, Theseus, on an island and Bacchus has come to her rescue. Bacchus is madly in love with her and offers to marry her. As part of his pledge, he promises her a crown of stars.' Rahnald raised his glass in a small salute as if to suggest the story was in some way analogous to Olivia's own situation. Was it? Did his brother fancy he was Bacchus in the story? Is that what he'd come for? To woo Olivia? Did Rahnald think she'd been left a wealthy widow? He would be disappointed when Logan informed him otherwise. His Bacchus-like ardour would cool quickly. It was time to clear the table. Logan arched a brow in his mother's direction, encouraging her to give the signal for her and Olivia to depart.

'Come, Your Grace.' The countess rose. 'The boys have so much to catch up on. I doubt we'll see them the rest of the evening.'

Olivia flashed him a look as she left. *Be nice* it said as if she guessed how this interview with his brother might go. He thought he also read a message of regret in those blue eyes, that perhaps she, like himself, had hoped the evening would end differently. Not with more wine drinking in the cellar, but maybe sitting before the fire in the library discussing the upcoming visit to the farms or ruminating further about the visits today and what might be done to expand the village.

'Here's to you, brother. Cheers.' Rahnald raised his glass of port after the ladies departed. 'You've landed a plum now.' He gave a sly smile. 'You lead the most charmed of lives. First the viscountcy and now the dukedom.'

Logan skewered Rahnald with a strong look and did not pick up his glass. He would not toast to anything nefarious. 'What is that supposed to mean?'

Rahnald adopted an expression of innocent

explanation as he waved his glass of port to indicate the whole room. 'All of this was never supposed to be yours except by the luckiest stroke of fate. You weren't the heir to either and yet fate has favoured you extraordinarily. Griffin dead from a fever that came out of the blue. Father gone. Then Adolphus without an heir.'

Logan held his brother's gaze. 'I do not call that lucky. I call it unfortunate. I would not wish any of them gone, certainly not Father or Griffin.' Although he did feel less friendly toward Adolphus after Olivia's confessions last night.

Rahnald raised a brow. 'And yet, here we are and you're His Grace of Darlington.'

Logan refused to be drawn down that path any further. Rahnald was a master of deflection and that was what he was doing now—focusing on Logan's situation instead of his own, a sure sign that something was afoot. 'Speaking of being here, Rahnald, what brings you to Darlington in the middle of winter? Travel is not easy on the roads.' And he'd come on horseback, without a carriage. Of course, Rahnald couldn't afford to keep a carriage in Town and probably couldn't afford to rent a private coach, either. He had to have wanted to come quite badly to brave the elements.

Rahnald sobered. 'Cannot I come and be with my family? As you pointed out at dinner, we *are* a family in mourning. We should be together at a time like this. Our cousin's passing is something of a shock.' He looked so sincere. 'And I thought you might need a hand?' He arched a brow in question, another sincere gesture of enquiry. 'You were certainly not planning on assuming the estates. This must have upended your schedule something fierce. I could help.' Then he added quickly, 'Maybe not with the estate business. I know I'm not up to your standards there, but perhaps with other business, like sorting through our cousin's papers and personal items.' He dropped his eyes. 'I am sorry I could not make the reading of the will. Did he leave me anything?' The last was asked offhandedly, designed in its phrasing not to be intrusive, but Logan had been dealing with Rahnald's strategies for years. Now they were getting somewhere. Was he looking for money?

'No, I am afraid not. Were you expecting something? I was unaware you and our cousin were that close?'

'I saw him more than you did in Town, is all.' He gave a shrug to indicate it was of no consequence. 'I suppose I was feeling suddenly nostalgic, wanting something to remember him by. After all, he was family. It's not important. Did he leave things in good order for you? Is our cousin by marriage well provided for? She's young and she'll want to start a new life when all this mourning is over.'

'Is that why you've come, Rahnald? To sniff after a wealthy widow?' Logan asked bluntly. Marrying money would be a long-term solution for Rahnald's chronic shortage of funds.

Rahnald's eyes widened in chagrin. 'That is insulting. How could you even think such a thing?'

'You were flirting with her at the table tonight. What was I *to* think, given your track record?'

Rahnald placed a hand on his chest in a show of exaggerated disbelief. 'My track record? What about *your* track record? If I'm a libertine, I've learned from the best. You who keeps a new mistress in Town every Season and never the same woman twice.' He shook his head. 'It galls me that Mother thinks you're reformed. Clearly, she knows nothing about last Season's opera singer.'

'*I* do not seduce grieving widows.' He was a rake, he was well aware of that, but he had rules and the women he engaged with had rules, too.

'*Seduce* is such a harsh word.' Rahnald shook his head. 'It implies something sordid, as if I wanted to lead her down an inadvisable path.' Yes, that was exactly what *seduce* meant, and yes, any path Rahnald was on was likely inadvisable, Logan thought. In terms of imparting a sense of responsibility to Rahnald, Logan had failed miserably. 'All I wanted to do tonight, brother, was make her laugh. Have you looked at her lately? That poor woman, young and alone, her husband suddenly taken from her. Who is there to comfort her? Her family has not come running to her side. She is surrounded only by her husband's extended family with whom she's had little to no contact. She needs a friend. She's desperate for one. If I can help by being that friend, then I will step into the breach. Her smile is payment enough for me.'

He was doing it a bit brown, even for Rahnald. Logan shot him a hard stare. 'Stay away from her. She's not what you think.'

The brothers locked gazes. 'Perhaps we should let her decide what suits. She is not your ward, Logan.' Challenge glinted in Rahnald's eyes. That was not exactly the chord Logan had wished to strike with him. He'd merely wanted to assert his authority, to let Rahnald know where the line was and not to cross it while he was a guest in this house. 'Or is she your inherited duchess?' Rahnald said with a burst of insight. 'Do you fancy her for yourself?' He sat back in his chair. 'I think you do, brother. The two of you came in together this evening, you'd been out driving, meeting tenants together. Everything was *we* and *us* and *our* when you talked about your day in the drawing room before supper.' He made a considering noise in his throat. 'Very good strategy, I think, giving her a taste of what life with you would be like. Something to tempt her with.'

'That is *not* what I did. It makes sense to have her come along. She knows everyone and I do not,' Logan barked, although his brother had not been entirely wrong. He simply hadn't done it with marriage in mind, but something else—building trust.

So that you could seduce her secrets from her.

But not with an intention to hurt her. That was where he and Rahnald differed. Rahnald used people for his own ends.

Rahnald looked dubious. 'Well, keep telling yourself that if it helps you sleep better. I saw how you looked at her tonight, and at me. In your eyes she was Miss Muffet and I was the spider that sat down beside her.' He chuckled. 'What she doesn't know is that the real spider is you.'

'All that education and the best you can do is resort to nursery rhymes?' Logan growled only to be met with a serene smile.

'I save my Titian for the ladies.' He held up his empty glass. 'Is this little interrogation by port over or should I have another glass?'

Logan poured a half glass. 'Did you see Cousin Adolphus in London?' His mother had been disappointed Rahnald had not come home to Hailsham for Christmas.

Rahnald smirked. 'I did. I saw him the day after Christmas Day. We went target shooting in Green's Park. It was cold. Our fingers nearly froze on the triggers.'

'How did he seem to you?'

'Fine. His usual self. He shot well. He had a new pistol he was trying out. We had a good time. We went drinking afterwards.' He gave a self-satisfied smile. 'Although I beat him. I'm the only one who's bested him in some time. I've been practising. Say, you and I should shoot while I'm here. We haven't shot together in ages. You were the one who taught me everything I know about guns.' How like Rahnald to challenge him one moment and then invite him to shoot the next as if no terse words had been exchanged.

'Who was he with? Did anyone go drinking with you?' Perhaps those same people might have gone out to the Hampstead house party.

'No, it was just us.' Rahnald gave a sad smile. Perhaps he'd not thought it would be the last time he saw his cousin alive. 'Why do you ask?'

Logan sighed. The long day was starting to wear on him. 'I just have a hard time believing an expert with firearms would be so clumsy as to shoot himself, and in the thigh of all places.'

So close to his groin, Logan thought silently, shifting in his seat uncomfortably.

Rahnald nodded and for once Logan felt in accord with his brother, and for once when Rahnald leaned forward it was with serious intent. 'Do you think it a suicide?' he asked quietly.

'Maybe. But there was no reason for it that I can tell. You say he wasn't depressed, and then there's the issue of that shot. Why shoot himself in the thigh? Gun suicides are usually to the head. It's instant.' Logan shut his eyes against such morbid recollections. He rubbed at his temples.

'Perhaps he shot himself in the thigh as a kind of self-flagellation over not having an heir, a type of penance,' Rahnald said quietly. 'Perhaps it was an act of self-emasculation in order to punish himself. One need not outwardly show depression.' Rahnald shook his head. 'I know it's a ghastly conjecture, but perhaps it was his fault they could not have a child.' He sighed.

'Yes, perhaps. It seems a bit dramatic, but one never knows what happens inside another's marriage. Not really,' Logan acceded but said nothing more, wanting to keep Olivia's confidences. Rahnald's thoughts certainly matched in their own way with what Olivia had told him last night; Adolphus raging over the lack of an heir, targeting her with his anger over his own impotence. And what a shock such impotence would have been for a man of Adolphus's extreme arrogance. 'Well, thank you for the insight. It's definitely something to consider.' Logan rose. 'It's been a long day. Can I see you up?'

Rahnald shook his head. 'No, I think I'd like to stay up a bit longer, perhaps walk about a little and stretch my legs. Good night, brother. I am glad to be here and I am here to help.'

'If you want to help, make it up to Mother for not coming home for Christmas.'

'I will,' Rahnald said solemnly. 'I have changed, Logan. You'll see.' Logan nodded, wishing he could believe it. Listening to Rahnald make such promises was like waiting for the other shoe to drop. One knew it would; it was just a question of when. And where. And how. Nothing was ever simple when Rahnald was involved.

Chapter Ten

Logan was still waiting for that shoe a week later as the calendar took them deep into February and he was finally to make his visit of the farms. The weather had conspired to keep them inside, which had served to set his nerves on edge. There'd been too much time for Rahnald to devote to entertaining Olivia, which his brother did assiduously when he wasn't exploring the house. Rahnald strolled the gallery with her, extolling the virtues of the English versus the Italian school in the afternoons and played two-handed whist with her in the evenings. It was hard to tell if Olivia was enjoying the attention, but every once in a while, she would laugh over cards and Logan had to resist the urge to shout at his brother, 'She has nothing, only a thousand pounds a year. She is broke.'

And to Olivia, 'He's a flirt. Once he knows you have no money, he'll drop you like a hot rock.'

But he did neither, because he had Olivia to himself when it mattered, like today: touring the farms, an activity that felt more like an escape from the confines of the house and Rahnald's pandering than a ducal obligation. Logan had enjoyed the day immensely even if they'd come home damp and muddy.

It was her company you enjoyed, the inner voice of honesty prompted as he turned the gig for home, unable to justify delaying their return any longer. *You could have seen the farms on your own; she'd briefed you well enough and you've been managing your own estate farms for years now.*

All true. He had not *needed* her company to the farms, but he had wanted it. That had surprised him. She had crept up on him. While he had been busy attempting to earn her trust, she'd been wiggling her way beneath his skin in much the same way he'd been hoping to get beneath hers. He refrained from thinking too much about what that might mean, although it was getting more difficult by the day to do that.

'You are a man of hidden talents,' Olivia

commented as they put the farms behind them, grey clouds threatening overhead. 'I never would have guessed you were an expert on crop rotation.' She was teasing but he sensed a probe beneath the joking.

'Why? Because I'm a man about town, a viscount with a certain reputation?' He slid her a smile as he guessed the direction of her thoughts. It was an assumption he was used to people making, and one he was happy to let them make. He did not need to be an open book for all to read, nor was just anyone entitled, in his opinion, to read that story. 'It's no more auspicious than you being Darlington's wine expert.' Yet, sitting beside her on the gig bench, he was cognizant that deep within him there *was* a need, an urge to be 'read' by her, to tell her his story, to show her he was more than the sum of Society page gossip—another need he was in no hurry to take out and examine too closely when it came to understanding his association with Olivia DeLacey Maddox.

She laughed. 'Fair enough, but in my case, I had help. I can't take credit for it all on my own. I had Moresby to coach me.'

'I had help, too,' he reminded her with a friendly chuckle. He liked teasing her. 'You didn't think I was born with an innate knowledge of farming, did you?' He sobered, remembering just how and why he was now conversant in agricultural practices. 'Like you, my education was something of a crash course and just as unexpected.' Thank goodness he'd been a fast learner. He'd not had long to learn before it was all suddenly dumped into his lap. He clucked to the horses, aware of the puzzled frown on Olivia's face. It was hardly fair of him to make such a cryptic remark and not explain it. 'I wasn't supposed to be the heir. I had a brother, Griffin, who was older than me by four years.' Perfect, wonderful Griffin, everything a viscount's heir should be. 'I worshipped him. He passed away the summer before he left for university.'

He felt Olivia's hand slip through his arm. 'What happened?' Her quiet tones hovered politely, nonintrusively, on the periphery of his memories, waiting to be invited in.

'An unexplained fever.' Logan shook his head against the remembrance. 'He and I had gone fishing that afternoon and swimming afterwards.' It had been hot that day, even in the shade. 'After supper Griffin didn't feel well, and by midnight he was burning up.' But only Griffin. Logan had felt fine but Griffin never recovered. 'Two days later he was gone.' Logan swallowed against the clogging in his throat whenever he thought of it. What kind of fever took a strapping seventeen-year-old out of the blue, without warning? It was a riddle he'd yet to solve, yet to find a reason for. 'I wonder to this day why it happened. Had he caught the fever from the swimming hole? From a bug bite in the water? Had there been something in the river? Perhaps there'd been a disease from one of the fish?' He'd racked his brain for days afterward, looking for reasons.

'Sometimes things just happen. We don't always get answers for them,' Olivia consoled. 'It might sound trite. In fact, I know it does, but it's true.'

'The thing is, Griff hadn't even wanted to go fishing. He was mooning about the squire's daughter and had wanted to walk to the village instead so he could walk her home from the vicarage after the ladies' meeting.' How differently things might have turned out if he'd let Griff go about his plans. 'But I pestered him into coming fishing with me.' Rahnald had been only eight that summer and Logan had deemed his younger brother too babyish to play with. He'd been desperate for his older brother's attentions. He'd missed Griffin, who'd been away at school, and who was going away again in the autumn. 'I often wonder if…'

'If it was somehow your fault? If you could have done something?' She filled in his unspoken thought.

He gave her a rueful smile. 'Yes, exactly that, although the doctors assured us there was no discernible cause.' She nodded and Logan realised she would know something about that kind of loss; perhaps even that kind of guilt. She'd lost a parent as well when she'd been young.

'I felt that way when my mother died. It was from childbed fever. There was nothing I could have done, but I felt there should have been. Perhaps if I'd gone for the doctor sooner, or if I had sat up with her at night longer, it would all somehow have gone differently, gone better, that she'd still be here.' She offered the story not for pity, but for commiseration, to be in the emotion of the moment with him. She offered more than the platitudes of the unknowledgeable. She offered the rare comfort of having walked that same path, too.

Logan didn't speak for a while, appreciating the permission to simply sit in the silence with the emotions that had been stirred. 'I still miss him. Griffin was one of my favourite people in the whole world. My father was the other and I lost him two years later.' He knew what it was to lose a parent, the aching, gaping hole it left in one's heart and the insatiable need to fill that hole, to prove oneself to the ghost of a beloved memory. 'It was too much, to be fifteen and in possession of a title, to take on the responsibility of a family. I outranked my mother in terms of legally recognised authority even though I relied on her guidance as I fumbled through the viscountcy, school and adolescence.' He gave a dry laugh at the last. 'Puberty, pimples and a peerage all at once. There should be a law against it.' The pressure of it had shaped him as he grew into it, had learned to cope with it and with the loss that had brought it all about. He was aware those lessons had turned him into a man who was determined to never experience such tragedy again and who had been, to date, successful in that regard.

He felt her gloved hand squeeze his arm. 'I'm sure you managed just fine. Your father taught you well. He would have been proud of you today.' Then she added, 'I was.' Surprisingly, those words mattered more. It mattered to him, he realised, that she was pleased. He was struck again, as he had been that day in the village, that this was her work, her efforts, that she was handing to him. It was not being handed over to him out of choice, but out of force. Capable or not, he was being allowed by the simple dint of being a male, to take her hard work from her. He'd not asked for it, but he would be worthy of it.

'I hope my father would be proud of at least how I've managed his estates, his title, his legacy. I don't pretend that he would always be proud of me, though,' Logan confessed. He turned the gig onto the road running up to Darlington. Soon, they'd be home and the magic of their outing would be gone. He'd have to share Olivia with everyone else, with Rahnald. 'My father never kept a mistress.' His father did not approve of keeping mistresses but for Logan it was the price of coping with loss.

'Ah, your father wouldn't approve of the raking. What a rare man he must have been.' Olivia arched a slim, pretty blond brow knowingly in his direction. 'Why do you do it, then?'

Of course, Olivia would ask. Their relationship was not based on easy questions. He'd asked difficult ones of her and now she was reciprocating in kind. 'It meets a need.' He slipped her a sideways stare, wondering if she would understand that need was more than mere physical satisfaction, that such satisfaction was merely an outward symptom. His mistresses fulfilled his need for comfort at a price he could afford. He left his mistresses; they didn't leave him; they didn't die. In his relationships with them, there were rules. Fate had no hold there, just the way he preferred it. He didn't want to lose anyone else he loved and the best way to ensure that was simply not *to* love. One could not lose what one did not have.

'You're a very complex man, Logan Maddox,' was all she said as the house came into view, the welcoming lights of evening shining through the windows although Logan had the distinct impression that he was already home and it wasn't a place but a person, someone he'd not known just a couple weeks ago. How was that possible?

What was he going to do about Olivia? Logan watched her over the edge of his newspaper that evening, the events of the day still warmly and deeply imprinted in his mind. She and Rahnald were playing yet another round of cards and tonight she was winning. Again. If Rahnald was 'letting' her win, she would not thank him for it. Did Rahnald not know her better?

You're being jealous.

Yes, he probably was. He'd been reluctant to bring her home today, to share her with his mother and Rahnald. He could not recall the last time he'd wanted a woman's company for any extended period. Usually, he spent a few hours with his mistress in the late afternoon before making the rounds of balls and routs, but never did he spend a night, and never did he have her accompany him on errands or did he ask for her opinion. A mistress might be a business associate, but she was *not* a partner. Nor did she expect to be. She understood her place and he understood her place in his life. But Olivia was not his mistress, nor his mother or a sister and because she was none of those, her place in his life was undefined. He liked order; he didn't like things or people that could not be classified. Hence the question: What to do about Olivia? How did he understand her place in his life?

His conscience nudged him. *You can classify her, you just don't want to. She is your cousin's widow. You can choose to make her off-limits.*

Or not. Rahnald did not see her as off-limits. The law didn't, either. It was seldom that the law and Rahnald were on the same side. Perhaps he would not have been tempted to such thoughts if he didn't know how unhappy her marriage had been; if she was truly a grieving widow. But something primal in him he couldn't explain or want to explain, needed her to know she deserved so much more than Adolphus had shown her, and he wanted to be the man who showed that to her.

But to what end? came the reminder. *She is not the sort of woman a man spends a few hours with and then leaves to go about his business. She is no man's mistress.*

Not that he was the one who needed that reminder. If anyone needed it, it was Rahnald, who had no compunction about taking what he wanted. Across the room at the card table set by the fire, Olivia laughed.

'You are growling, my son.' His mother's soft tones broke into his thoughts.

'He's letting her win.' He glanced over at his mother, who met his gaze above her embroidery hoop.

She frowned at him. 'Perhaps she is a good card player. You do her a disservice to doubt her skill. Don't you think she's capable of besting your brother?' She made a tsking sound. 'I thought you were more progressive than that. I thought your father and I raised our children better, to believe that a woman can be the equal of a man in any skill she sets her mind to.'

'It's not her skill I'm doubting. It's my brother's motives. He is letting her win.' Logan grimaced.

His mother rummaged through her embroidery bag for threads. 'Can you not accept that he's changed, that he's grown up at last? You grew out of your wilder tendencies. Why shouldn't he?'

He gave his mother a half smile. 'I think you might be biased by a mother's optimism, always willing to see the best in her children.'

His mother smiled. 'Perhaps the world would be a better place if everyone did that, if we all looked at each other and saw our best instead of our worst.' She selected a strand of red silk floss. 'I worry for you, Logan. You've become a cynic. You're not old enough for such negativity. Life is not a set of tasks to be checked off. At its best, it's messy and it's vibrant and it fills you up. It doesn't let you stay empty.'

'It steals your objectivity is what it does,' Logan countered. 'All that vibrancy, all that feeling, overwhelms one and blinds one to reality. It leaves one open to loss.' Loss was bad business, emotionally or financially. Loss hurt.

'Your father didn't think that, Logan.' She took out her little scissors and cut the floss. 'His great gift was finding the balance. I have hope that you will find that balance in time, too. I'd like you to live your life for something more than the estates.'

'Am I not the embodiment of a title? Now the embodiment of two titles?' This was an old discussion between him and his mother. His life was not his own. It belonged to Hailsham and to Darlington. Everything he did needed to put those entities first.

'There's a *woman* out there, Logan, who will love you for the man you are and not the titles you possess. But you have to look for her.'

He offered a placating smile. 'I'll go to London in the spring, Mother, and make a discreet but concerted effort.' Time was of the essence, mourning rituals be damned. Darlington was running out of males.

She shook her head. 'I don't think that woman will be found in London's ballrooms.'

Logan chuckled. 'Where do you think she is?' Knowing his mother, she had a list tucked into her embroidery bag. But to his surprise, she only shrugged.

'I don't know. I only know that the right woman can show up in the most unlikely of places. You just need to be open to her.'

From across the room, Rahnald laughed too loudly as if he wanted to draw everyone's attention. '*And* be open to your brother?' she asked. 'We're all the family each other has. It would be a shame to spend what time we have together in animosity.' Her eyes grew misty and Logan knew she was thinking of the overpopulated family graveyard at Hailsham. His father's grave, Griffin's grave and the four white crosses that belonged to the two brothers stillborn between him and Griffin, and the sisters who had died in infancy between him and Rahnald. It was no wonder his mother was soft on Rahnald. He'd been something of a miracle born after she'd given up hope of having another child.

Rahnald and Olivia came to join them, their card game finished. 'She's cleaned me out of pennies,' Rahnald announced and Olivia's colour was high. The bastard had been flattering her again.

You're worried that she liked it.

Yes, he was worried she'd liked it. Too much of liking it and Rahnald would turn her head. Away from him. Was he jealous? Perhaps. But neither would he compete with Rahnald and turn this into some kind of contest. Olivia would not appreciate being made an object of male competition.

'I think you're taking it easy on me.' Olivia laughed off the compliment. Well, that was something, Logan thought. She wasn't entirely oblivious to his brother's wiles.

His mother rose, gathering her embroidery. 'I think we should have an early spring picnic tomorrow. You boys can set up the shooting targets and show off your prowess while Olivia and I sit under lap robes next to a brazier.'

'It will likely rain.' Logan politely dismissed the idea.

'Nonsense. The rain will hold off,' his mother insisted.

'How do you know that?' Logan laughed. His mother was a font of never-ending optimism when it came to Rahnald, to love and even the English weather. Perhaps he'd been like her once, before he'd seen the error of his ways.

'Faith, my son,' then she added, 'and my joints have stopped aching.' She slipped her arm through Rahnald's. 'Escort your mother upstairs, young man. I'm going to need my rest. We have a big day planned.' Logan hoped for her sake the weather didn't disappoint her. She'd had enough disappointment.

And yet, her optimism persists...

It wasn't until after Rahnald and his mother left that Logan realised what she had done; she'd arranged for him and Olivia to be alone. Bless her. Olivia's last memories of the evening would not be of Rahnald and the card game, but of him and whatever he decided to do with the opportunity.

Logan busied himself helping Olivia pick up the cards. 'Are you enjoying my brother's company?' He wanted to kick himself. He was usually smoother than that, much smoother. The last thing he wanted was her thinking of Rahnald.

She smiled. 'He is fun.' She cocked her head, thoughtful for a moment. 'He makes me laugh. He reminds me I'm alive. I think that gets lost in the ritual of mourning. Perhaps his ideas about mourning aren't so radical after all.'

'Perhaps not,' Logan acceded. 'If it makes you happy, then I'm glad he's here.' That much was true. Her happiness had become important to him over the weeks he'd been here, if only because she'd endured so much unhappiness with his cousin.

'Does his being here truly not make you happy?' Olivia queried.

'Not unhappy.' Logan put the cards in the carved wood box that contained game pieces and set it on the console beside the decanter set. 'Worried.'

'How so?' Olivia settled in a chair before the fire, inviting him to come and sit, too.

'In the past he's had a habit of only showing up when he's in need.' Logan refused to take the opportunity to speak poorly of his brother by offering details, of which there were many.

He furrowed his brow. 'He hasn't needed any money for a long while, longer than usual for him.' That perplexed him. What had changed? Had Rahnald finally learned financial management? Had all those lectures finally borne fruit?

'Isn't that a good thing?' Olivia asked with a laugh.

'It should be, shouldn't it?' Logan offered her a smile. Perhaps his mother was right and he had become too much the cynic. Perhaps he should accept this current development at face value and not ruin it with worry.

'I would be relieved if my sisters and father stopped asking for money.'

That was interesting. Her family had been mentioned quite significantly in the will, but Olivia had yet to discuss them in any detail. 'Tell me,' he asked. Everyone had a story to tell, even her, or perhaps especially her. Another sign that he was indeed teetering on infatuation with her.

'I have three sisters.' She gave a self-conscious laugh and he had the suspicion that while she was used to listening to others talk about the personal aspects of their lives, she was not used to sharing such aspects about her own. 'Delia is seventeen and will be out next year, Emilia is fifteen and Lydia is twelve.'

Twelve. Logan thought about the condition of the will that discontinued the girls' finances if Olivia remarried before they'd all turned twenty-three or were married themselves. On the one hand, his cousin's offer to support the girls that long was quite generous. On the other hand, it was a social death sentence to Olivia herself. Olivia would be almost as old as he was now by the time Lydia's funding ran out. That seemed more than unfair to Olivia; it seemed downright cruel. It stole her chance of a marriage, of a family.

He thought of how right she'd looked with a baby on her lap. Adolphus was holding her youth hostage with her sisters as ransom. Why would his cousin do that to her? Punishment? It didn't seem out of the question. Revenge? To control beyond the grave what he'd not controlled in life?

Unless she married a man who'd be willing to take those finances on. She would need a man of extreme means.

'Would you like your sisters to come for a visit?' Why hadn't he thought of that before? Perhaps having them here would ease her transition, and family visiting didn't break any mourning rules. He was just congratulating himself on his inspired idea when she shook her head.

'No, but thank you. It's a kind idea. I love my sisters but sometimes they wear on me. They have rather idealised ideas about life.' She grimaced. 'My father has spoiled them and they don't always appreciate my efforts to un-spoil them. I think it's a lesson they might have to learn for themselves. I just hope it won't be too hard.'

Logan nodded. 'I admire your discipline in that regard. It's my greatest regret with Rahn-ald. I was too soft-handed. He was young when my father died, and I confused pity with love. I let him get away with all sorts of things. I felt sorry for him and I kept cleaning up his messes instead of making him take responsi-bility for them. And now I am still doing that. If I'm frustrated with his inability to grow up, it's my own fault.'

'You were young, too. What does an ado-lescent boy know of being a parent?' She of-fered the question as absolution, holding his gaze with hers, letting him see the tenderness in her eyes as she searched for that adolescent boy in his. On the mantel the clock chimed, breaking the moment, the spell.

Half past midnight. They'd talked for an hour. It felt like minutes. Logan shifted in his chair and rose. 'We should go up. Thank you for the chat. You're a good listener.'

'So are you.' She smiled and Logan felt as if she'd bestowed a great treasure on him. After two weeks of watching his brother dance attendance on her, he'd take it.

Chapter Eleven

The countess's joints were right. The rain had stopped and a winter picnic was underway on the south lawn. Perhaps excited over the prospect of something new to turn their attentions to, the servants had outdone themselves. Olivia had awakened to discover the footmen had laid down impromptu planked flooring to mitigate the waterlogged grass and erected a canopy with curtains drawn on three sides to keep out the cold. Old items from the attics had been brought down to furnish the pavilion: mismatched chairs stored away, a faded carpet that wouldn't be the worse for the mud, a scratched table and a coal brazier to warm the space. The maids had been busy, too, laying out baskets of food on the table: trays of sandwiches, a bowl of oranges, jugs of hot tea and warm, mulled wine. There were desserts galore to tempt any sweet tooth. Cook's carefully iced petits fours, lemon squares, raspberry jam tarts and a tower of chocolate truffles.

'Such luxury!' Olivia exclaimed when she saw it all. 'It's the perfect little camp.' She took a deep breath of the fresh, rain-scented air. It might be February, and there might be grey clouds overhead, but it felt good to be able to be out of the house, to be out of doors. She stopped one of the maids returning to the house. 'Tell Cook it looks delicious. Tell everyone thank you for their efforts.'

'They are happy to make such efforts for you.' The countess joined her. 'As I've noted before, they care for you.'

'As I care for them.' Olivia moved to the table to hide the rush of emotion brought on by the words. It would be hard to leave here, to not have the running of the house. Perhaps she was doing herself no favours by lingering. Perhaps she should move to the dower house sooner rather than later. Maybe lingering was making leaving worse. She began to assemble a plate, starting with the chocolates first. Today she'd eat chocolate whenever she felt like it, even if it wasn't quite noon yet.

'Transitions are always hard, even when we've been raised to expect them,' the countess said kindly, filling her own plate. 'I may not have been as young as you when I lost my husband, but I have been through it, and the transitions that follow. I am here to listen if you want to talk about it, and even here to advise if you wish it.' She gave a little laugh. 'My sons are not so keen on my advice.'

'Thank you. You are generous, my lady.' Olivia offered a smile of gratitude and took a seat, balancing her plate on her knees. She liked Logan's mother. Her own mother had died when Lydia was born and she missed the idea of having maternal guidance through life. A girl never really grew out of needing a mother: to see her through adolescence, to usher her through the intricacies of a Season and into a good match, to see her through pregnancies and children. How might her own choices have been different if she'd had feminine guidance?

The countess took the chair next to her and put a gentle hand on her knee. 'Women must stick together, my dear.'

'Safety in numbers?' Olivia laughed, her

eyes drifting to Logan as he stepped beneath the canopy.

'No, power.' She winked covertly at Olivia and smiled harmlessly at her son.

'I don't know if I like the idea of the two of you collaborating together,' Logan teased. He looked good today, different, although he wore his usual dark colours. There was nothing new about him but he looked relaxed, or was it simply that she was looking at him afresh, after yesterday's discussions? It was a good look for him. A dangerous look for her. He was no longer merely an attractive man to be handled with caution but a multifaceted human being with thoughts and feelings that ran deep. She could care for a man like that. A man like that would be hard to dismiss.

Rahnald sauntered into their little camp, curls askew in a rakish tousle, carrying a case at his side, a wide smile on his face. 'This is cosy.' He swept her and his mother a bow. 'Ladies.' He bowed in Logan's direction. 'Brother. Good morning or should I say good afternoon? Shall we shoot? I see the targets are set up.'

He set the case on the table and undid the latches. 'I've brought my guns.' He held one aloft. 'A cased pair of percussion pistols. Have you ever seen something so pretty?' He passed one to Logan for inspection.

'Bond?' Logan asked, letting out a low whistle. He glanced in her direction, including her in the conversation with his explanation. 'William Bond's family are one of the best gunsmiths in London.'

Rahnald came to stand beside her, the other pistol in his hand, not willing to be outdone by his older brother. 'See the twist-sighted barrels, the engraved dolphin hammer.'

Olivia laughed and pushed the gun away. 'You might as well be speaking a foreign language to me. I don't know a thing about firearms, but you Maddox men know enough for all of us.' Adolphus had been a collector of firearms, sometimes travelling days to make an acquisition. He'd been an avid hunter and marksman. In the early days of their marriage, he'd hold forth on the merits of different guns, their firing mechanisms and other technologies for the duration of a meal. Later in their marriage he'd loved his guns more than he'd loved her.

Rahnald clapped Logan on the shoulder. 'C'mon, brother. Let's go shoot.'

'You have to forgive them their eccentricities.' The countess watched her sons go with a soft fondness in her eyes. 'The Maddox men have shooting in their blood. My husband was an excellent marksman, but Logan is even better than he was.' She nodded toward the targets where the men were counting their paces. 'Competition is in their blood, too. Just watch. It will start out friendly enough but give it a couple rounds and it will turn deadly serious. Rahnald can't stand to lose to Logan but as good as Rahnald is, Logan will always be better. Logan taught him everything he knows about shooting, but some things can't be taught.' She smiled proudly at her handsome sons as they sighted their first targets. 'Get ready to clap, Olivia. A man never gets too old for female approbation.'

It was quite possibly the best day she'd had in weeks, or months. The afternoon passed pleasantly, watching the men shoot targets at varying distances, sipping mulled wine and eating delectable chocolates while she laughed with the countess, who insisted on regaling her with stories of Logan—and Rahnald, but mostly Logan, she noticed—growing up.

'He was a precocious young boy and a rowdy youth, always up for a prank or an adventure, but kindhearted. A sweet boy, really. We would go for walks and he would reach up to take my hand and say, 'I love you, Mama.' Or he'd pick me daisies.' The countess smiled, remembering. Olivia could imagine that boy, the same boy who'd adored his older brother, the boy Logan had told her about yesterday. 'But his brother died and then his father, and it changed him.' It had. He'd tried to defend himself by exchanging loving relationships for business contracts with mistresses. *It fills a need for me*, he'd said. It had not taken much to figure out what that need was. A man like Logan would be desperate for control over a life that suddenly seemed to be out of control.

'He still loves me, I know he does, but he doesn't say the words anymore.' The countess's gaze was far away, seeing the past. 'Something in him broke when my husband died.' She bit off a length of thread. 'But I best mind my tongue or I'll be saying too much. Logan would not appreciate that.' No, he wouldn't, Olivia thought. Logan wanted to be in charge; it was his best weapon, his best chance of protecting those he loved: to stand between them and whatever monsters threatened.

He is extending that protection to you.

Was he? Or did he still see her as a problem to solve instead of a person? It would all be easier if it was the former. She had no room in her life for a relationship and neither did he. The only difference was that he'd decided there was no room by choice, and he'd made that decision long before he'd met her. For her, she simply couldn't choose otherwise. Adolphus's secrets, Adolphus's will, her family's circumstances, had all made the decision for her.

She let her gaze drift out to the targets. The two men were what seemed like miles away from the bull's-eyes. Logan turned sideways and extended his arm, presenting a lean silhouette. Her breath caught as his hand flexed around the butt of his pistol, his gesture unequivocally…sexy. It was not a thought worthy of a new widow, but she wasn't that newly widowed. She'd been widowed long before Adolphus had actually died.

Of course, she understood the attraction that seemed to flare when they were together these days. It was all about proximity, *enforced* proximity. They spent their days doing estate business together; they spent every day sharing a house, sharing meals, sharing the late hours of the evening engaging in personal conversation. All of that activity could not pass without effect. It was only natural to speculate. And yet, she did not speculate in the same way about Rahnald with whom she'd spent considerable time the past two weeks as well. Rahnald made every effort to engage her, he seemed to crave her attention and she gave it in a most neutral way, although she sensed he wouldn't mind if she was a little less neutral about it.

Out on the field Logan's shot found its mark. Rahnald's missed by a few inches but it seemed like feet compared to Logan's. Rahnald made a disgusted sound and the men walked toward the canopy, their shooting display done at last. 'That was very impressive,' Olivia complimented Logan quietly as the countess soothed Rahnald's disappointment with effusive praise. 'How do you do that? Hit targets at such a distance?'

'Shall I show you? Come on.' He put a hand at her back and ushered her toward the field, pistol in the other hand. She might have followed him anywhere just to feel his touch at her back, warm and commanding. Out on the field they took up a spot several feet from the target. He put the pistol in her hand and stood behind her, his body wrapped about her as his hands moved hers into position on the weapon. His mouth was at her ear as he murmured instructions like a seduction. 'Line up the target through the sight, just like so. Remember, the gun will recoil, or jerk in your hand after it fires. You have to hold on to it. The steadier you are, the truer your aim. Letting it have its way will send the bullet wild.' His finger closed over hers on the trigger. 'Ready, aim, steady now, fire.'

For a moment the gun was like a wild thing in her hand, but the force of Logan's grip kept it steady, and when she looked at the target, she saw a hole. 'We hit it,' she said with a sense of irrational pride.

'We did. Good job. Would you like to try again? This time on your own?' He reloaded the gun. 'For your next lesson, I'll teach you how to load it.'

He passed her the gun and stepped back. 'You can do it. Use two hands on the butt if you'd like.'

Olivia drew a deep breath and steadied her arm. The gun was heavier than Logan made it look. She didn't want to disappoint him. She felt compelled to be successful. She fired, her shot hitting the inner circle of the target, at least.

'Well done,' Logan praised. 'A few more lessons and you'll be an expert shot.' His praise warmed her. Since when had his words come to mean so much to her? A fat raindrop fell out of the sky and Rahnald called from the canopy that he was going to escort their mother back up to the house.

Logan raised his dark head to the sky, searching the clouds. 'Would you like to go back, too? Once the skies open up it may be a while before we can get back without being soaked.'

'Let's take our chances and stay a while longer.' She should not tempt fate by being down here alone with him but should-nots held little sway here.

Their little pavilion was warm from the heat of the brazier and well insulated by the thick curtains. Logan drew the last curtain across the entrance, and the space took on a new, intimate quality. 'It feels like a sultan's harem,' Olivia said, taking a seat on the low daybed that had been dragged out to act as a sofa of sorts and lined with pillows and blankets.

'Know a lot about harems, do you?' Logan

laughed and poured two mugs of the warm mulled wine. He brought one to her and sat down beside her instead of taking a separate seat.

'Only what I've read. But before you ask, I do read a lot. Books are good company.' Better company than Adolphus. Better company than being alone in the country. But she didn't add that; didn't want to change the mood. She liked this banter with him. It was different than the amusing flirtation of Rahnald. This seemed more natural, more sincere, although she knew better than to tempt herself with it. What did she think she was playing at? And yet, she couldn't seem to help herself. 'Tell me something about you. What do you enjoy besides shooting?' She smiled and he smiled back. This was bad, very bad. The only consolation she had was that it couldn't lead anywhere.

I enjoy you.

The words flared to life in his mind instantly at her prompt.

Tell me something about yourself, she'd said.

Did she have any idea how seductive he found those words coming from her lips?

This idea that *she* wanted to know him. What should he tell her? That he found her to be beautiful and strong; that she deserved a lover who would wipe away every trace of disappointment she suffered at his cousin's hands, that he could be that lover, that he *wanted* to be that lover? What would she say to that? Now was not the time or place to find out. 'I race carriages. Well, I don't do the actual racing but I run a carriage racing syndicate of what you might call 'professional' whips. We travel from location to location and sponsor races with local driving clubs.'

'Fascinating, and there's a market for that?' With a simple question and a tilt of her head in interest, she had him talking nonstop about the syndicate, about the annual race in Benson, about the last race of the season this past November in Wallingford.

'It sounds very exciting, and very dangerous,' Olivia said at last. She cocked her head and he felt the considering weight of her stare. 'Guns. Carriages. Do you like danger? Risk?'

'I'd never thought of it that way before.' Logan furrowed his brow at her insight. It was becoming unnerving how well she read him, especially when he considered himself a very closed book. 'Once upon a time, I might have said yes.' He gave her an endearing wry smile. 'As my mother has been fond of mentioning, to my extreme embarrassment, I had my wild days. But now my thrill is in the challenge of doing something, building something. Now, my friend Carrick, who helps me with the syndicate and runs the carriage works in Benson, *he* likes danger. At least he used to.' He wasn't sure what Carrick liked these days except his new wife. He was happy for Carrick, but he felt as if Carrick's marriage was another form of loss for himself. Carrick had moved on and Logan wasn't sure yet if their friendship would survive it; at least not in the shape it used to be.

'Used to?' she asked. 'He doesn't anymore?'

Logan shook his head. 'He's married now. Got married over Christmas, a quiet, quick affair. I stood up with him at his wedding.'

'Are you disappointed he's married?' she asked softly.

He thought for a moment. 'No, not really. I just miss him. It will be different now. I have to share him with his wife, with my racing syndicate.' He was quiet for a long pause, reflecting on why that was. 'We met in school and for a while there was just the two of us. We'd both lost our fathers at the same age. We formed a bond over that. We were both affected by that in similar ways. He was someone who could truly understand what I was going through.'

'I envy you that friendship. That sounds special indeed.' She murmured with a smile that was reflected in the depths of her eyes. The sincerity of it was too much and he looked away, glancing down to see that during the course of the conversation their hands had become intertwined although he could not recall having reached for hers. Had she been the one who'd reached for him?

He made no move to disentangle them. It felt good, to touch and be touched. He was always touching something, someone. But to *be* touched by someone else, that was a luxury to him, something he craved. It was what he paid his mistresses for—the pleasure of being touched. But there was nothing quite equal to the pleasure of unsolicited touch, to be touched as Olivia was touching him now with gentleness, with kindness and caring. His father had touched him like that whether it was a hand on the shoulder as they tromped through the woods at Hailsham, or a pat on the leg as his father gave him a riding lesson on his pony in the paddock.

Casual touch fell out of a man's life experience at far too young of an age. At school, touches became punches in the yard. Touch wasn't for affection anymore; it was designed to convey power, to tell others who was in charge. Even the way a man touched a woman in public was designed to communicate the same; a touch at the elbow to guide or a hand at the back to direct, but never just to say *I am aware of you; I am here beside you.* And heaven forbid a woman touched a man. Society had made it so that there was no reason to. She had no power to convey. She would never attempt to overstep herself and offer guidance to a man.

'I've lost you, Logan. Where have you gone?' she enquired softly. He let his eyes drift over her face, slow and intentional, his mood shifting to something less friendly and rather more...well, just *more.* What would she say if he told her what he was really thinking? Not of his friend, but of her, how she'd got under his skin in the past weeks, become a companion whose company he coveted, a presence he sought whenever he entered a room? How his fingers wanted to touch her, his tongue wanted to taste her, because taste was just another form of touch, after all. It must have shown in his eyes.

'Are you thinking of your friend?'

'No.' He brought his hand up to her cheek, letting his thumb caress the arch of her cheekbone. 'I'm thinking of you.' He leaned forward, his rakish instincts taking over. He let his mouth brush her ear with seductive words. 'Does that shock you?'

It did. He could feel her pulse hitch, saw her breath catch, heard a soft sigh escape her as his mouth captured hers. And then he was lost in her. She tasted of warm wine, spiced with nutmeg and cloves, a dash of cinnamon and the elusive undertone of citrus. She smelled of peace and felt like comfort. He was not so much lost in her as he was finding something he'd not known he was looking for. His hand was in her hair, tugging it loose, deepening the kiss, consuming her mouth, devouring her throat as she arched against his mouth, murmuring the most delightful sounds. He was hard and hungry and she was an easy feast for the senses. No. He drew back. He would not take advantage of her, no matter how much he ached, no matter how much she thought she wanted more. She was vulnerable and no match for him.

She looked at him with wide eyes. 'Why did you kiss me?' Her long fingers trailed unconsciously over her lips, tracing where his mouth had been.

'Because you deserve more.' More than what that lout of a husband had given her; more than what life had allowed her. She deserved passion, real, burning passion.

'Then why did you stop?'

'For the same reason.' And it had taken all his willpower to do it. Next time he might not be able to give her that choice, now that he knew how she felt beneath his fingers, beneath his mouth, how her breath caught when he touched her, how her tongue tasted against his, now that he knew how much he needed her. He'd started that kiss with the intention of giving her something *she* needed, but dear Lord, he'd got far more than he'd bargained for.

Chapter Twelve

❧❧❧❧❧

Dear heavens, she'd kissed the duke and it had been divine. No, not *it*, *him*. He had been divine. Now it was all she could think about, *had* been all she could think about since she'd come back to the house, dressed for supper, gone down to the drawing room and into dinner. How had she managed all that when she could remember none of it—not what had been served for the first course or the second, not how her maid had done her hair, or if she'd had sherry for her preprandial drink.

All she knew was that kiss. It had become the sum of her world, every aspect of it etched into her memory with the finest care for detail. And what details they were! Shocking in their intimacy. He'd touched her, tasted her, nipped her, caressed her, drank from her, all with his mouth, his fingertips, and she'd done the same of him. Never had she experienced such a kiss. She'd not known there *were* such kisses, kisses that obliterated reality and reason. Even now, hours later, looking at Logan at the head of the table was enough to conjure the feel of his hand at the back of her neck, his fingers in her hair. His touch had felt... Well, it had just *felt. She'd* felt. Alive. For the first time in years. At his touch she'd become a person again, not merely a disappointment or a duchess, not a vessel in which a seed had failed to grow or the embodiment of a title—a placeholder in Darlington history.

And then he'd stopped. *Because you deserve more.* She understood what he meant, both in his reasons for starting and for stopping the interlude on the daybed. He'd wanted to show her her worth, to show her what Adolphus had not, to show her she was a woman worthy of passion, of reverence. And she'd burned at the first stroke of that reverence. But to what end? They both knew the answer to that. There was no future in burning. Burning consumed and then it was over, leaving nothing but ash. He'd played the gentleman and she ought to thank him for it. Perhaps later—much later—she would. But for now, stopping had only fanned the flames of her curiosity. He'd shown her a glimpse of what could be, of what real passion tasted like, felt like. How could he *not* expect her to want more?

Moresby served the third course and she glanced to where Logan sat, groomed and immaculate in his dark evening clothes and onyx stick pin winking in the perfect folds of his neckcloth. He looked cool, calm. She envied him that calm. How did a person learn to separate themselves from such emotion, such passion, so that they could rejoin reality and appear unaffected? Unchanged? Was he indeed unaffected by the interlude? Lost for a moment only, as if he had not even been the least bit singed by what had occurred on the daybed; as if he'd not drunk from her lips like a man fresh from the desert; as if he'd not groaned his want against the tender flesh of her throat until they were both panting with it.

It is nothing but physical pleasure for him and he is a master of it, her inner voice warned gently. *Do not forget what he is. He gave you a gift today. Nothing more.*

His gaze moved in her direction as Moresby put the third course before them. A green flame burned in his eyes, there just for her, and she felt her skin heat with remembrance, with appreciation, with want, coming alive again. Was this how he teased his London women? Seducing them with a gaze at dinner parties? Keeping them on tenterhooks with a sweep of his eyes? Promising paradise with a secret look? A trill of desire travelled down her spine. *Was* he promising her more? Or was she, too, just another of his London women? A game with which to pass the time? She couldn't believe that. All those conversations: in the wine cellar, on their drives, late at night after the house retired, consulting her on the books. All of that couldn't possibly have been only for the sake of a game. Did it matter?

Those possibilities occupied her through the last course and into dessert. What would she do if her curiosity got its wish? Would she take the 'more' knowing full well it meant nothing and led nowhere? He could promise her an experience nonpareil and nothing beyond that whether it was a game or something more real. That was what made the offer in his eyes so tempting. She could have him once, without risk, without doing any harm to other promises she made, to secrets she'd promised to keep even from him. She *could* have him. He was offering himself to her and no one needed to know. What delicious madness this was. Her mouth was suddenly dry at the prospect of it all. She reached for her wineglass and found it empty.

'More wine, my dear?' Rahnald's offer sliced through her thoughts. He filled her glass and cut her a look. Did he suspect anything? He'd been staring between them all night. Had his lighthearted flirtation been intended to be taken more seriously? She feared she'd misread him, the poor lad. Well, he wasn't really a *lad*. He was older than she was, but he appeared as a boy beside Logan. Rahnald shot an unfriendly look in Logan's direction and she felt a moment's guilt. She did not want to be a source of conflict between the brothers. She'd not meant to encourage either of them. She was in mourning; she'd not meant to encourage *anything*. And yet, *something* had most definitely stirred between her and Logan today.

Not just today. That something had been simmering since the night they'd drunk wine together in the cellar; perhaps even before then. Perhaps it had been there, dormant, beneath the sparring and testing that had defined their earlier conversations; like subtly recognising like as they'd slowly, carefully, opened themselves to each other, discovering similarities like the tragedy of losing a parent young; a tragedy that had shaped them both, encouraged both of them to take on the enormous responsibility of caring for the family, a responsibility that required them both to set personal needs aside.

Such similar depths had not been what she'd expected to discover about the rakish viscount with a reputation as long as the trailing ivy that covered Darlington's west side. That discovery changed everything, especially how she saw him, how she felt about him, how she might come to feel about him.

She took her newly filled goblet from Rahnald and sipped. Oh, this was dangerous ground! If she had any sense at all she'd pack a bag and move to the dower house tonight. But any sense she possessed had been left on the daybed to die at the hands of a maestro, done to death by kisses and curiosity.

Dessert had barely been swallowed when Rahnald threw down his napkin on the table. 'I will excuse myself early. I have things to attend to.' He flashed his brother an angry glare and pushed back from the table to his mother's consternation.

The countess rose, the instinct to console and comfort in her eyes. 'Rahnald, what is it?'

Rahnald jerked his chin in Logan's direction. 'Why don't you ask him?' He departed. The countess threw Logan a long-suffering glance and hurried after him. Guilt nagged at Olivia. This was not what she wanted. Rahnald's tantrum reminded her just how dangerous it was to play with fire. More people got burned than just the person holding the match. She had to end it now before the flame between her and Logan got out of control. Better to nip all those fantasies in the bud before it was too late.

Too many people were counting on her not to lose her head at the first opportunity. Nothing could come of this except misery.

But first, before the misery there would be great pleasure.

And yet, was this not the same mistake she'd made with Adolphus? Hadn't he, too, offered great pleasure only to have it be an illusion? Perhaps such temptation ran in the Maddox family. *And perhaps, maybe this time it would be different*, her curious mind whispered defiantly.

She rose and Logan rose with her, something feral glinting in his eyes that was both exciting and perilous. 'I should go up. It's been a busy day.' She made a flimsy excuse.

Coward, her curiosity scolded. *If you're going to walk away from him at least give him the courtesy of an explanation.*

She grabbed at her courage before she lost it altogether. 'Perhaps I might have a word first, though, Logan?' What to tell him? That he was too dangerous, that she was too scared, that she feared he would be too much like his cousin? That she wanted him anyway.

He stepped close to her, reaching for her. 'You can have all the words you want, Olivia, after this.' He seized her then, dragging her against him, his mouth on hers, rough with want as he danced them backward to the wall, leaving a ragged kiss on her lips, his voice a rasp at her ear. 'I've wanted to do this all night. I envied every morsel of food that passed your lips, every swallow of wine on your tongue, minx.'

His words filled her like a heady elixir and just as intoxicating; to have this man in her thrall was potent indeed. She would not last long. Already she was burning for him. 'This cannot happen,' she cautioned with a gasp.

'Yes, it can, and it is, unless you tell me you don't want this.' He was all fire and flame, want naked in his eyes.

'I can't be a game to you, Logan. I don't know how to play such games.' They would break her. It would destroy her if her judgment failed her again. She'd have no excuses this time. This time she'd known better. She knew now what men were capable of and of what they were not.

'You are not a game, Olivia.' Logan's mouth was at her throat. 'I promise.' Oh, how she wanted to believe that.

Her head lolled back against the wall at the pleasure of his touch, a groan escaping her. She had to give this up. 'We can't.'

'Give me one reason why.' Logan's voice was a husk against her skin.

'Your brother.' She managed the words between rough kisses, giving as good as she got, her hands raking through Logan's hair.

Logan drew back. 'What does Rahnald have to do with this?'

'He knows,' she hissed. 'His feelings have

been hurt.' She was starting to care quite a bit less about those feelings and more about her own feelings at the moment.

'His feelings?' Logan chuckled, teasing her ear with his teeth. 'He's a flirt and a grown man, Liv. He'll get over it. It was nothing to him.' *Liv.* She'd treasure that.

'And to you? Is this nothing to you?' she queried, her hands digging into his shoulders, seeking something steady on which to anchor herself. She could not be another of his endless women.

'This can be whatever we make it.' He kissed her again, this time his pace slowing, the kiss deliberate. 'I want you. Do not doubt it.' It was a veiled invitation. He was leaving it up to her but he had her at a disadvantage. How did anyone say no to him when he had them up against a wall, the taste of him on their tongue? The touch of him on their skin? The promise of more in his eyes? 'Shall I come to you tonight?'

'Yes,' she whispered before she lost her nerve. Her heart was pounding with excitement, her body trembling with anticipation. By the time she made it to her room, her mind was a flurry of chaotic thoughts. This was madness, sheer insanity.

If she'd been in her right mind, she might have seen the signs sooner. As it was, her mind did not register the subtle clue something was amiss; her usually closed door was ajar, her maid nowhere in sight. Inside, her eyes took a moment to adjust to the shadows. Her breath caught. There was a man at her dressing table bent over her drawers. That was when she screamed. The man turned at the sound and she nearly dropped the lamp in her shock. This was no burglar.

The next moments were a blur. Logan's feet pounded on the stairs. He was beside her with admirable speed, concern on his face, quickly replaced by disbelief. 'What is going on here? Rahnald? What is this? What are you doing in her room?'

Rahnald gave a harsh laugh and strode forward, menace in his expression. 'What *is* going on here? That's what I would like to know. I thought the table was going to incinerate every time you looked at each other tonight. Then there was that little shooting display today. You were all over her. 'Put your hand here, wrap your hand here, watch out for the recoil. Let me show you how.' You practically had her ear in your mouth whispering your so-called instructions. How long has this been going on behind my back? Dammit, Logan. We're brothers and you *knew* I wanted her.'

'And I told you to stay away from her,' Logan growled as the brothers circled each other.

Olivia moved to step between them, shame and anger staining her hot cheeks. She did not want them fighting over her. She definitely did not want them fighting over her *in* her bedroom. She could just see it as headlines should anyone find out: *Brothers Brawl Over Duchess in her Bedroom!*

'Stop it, both of you. I am not some prize to be fought over and won.' But they sidestepped her, conveniently ignoring her request.

'You need to have everything, don't you? You have our cousin's dukedom and now you want his wife, too?' Rahnald raged, putting up his fists.

'How dare you cast aspersions on her honour. You insinuate too much.' Logan's fist jabbed but Rahnald darted beyond its reach.

'What is going on here?' This time it was the countess who asked, running into the room in her nightgown, a shawl about her shoulders. 'Olivia, dear, come away or you'll end up being the one with a black eye.' She tugged at Olivia's arm, dragging her out of the circle of influence. 'You boys should be ashamed of yourselves, fighting in a lady's bedchamber.'

Logan lowered his fists. 'Get out, Rahnald. There will be a room for you at the White Stag.'

Rahnald sneered. 'And I must do as I'm told because this isn't *my* house. I have no authority to countermand you because you control everything I have. How convenient for you that you must always be obeyed. Don't worry. I'll leave immediately. Have my things sent down if you want me gone so badly.' He shot a look in Olivia's direction as he stormed out. 'Take care of yourself, my dear. You do not know what you're surrounded by.'

'Logan, will you please reconsider? It's late. Perhaps we can sort through this in the morning,' the countess pleaded.

'No, I will not. He has offered not only myself but a woman under my protection grave insult in her home,' Logan said grimly. 'I will not tolerate his temper tantrums. He's a grown man.' Then he softened. 'Go to bed, Mother. We'll discuss it in the morning.'

The countess dismissed, he turned his attentions to her.

'Are you all right?' Logan pushed a hand through his hair.

'Yes, I was more startled than anything.' She moved to the dressing table, her nervous hands straightening the little bottles on top. Downstairs the front door slammed, announcing Rahnald's departure. Only then did she realise Rahnald had not answered the question. What had he been doing in her room? There were only two reasons someone crept into a lady's chamber: a rendezvous or he was looking for something. Had he come to lie in wait, upset about her and Logan? But he'd been looking through her dressing table, to kill time until she arrived, or had he been deliberately searching for something? But what? She'd never met Rahnald before this visit.

But he knew Adolphus. Hadn't Logan said Rahnald saw him in Town often? The ghost of Adolphus whispered: *Keep my secrets.*

She thought of the journal left below in the cellar. Her hands trembled, knocking a vial over as she tried to stand it up. Did Rahnald know of it? Had he come searching for it? Or flirting for it? Had he thought to claim it first through friendly means and when that had failed, he resorted to more nefarious stratagems? Then, when he'd been caught, he'd deflected with jealousy, playing the jilted suitor, the wounded brother.

Your imagination is too vivid; it's running away with you. Surely, Rahnald is no threat. He is nothing more than the jealous boy he seems.

Yet, Rahnald's words haunted her. Had he meant danger from Logan and his rakish ways? Or had he meant something more?

Logan's warm grip covered her hands. 'You're shaking. What is it? You're pale as if you've seen a ghost.' He wasn't off the mark.

She forced a smile. 'I was just thinking instead of you coming to me tonight, perhaps I should come to you.'

'Perhaps that's not the best idea given the circumstances.' Logan ran his thumbs in a soothing motion over her knuckles.

She shook her head. If she stayed in this room tonight, she would torture herself with scenarios, worrying over the journal: Had Rahnald come hunting it? Should she tell

Logan, or was she hunting ghosts of her own, seeing trouble where there was none? *Making* trouble? If she made any unjust accusations, she would only cause more difficulty between the brothers. 'I do not want to be alone tonight.' She wanted oblivion. She wanted to be safe from a past that held her prisoner. She could find both in his arms.

Logan held out his hand to her. 'Come with me, then. We can't stay here.'

Chapter Thirteen

Logan ushered her down the hall to his rooms, thankful that he had not yet taken up residence in the ducal suite, which adjoined her chambers. When he'd arrived, he'd been placed in a guest suite and it had been too much trouble to move once he'd unpacked. He'd also felt it was unseemly, an invasion of her privacy to move in next door. Now he was doubly glad he had not. He could not think of a worse place to practise pleasure than in his cousin's bed knowing the sort of memories it must hold for her. She would find nothing but ghosts there.

Inside his rooms, the door shut behind them, he directed her to a chair before the fire. He poured her a drink and pressed it into her hand as she sat. 'Sip this. It will help.' She was still pale, perhaps more shaken than the episode warranted. Still, it was likely to be unnerving to discover a trusted house guest discreetly ransacking one's dressing table. As an evening of lovemaking went, this one was veering in an unhopeful direction. It had started out well on the daybed, progressed rather spectacularly in the dining room, and now the bottom had fallen out of a very enjoyable day, thanks to Rahnald and his antics. Whatever had possessed his brother to lie in wait for her in her bedroom? Had he been looking for jewellery to steal? Was that how Rahnald was making his funds last these days? Perhaps women voluntarily gave up their jewellery but since Olivia was not inclined to give in to his flirtation and be cajoled out of hers, he'd resorted to thievery? Unfortunately, Logan couldn't put it past him.

Logan sat down in the chair opposite and stretched out his legs. 'Do you want to talk about it?'

She shot him a sharp look, her words sharper. 'Is that what we came here to do? To talk? I was under the impression we were going to do something else.' That something else was looking less likely from where he sat.

'You've had a fright. A man doesn't take advantage of a woman when her feelings are vulnerable. I'm a possessive lover, my dear. I don't like to share with anyone or anything. When I take you to bed, I want all of you—your body *and* your mind. I tolerate no wandering thoughts.' He took a sip from his tumbler before adding, 'Besides, I make it a habit not to seduce desperate women.'

Those words riled her. 'I am *not* desperate for a man.' Her blue eyes flashed. 'How dare you suggest such a thing when you know better.'

He cut her off. He did know better. Men had failed her—her father, her husband—the two men who should have protected her. 'I do not suggest your desperation stems from a want of men. Something else has made you desperate and it has upset you greatly, far more than my audacious brother importuning your dressing table should have.' She was a strong woman. She ran an estate, oversaw a dukedom, ran her family home from afar, had survived a disastrous marriage, had chosen obscurity in the countryside for the foreseeable future so that her sisters might have the futures they required.

She was not upset only because Rahnald

had snuck into her bedroom. There was something more at work. It was a maddening reminder that while they had made inroads in their friendship, he still did not have her trust entirely.

I cannot be a game to you.

Not even in seduction had he won her trust. Even in the throes of passion, she still had her doubts. For a man of his reputation, it was a lowering realisation. He'd not yet won her body or her mind.

'Do you know why he was there?' Logan asked the question gently in the darkness. Perhaps Rahnald had not been looking for jewels. Perhaps Rahnald had thought to plan a little seduction of his own. His interest in Olivia had been obvious since his arrival. But Rahnald was always interested in a pretty woman, and always obvious. It was hard to know when he was in earnest and when he was playing. Perhaps he should have told Rahnald the truth straightaway that first night, that Olivia had no money to speak of.

Olivia shook her head. Logan stared into the flames. 'Let me be indelicate for a moment.' So many of their conversations trended that way.

What did that say about the nature of their association? 'A man goes into a dark room not his own for very few reasons. Either to meet with someone clandestinely, or because he's looking for something. Since you were downstairs kissing me against the dining room wall, I'd prefer to think it wasn't because there was an arrangement.'

'You know there wasn't.'

'As I said, allow me to be indelicate as we ponder these current events,' he said with apology. 'That leaves us with the other option. Was he looking for something? Had he asked you for money or for jewellery while he was here?' He would expire of abject embarrassment if Rahnald was preying on lonely, destitute widows. But again, she shook her head. He tried a different question. 'Did you see anything missing from your dressing table tonight?'

'No.' She was being extraordinarily uncommunicative, and it did put him on alert. She wasn't even trying to help. Was she protecting herself? Protecting Rahnald? If so, for what reason?

'Perhaps you might take a moment tomorrow in the daylight to do an inventory and let me know?'

* * *

'I could do that.' She gave him a brief smile and sipped some brandy. He was being generous with her, she knew. Her answers had been unsatisfactory. He was trying to sort through what had happened, and he was counting on her to be his partner in this little mystery. She was not complying. She returned her gaze to the fire. It was easier to look at the nonjudgmental flames than to look at him. She was afraid she'd give something away and he would seize upon it. 'What will you do?'

'About Rahnald?' He shrugged. 'I suppose I'll ride down to the inn tomorrow and try to get answers out of him. If he has taken anything, I'll retrieve it for you.' He offered her a reassuring smile. If only it was that simple. Maybe it was. She liked Logan's theory that his brother was a petty thief, paying his way by stealing jewellery from besotted women. She would like that to be true very much. It would mean the journal was safe. It would mean no one had come looking for it yet. It would mean she didn't need to tell Logan about it.

That last bit was becoming trickier. The longer it went on, the harder it would be to tell him, and the more likely it would be that

Logan would feel betrayed. Just as there were things that should not be shared early in a relationship, there were things that could be shared too late and be just as damaging. She feared the journal might be one of those things. She preferred not to have to tell him at all.

Because he's kissed you? Do not confuse an affair with love or a relationship. He's promised you none of that because he can't and besides, you're not looking for those things because you can't have them without jeopardising your sisters, came the swift reminder.

Logan let out a long sigh. 'I am so incredibly sorry about this. I cannot apologise enough for my brother. I should not have allowed him to stay. I knew something like this would happen. It always does. He came into your house...'

'*Your* house,' she corrected. They both needed to get used to certain realities. None of this was hers anymore. 'Of course he came here. He's family. This is his home, too. You needn't apologise for him. As you noted earlier, he's a grown man. He is not your responsibility.' Perhaps he needed to hear that. There was a weariness in his voice that affirmed his words. This wasn't the first occasion. He'd been picking up the pieces for Rahnald for a long time. They had that in common, she supposed. She'd been picking up her family's pieces for a while, too. Only in her case she wasn't sweeping up the pieces as much as she was holding the pieces together. She knew firsthand what a wearying task that could be.

'Will your mother be all right?' she asked quietly, reaching out to put a comforting hand on his knee. Perhaps they should check on her. The woman had been distraught over her sons.

'She'll be disappointed. But she'll be fine. Deep down she knows what Rahnald is. Unlike me, though, she's endowed with an extraordinary sense of optimism. She believes people can change.' He gave a dry chuckle. 'Maybe they *can* change, but most don't choose to. People like themselves just the way they are, flaws and all.'

'Do you have flaws?' She couldn't help but ask. The evening's interruption had been dealt with as best it could be and now in the quiet dark of the room with only the fire to play chaperone, the mood of the daybed was returning. Where there was privacy, there was intimacy, a chance to explore one another through talk and perhaps something more.

'Hopeless causes,' he answered with a dry

laugh. He slanted her a look and a devastating smile.

'Does a cynic have such things?' She sat deeper in her chair, settling in for the duration. 'I would think not. You see Rahnald plain. You know he won't change. You said so yourself.'

'Ah, but that's where you're wrong.' He gave an elegant wave of his glass. 'I *do* see him plain. I *know* he won't change. He does not surprise me. And yet, I keep cleaning up his messes. That, my dear, is the very definition of a hopeless cause. My mother, on the other hand, keeps thinking he will mend his ways and *that* is what drives her continual investment in him.'

She crossed her legs and tucked them up beneath her, letting her gaze hold his. 'Either way, it sounds like love to me.'

Logan's eyes glittered. 'Love is for fools.'

'Spoken like someone who has been hurt.' By a boy who'd survived an accumulation of losses: a father, a beloved older brother, the abuse of his hospitality by a younger one. Why was it that the people one loved the most had the power to hurt them the most? She often felt that way about her sisters; yet one more thing she and Logan had in common.

'No, it's spoken like a man of *reason*,' he amended, laying out his argument. 'Seeking out hurt is not rational. If love hurts, it stands to logic only fools would seek it. A rational person would run from it as fast as he could.' Then he added. 'Or she?' He took another swallow. 'You once believed in love at first sight, but now?'

'I was infatuated. It is not the same thing, although it can look like it. No one tells you that growing up.' She sighed. 'I was attracted to what Adolphus could do for me and my family at a time when we needed that help desperately. But I never loved him. I wanted to. I tried to. It took me a while to understand the difference between loving him and loving what he offered.'

'And by then it was too late?' Logan postulated softly.

'Far too late. For both of us.' She gave him a rueful smile. There had been more than one tragedy in her marriage. She had suffered in obvious ways: an innocent's dreams of a Society marriage torn apart; the inability to conceive a child regardless of who was at fault for that; the additional inability to satisfy her husband and hold his attention, to keep him at home. She'd borne the brunt of her husband's disappointment: his absences, his black moods and once even the bruise of his hand. Adolphus had suffered, too. He had his own tragedies, things the marriage had not provided for him that he'd hoped for. Whatever those tragedies were, he'd borne them alone and in silence away from her until they'd killed him one way or another. She'd been denied much and she'd deserved better than what she'd got, but he had suffered, too, and she did grieve that even if she didn't grieve him. 'In answer to your question, I still believe in love. I still hope for love. I simply haven't found it yet.'

Logan rose and brought the decanter over to their chairs. He poured a bit more for each of them. 'May I ask a difficult question? Why do you suppose my cousin picked you, then, if love was not at the heart of it? I do not mean any insult by it.'

It was a question she often wished she'd asked herself sooner. 'I have an old and distinguished name. My father is an earl and despite my lack of a dowry, I was a diamond of the Season. Adolphus was a man who felt entitled to the best and I was the best.' She paused and smiled coyly. 'I don't mean any arrogance by it. He hadn't needed the money. He could choose a bride of his own preference to some degree, assuming the family and lineage were right. Mine was.' She'd been just so glad to find a man who would save her family she hadn't questioned the rest or noticed what was missing. She couldn't say that out loud or Logan would want to know what *the rest* was, although he might assume it was simply Adolphus's intimate performance issues.

Logan laughed. 'Plain speaking requires some tolerance, doesn't it?' He thought for a moment. 'So he chose you for your pretty face and your distinguished name. Fair enough. He wouldn't be the first man to wed for those reasons.' Guilt dug at her. It wasn't fair enough. There was more she could tell Logan but she was deliberately choosing not to. What seemed unfair in the moment was choosing to be loyal to a man who'd not loved her and deceiving a man who showed her consideration. She yawned, the late hour and the brandy starting to work their magic on her worried mind.

'Would you like to go back to your room?' Logan solicited on cue.

No, she would not. If she did, her mind

would come alive again. She'd get no sleep. No oblivion, no momentary escape. 'Do I have a choice?' He'd made it clear there would be no second act to follow the dining room tonight despite their hastily made plans.

'There is always a choice, Liv. You may sleep here. I will not importune you.' She did not think anything he did ever importuned a woman. 'Let me help you with your gown.' He decided for her, or was it that he'd simply read her decision in her face? He drew her up and turned her around, deft hands working the laces of her gown, his touch warm, competent, assuring…alluring, too, despite the lateness of the hour and the disappointments of the evening. Perhaps the allure was that his touch promised there'd be another time, a better time.

The bed was already prepared, the servants having pulled back the covers and passed a warming pan over the sheets. The pillow smelled pleasantly of him—bergamot and citrus as she slid in. She reached out a hand, taking his. 'Come join me.'

His eyes darkened and he hesitated. 'I thought we'd decided.'

'Come sleep beside me. I will not have you sleeping on the floor in your own room.' For a moment she thought he would refuse. Then he smiled and shrugged out of his jacket and waistcoat.

'My mother told me never argue with a lady.'

'She's very wise, your mother.' Olivia laughed. The bed took his weight, although she noted he did not undress further. He rolled toward her and tucked her into the curve of his body, an arm wrapped about her. She closed her eyes and savoured the luxury of being held. Had anyone truly held her? Just held her? His hand stroked idly up and down the length of her bare arm. At this rate she'd be asleep in minutes. But wasn't that what she'd came for? To find oblivion and safety in his arms? She'd just not expected to find it in this particular way.

'Liv,' his voice was thoughtful at her ear. 'I just had an idea. When you do your inventory tomorrow, check my cousin's room. It adjoins yours. I am wondering if Rahnald was in there, too.'

Olivia's eyes flew open in the dark. 'Why?'

He pressed a kiss to her ear. 'Just something he said when he first arrived. He'd asked if Adolphus had left him anything. He seemed to expect it and was disappointed when I said no. I wonder if he wasn't looking for jewellery. Maybe he was looking for a memento.'

Or a journal came the unwanted thought as sleep claimed her at last.

The journal wasn't there. Rahnald paced his cramped room at the White Stag Inn. Tonight had been the final straw; that and being caught, of course. He'd not planned on that. He'd thought he'd have more time, that his brother would linger in the dining room. Perhaps his perfect brother was losing his touch. As for himself, he might also be losing his touch. He'd spent two weeks searching the house and had nothing to show for it. He'd been so sure the journal would be here, that Adolphus would have kept it here if it wasn't on his person.

This all would have been so much easier if Logan hadn't decided to seduce the duchess. Rahnald had been hoping on a little flirtation to ease the way, to create a situation where he could ask intimate questions outright. She might have told him where the journal was, *if* she knew about it. He wasn't sure about that. Would Adolphus have confided in her?

There was no love lost between them, mostly because…well, because Adolphus didn't love her. But one could trust without love and perhaps he'd trusted her.

Rahnald leaned against the fireplace mantel, racking his brain. If it wasn't here, where was it? Darlington House in London? Had Adolphus had it with him the day they'd gone shooting? And if he hadn't found it? Who had? People were looking for the journal. He'd have to try again and he'd best be on the road early before Logan came looking for him. There was a bit of petty revenge in that. Logan would have to tell their mother he was gone. Mother would be disappointed; he did regret that. He didn't like disappointing her. But this wasn't really his fault. This was Logan's fault. Logan was the one who threw him out. Logan had overreacted, all for the sake of a woman he didn't mean to keep. He never kept any of them, not even that Italian opera singer the whole ton had been mad for.

That gave him pause. If the duchess knew about the journal, had she told Logan? Or was she keeping mum about it? Logan wouldn't like that. It would probably ruin their relationship. He chuckled. He'd like to ruin their relationship, or what passed for a relationship with Logan. It would almost be worth it to wait for Logan to show up and tell him all about the journal. But then Logan would want to know why he knew about it and why he cared.

Because that journal is my meal ticket for the rest of my life, dear brother. Those of us who don't have titles have to resort to other means to make our way.

Chapter Fourteen

It took a Herculean effort of will to even think
of leaving his warm bed *and* a warm Olivia
in order to make the trip to the village. A man
did not give up the best night's sleep he'd had
in years for just anything, and yet, that was
exactly what Logan needed to do. He groaned
and flung back the covers, hoping for a burst
of energy.

What he got instead was the drowsy temptation of Olivia's murmured words, 'Don't go.
Do you have to leave?' Her arm reached for
him and he allowed himself to be tugged back
under the covers, his hard-won progress in rising forgotten.

'Did you sleep well?' he murmured against
her hair.

'Brilliantly.' She sighed and scooted into the

curve of his body, her buttocks nestled against his groin as she drowsed. Did she have any idea how dangerous that was to his self-control? But sweet heavens, how he liked having her there. He liked it enough to endure the temptation of her as he passed another half hour in a delicious state of early-morning half-sleep. He could get used to waking up like this. The thought ought to scare him; maybe later it would.

He would pay for that morning idyll, though. Rahnald was gone when Logan arrived at the White Stag Inn later than expected. Fate was not smiling on him, Logan groused over a plate of Paddy Trask's 'morning hash.' Fate owed him a visit with Rahnald. But Fate had favoured the wrong brother, in his opinion.

'Is the hash not to your liking, Your Grace?' Paddy Trask looked up from wiping down a table, catching his grimace.

'It's not the hash that has me frowning. It's my elusive brother,' Logan confessed, making sure to shovel a huge bite of hash into his mouth to prove it. The hash *was* good; eggs and fried potatoes mixed together with pork sausage in the sausage's own drippings.

'Ah, he headed out early this morning before we even had breakfast started.'

'Did he say where he was going?' Logan enquired, taking a hot, healthy swallow of coffee. He'd headed out while Logan had been indulging himself in bed with Olivia in his arms.

'I think he mentioned London, but nothing specific.' Paddy Trask raised a bushy eyebrow. 'An awful time of year to be in London, or to be on the road at all. It's time to be curled up next to one's own fire, if you ask me. The former duke, your cousin, was a gallivanter, too, always off somewhere, anywhere but here.' He paused. 'Meaning no offence, Your Grace.'

'None taken, Trask.' Logan rose and placed some coins on the table. He agreed with Trask's sentiment completely. He'd like to be back in bed snuggled up with Olivia.

'You don't need to pay for that,' Trask sputtered. 'I haven't thanked you proper yet for sending the wine and such down in payment for the welcome party. It was most unexpected.'

'But not unwelcome, I hope?' Logan clapped the man on the shoulder. 'You're a man with a family to support. You can't be giving your goods away for free no matter how much you might wish to.'

The inn door opened, bringing a rush of cold air with it, and a man covered head to toe against the elements, a satchel slung across his body. 'Mail's here,' he called out, spilling a pile of letters on the bar. That got Logan's attention. Maybe Fate was smiling on him a little, if there was a letter from Hampstead Heath. Enough time had passed for one to arrive.

Logan strode forward. 'Is there anything for Darlington Hall? I am going that way.'

'Yes, sir, there is, right here. I appreciate it. It will save me a trip out there, although I'll miss a glimpse of the new duke.' The mail carrier grinned cheekily, passing Logan a letter. 'Wait, there's a couple more.'

Today wasn't his lucky day, Logan thought, scanning the letter. It was not the one he was hoping for. This one was for Olivia, perhaps from her sisters. The carrier passed him another and his pulse quickened. This was it. He tucked the letters inside his coat and prepared for the cold ride home. It had begun raining and he regretted not bringing the coach in hindsight, but at the time riding had been quicker than waiting to have the team harnessed and hitched. It was only a distance of two miles. Still, he was damp when he arrived home.

Olivia was in the breakfast room when he strode in. 'You're soaking!' she exclaimed, seeing him. 'Quick, Moresby, get His Grace a towel and something warm to drink.' She stripped him out of his wet greatcoat and sat him down in a chair near the fire. He let her fuss over him. It was rather novel, being fussed over instead of being the one doing the fussing. And scolded. Particularly the scolding part. 'If you catch a cold, it will be what you deserve. You should have taken the coach. What sort of fool goes out riding on such a morning?' She pulled a hassock up and sat before him.

'This sort of fool, apparently.' Logan accepted a hot drink from Moresby. 'I wanted to catch my brother. I thought I would be early enough.' He'd actually hoped to roust Rahnald out of bed. Rahnald was not known for early rising.

Something flashed in Olivia's eyes. 'And did you see him?'

'No, he was already gone. Much to my surprise and my chagrin.' He leaned forward, allowing Moresby to drape a blanket about his shoulders. He reached a hand to her cheek. 'I did not take leaving you lightly.'

She captured his hand and held it against her cheek. 'I missed you, too.' Something was bothering her. She seemed fragile. He was not used to seeing her that way. 'Did you look through your dressing table?'

'Yes. Nothing was missing.'

'And my cousin's room? Did it seem as if Rahnald had been in there, too?' This had been his brainstorm last night before he'd fallen asleep.

'Yes. Nothing was gone that I could tell, but someone had been looking through things. The picture on the wall over his safe was crooked.'

'Well, that doesn't help,' Logan sighed. 'I had hoped we might have some answers this morning.' He reached for his coat where Moresby had draped it. 'Perhaps we might have other answers on a different topic. The mail came while I was at the inn.' He smiled at her, hoping to relieve her of her anxiety. 'There's a letter from your sister and I have one from the coroner at Hampstead Heath.' He passed her one of the letters. 'What? Aren't you going to read it?'

'It's from Delia. She'll be complaining that

she's in mourning for the duke. She hates wearing black.' Olivia smiled and tucked the letter away. 'I'll read it later. I'm much more interested in what the Hampstead coroner has to say. Shall I give you a moment with it?'

'No, stay, please.' Logan ran his thumb under the seal and read the letter. It was not long, and it left him with more questions, but he understood the coroner may not have wanted to commit too many details to paper. The mails were more reliable than they were discreet, and that wasn't saying much. He passed the letter to Olivia. 'The coroner removed a thirty-six-calibre bullet from Adolphus's thigh. He says I am welcome to come and see it.'

She puckered her brow. 'What would seeing the bullet tell us?'

'I'm not sure seeing it tells us anything we don't already know from the letter, but this is an interesting development.' How much to tell her? He didn't want her to worry, and yet this was definitely a wrinkle. Perhaps she deserved to know. 'A thirty-six is American-made ammunition. It's most commonly used with an American-manufactured revolver put out by Colt and Paterson.' He paused, letting her take in the information before he added, 'Adolphus didn't own a Colt-Paterson. There isn't one listed in his gun collection.'

'No, he collected European firearms exclusively,' Olivia said absently. He could see her mind, the very moment it reached the same conclusion he had. 'If he had shot himself, the bullet would have come from one of his guns.'

Logan nodded slowly. 'It would seem so.' She sucked in a sharp breath and he was quick to caution her. 'There could be several explanations. Perhaps he was trying the weapon out. Perhaps he was considering a purchase. We don't know for certain that it means someone shot him. It only means we know the type of gun the bullet came from.' But neither did it mean that someone *hadn't* shot him. It left the door wide open for that theory instead of shutting it down. He'd rather hoped the coroner in Hampstead Heath would have been able to assure him Adolphus's death had been self-inflicted. The coroner could not give him that assurance. 'We don't know enough to conclude someone would shoot Adolphus.' Although, one did not need a reason for an accident. It was only an intentional shooting one needed a reason for. 'Perhaps someone at the party was careless.'

'And maybe it's something more,' Olivia whispered, pale.

She had to tell him. She could not in good conscience ignore what the coroner's letter pointed to. Logan's logic was solid but it was flawed. He had more angles, more 'what-ifs' to account for than she did because he didn't know as much as she did. She could eliminate some of his options because she knew better and she had to help him know better, too.

'Olivia, you don't know that.' Logan cautioned. 'Do not leap to assumptions.'

'I do not leap, Logan. I would prefer for Adolphus's death to be self-inflicted. Everything would be much simpler. But I know something and I've been holding on to it, hoping it wouldn't matter.' She rose from the hassock and paced before the fireplace. 'Before he went to Hampstead Heath, Adolphus sent me a package. It was a journal full of fictional names from literature, obviously aliases for something. I didn't know what to make of it.'

Logan's face went hard. She hoped it was in

thought and not in anger. 'Was there a note? Anything with it?'

'Yes, a short note. All it said was 'keep my secrets.''

'And where is this journal now?'

'In the wine cellar. I was hiding it the night you found me down there.' She winced. It was yet one more lie of withholding that she'd told him. How many would he tolerate before he decided he'd had enough of her? That he need not be responsible for her? That he would not protect her or her family when the secrets came to light.

'Then let's go get it,' Logan said tersely.

The journal was right where they'd left it, buried in the basket on the table from the night they'd drunk wine and talked. Logan lit a lamp as she took it out and opened it. 'Just names and dates.' She stepped back to give him time and space to study it.

His long fingers turned the pages, green eyes scanning the lists. At last, he closed the journal, his hand splayed on the cover, his head bowed for a long moment. 'If I had to make an educated guess, I would say Adolphus was part of a secret society, hence the aliases.' He sighed. 'The other guess is that he made up the names himself and assigned them to people he didn't want to list directly.' He shook his head. 'But that seems far too intellectual for my cousin. A lot of work. In either case, the list will only have meaning to those who constructed it.'

'A secret society?' Now that Logan had said it, it seemed obvious but not necessarily plausible. 'Why? Aren't those usually political or religious? It reminds me of the Knights Templar.' None of which suited Adolphus. He was neither political nor religious. And yet, there was no doubting he had secrets.

Logan put the journal back into the basket and covered it with the linen. 'A secret society could be for anything. For a hobby, a belief, a practice.'

She thought about that for a moment. 'Adolphus loved his guns, his shooting and his hunting. I don't know of anything he loved more that would have prompted him to be interested in a secret society.' But that didn't quite ring true, either. 'There are nonsecretive outlets for those activities, though. He has memberships at shooting clubs in London and hunt clubs.' She knew; she'd paid his membership bills. The amount he'd spent every year on membership fees for clubs would have put new roofs on an entire village.

Logan put the basket on his arm as they prepared to go back upstairs. 'Well, there's usually a reason the club is secret.' He looked suddenly a bit uncomfortable as they climbed the stairs. 'There's something that the club does that is, shall we say, 'outside of proper society'?'

'You mean illegal?' she said as they shut the wine cellar door behind them. 'Like poaching?' She was trying to imagine what sorts of illegal things a hunting club might get up to, and how it would be accomplished. Riding through forests on horseback and firing guns was hardly a discreet activity. One had to be discreet to be illegal, didn't they? Otherwise, they'd be caught. Easily and often.

'Illegal or illicit,' he said tersely.

'Illicit? You're trying to spare my feelings but I fear you may have to speak more plainly.' They did not return to the breakfast room but went instead into the estate office and closed the door.

'I will not say.' Logan was resolute. 'I would not bring you more hurt than you've already suffered, unnecessarily. Anything I say now would be speculation only and add to your worries perhaps without cause.' He took up the chair behind the desk, drew out a sheet of paper and began to write.

She took the chair opposite and sat quietly but rigidly, fixing him with a stare. 'Do not dismiss me, Logan. I am part of this discussion, this investigation and whatever decisions you are making now.'

Logan looked up from the paper. 'It is best you let me take things from here, Olivia. If it is nothing but a bunch of bored aristocrats with nothing more than an exclusive club, trying to make their lives a little more interesting by calling it 'secret' than that's it. But if it's more sordid than that, deeper than that, then it affects the whole dukedom and must be dealt with swiftly, which is something you are no longer poised to do. I will tell you if I learn anything.'

'I want to be part of it, Logan. I need to be. He was my husband, and what he's done, as you point out, affects us all. It happened on my watch.' She infused her voice with a quiet steel. 'Women have pride and guilt as much as a man.' She was suffering from that guilt now. She clasped her hands and drew a breath. 'Logan, there's more I haven't told you.'

Logan stilled, all of his attention patiently riveted on her, no condemnation in his gaze. Perhaps that would come later. 'Then you'd best tell me all of it now.' There was a warning in that. He would not tolerate any further withholding.

'When Adolphus proposed, he asked me to keep his secrets. At first, I thought it was romantic nonsense, the things a suitor says to appear dashing or mysterious, or even appealing. At worst, I thought there might be an illegitimate child sequestered on the estate. It seemed very gothic to me at the time, something one might read in a novel. Later, after I knew about his…um…performance issues, I thought perhaps that was the secret and it might have been one of them, at least. But then the journal arrived and I knew there was more. Bedroom issues harmed no one but the two of us. However, if I've kept dangerous, *illicit* secrets that have harmed others, then I've been complicit in evil. Then it is I who must make amends, not you.' She paused and drew a breath. 'I lie awake at night wondering what secrets I have helped to keep, Logan. What sins have I committed?'

'You were not his keeper, Olivia.' Logan's

eyes glittered with anger, not with her, she sensed, but for Adolphus and the situation he'd put them in. 'But because you're not, it would be best if we distanced you from the situation.' It would be easy enough to walk away from this mess, to turn it over to Logan as she'd turned over the journal. He was the duke now. He had legal authority, a title, power, to get to the bottom of this.

'I volunteered for the role, anyway, when I agreed.' She looked down at her hands, a thought coming to her. 'I wonder if Adolphus meant for me to keep the secrets from you most of all. As duke you can address them in ways I cannot. It makes his secrets, whatever they are, safe with me. I have no way to expose them or address them even if I wanted to. Even if I were appalled, I'd be powerless to do anything but keep them hidden away. Not so with you. Perhaps he feared that.'

'Then it is doubly unfair—' Logan met her eyes '—that he has put you in a position where you have no choice but to comply, and to ensure that is indeed the case, he has held your family hostage in exchange for that compliance. I am starting to understand the settlements from the will better. All that altruism toward your sisters seemed out of character for him. I see now what he was getting in return.' He eyed her sternly and she braced.

'I wish you had told me everything from the start.'

'One does not tell a stranger her husband was a lout who loved his guns more than he loved her, especially when that stranger is her husband's cousin. Both propriety and discretion counsel against it.' Yet, she'd told him other things, intimate things.

'And when that stranger is a man perhaps reticence is doubled?' Logan raised a brow.

'Trusting men has never really worked out for me,' she conceded. It may still not work out for her, because she was desperately tempted to trust this one, with her body, her secrets, her family's future, despite the lessons she'd learned, and despite understanding that nothing could come of this except heartbreak.

'You can trust this man.' Logan picked up his pen and resumed writing.

'What are you going to do?'

'I am going to London. It's the last place my cousin was before the house party, and then I'll drive out to Hampstead and visit with the coroner. I will keep you informed. Surrey is not so far from London that a letter can't travel quickly.'

'No need for a letter.' Olivia rose. Sometimes the best way to win an argument was to make a statement and then leave the room. 'I am coming with you. I'll send someone on ahead to alert the staff at Darlington House.'

Logan's dark brows went up but he did not protest. 'Send word to Hailsham House instead. We leave in the morning.' Their gazes locked over the desk. 'If you insist on coming, I want you on my territory.' The flame in Logan's green eyes sparked a little trill of fire that ran the length of her spine, warm, delicious and decadent.

On his territory for protection. For pleasure.

Chapter Fifteen

Every rose had its thorns. The more beautiful the rose, the pricklier those thorns were, and Olivia was a beautiful rose indeed. Logan hazarded a look across the wheel well at Olivia dozing with her head against the upholstered padding as the Maddox travelling coach made the journey to London.

Early on, he'd tried not to stare, tried to ration his glances for his own sanity. Did she have any idea what she did to him? He was just starting to understand what those things were: she stirred the protector in him in a way a weaker soul couldn't. He admired her strength, wanted to protect that strength. He did not want her strength, her loyalty, broken on the altar of Adolphus's vanity. Adolphus had already taken so much from her and now his fingers were grasping for more from beyond the grave.

He'd like to have a word or two with his cousin. It was too late for that now. But there had been a time when those words might have mattered. That particular piece of guilt had been eating at him since the night in the wine cellar. He could have spared her; he could have been present for the years of her marriage. She need not have been alone. Perhaps he could have stopped Adolphus from his barbaric behaviour toward her.

Instead, he'd avoided Adolphus, distanced himself from the dukedom for his own selfish preferences, thinking he would never come to regret that distance; never questioning why the duchess didn't come up to Town; why, despite the rumoured grand love match, she was never at her husband's side. It had been easy to believe it was because of mourning, and all the while she was suffering with no one to turn to.

You can't save them all. You had your concerns to look after; an estate to run, Rahnald to extricate from scrapes. Don't confuse guilt with jealousy simply because it's the easier cross to bear. Regret isn't a sin but covetous-

*ness is. Perhaps you simply wish you'd seen
her first?*

The voice in his head was brutal today. Seen
her first? What did that mean? Before Adolphus? Or before he'd packed away his belief
in love? Before the people he loved had left
him? Before he'd learned how dangerous love
could be, how hurtful? How it made one overlook another's faults to their own detriment?
Or before he'd become this man, the man who
raked through London, collecting and discarding mistresses with urbane elan, leaving his
money behind but not his heart; claiming pleasure without paying the price. Before he'd decided he would marry because it was practical
and nothing more. Oh, that man would have
been head over heels over this woman who
slept across from him.

But she hadn't been that woman back then,
the voice reminded him. *What draws you to
her now had not bloomed in her then. Face it;
it's simply too late for you. You don't believe
in love anymore. But she does. You can give
her much, but you cannot give her something
you don't believe in.*

She's not looking for that from me, he answered the voice defiantly. What was she look-

ing for from him? Or had he led her down
this dark walk of seduction because of what
he needed? When had this stopped being about
what he could give her and had become about
what she gave him? That was frightening indeed.

The scenery outside changed, becoming
more urban as they approached London. He
would have to wake her soon. Sleeping Beauty
was running out of time. They all were. Aside
from whatever mystery Adolphus had left behind, he had the dukedom to think about as
well. It was a gift to have the winter to slowly
slip into it, but spring would be here within
weeks, the Season looming.

When he next came to London it would be
as an eligible duke, taking up official residence
at Darlington House and looking to make a
discreet match that didn't offend the sensibil-
ities of mourning protocol while not leaving
the Darlington cradle unguarded. By this time
next year he'd be a married man and with luck,
a father-to-be. It would be two more items he
could check off his list of responsibilities. And
Olivia? Where would she be this time next
year? Coming out of mourning, tempting him
from the dower house? Or a princess locked in

her tower until the spell was broken when her youngest sister married.

Logan gave a self-deprecating chuckle. He was being fanciful today, thinking in children's tales. Hadn't he just chided Rahnald for such thoughts? Rahnald. That was something else to add to his current list of tasks; making amends with Rahnald while trying to figure out what he was hiding; what had prompted a little 'light larceny,' as Logan was coming to think of the episode.

'We're nearly there, sir. North Audley Street, coming up,' the coachman called down in preparation. Or perhaps warning. Logan leaned over and gently shook Olivia's knee. 'Wake up, we're there.'

Hailsham House stood at number eight, four columned and pristine white, storeys tall. The knocker was even on the door, along with a mourning wreath. The staff had worked fast, especially given that he'd not been in residence since August. He'd spent the autumn and Christmas at the family seat. He made a mental note to show his appreciation, perhaps with a small bonus for their timely accommodations despite his surprise arrival.

He handed Olivia down from the coach.

'Welcome to Hailsham House.' Did she understand why he'd brought her here? Here, she could be safe. If someone was indeed looking for the journal, they would go to Darlington House and if she was there, it would put her in their path. He wanted to be discreet as long as possible, and if there was need for it, he wanted her to be safe and removed from the situation for as long as possible.

'You've shown me your housekeeper, now I'll show you mine,' he teased at her ear as the front door opened on cue. 'And my butler,' he added, nodding to Ayles, who stood with stiff correctness at the door.

'Welcome home, Your Grace.' Ayles bowed.

Logan handed Ayles his hat. 'Thank you, Ayles, and thank you for being ready on short notice.' He glanced in the housekeeper's direction to include her. 'Make sure the staff knows I am appreciative, as is Her Grace. Ayles, and Mrs Dondridge, this is Her Grace of Darlington. She will be staying here while we settle some estate business but we will not be receiving due to mourning. Mrs Dondridge, perhaps you could show Her Grace to her chambers so that she can refresh herself and please defer to her on any housekeeping decisions that need to be made during our stay.'

Olivia threw him a querying look that said, 'And what will you being doing?'

'I will see you later, Your Grace.' He offered Olivia a bow. 'I have some business to take care of before the day ends and I'll need to make a stop at my club,' he explained in the most benign terms possible as he made his escape back into the coach. There would probably be a price to pay for leaving her so abruptly after their arrival. Still, he'd allowed her to come to London. That was as far as he'd let her go. He wasn't about to let her come along asking questions until he was certain it was safe to do so—as in, he was certain Adolphus's secrets weren't dangerous or damaging.

He was not sure that would be the case, though. Logan leaned back against the seat and closed his eyes, permitting himself a moment's rest for the short journey to Darlington House. Olivia was in safe hands for the time being. His staff was loyal. Thank goodness for that. He did not like how this was shaping up. He'd done his best to spare Olivia the details but secret societies were dangerous entities, often engaging in risky, debauching activities that if Society knew about them, the members would suffer. He knew, too, just how alluring such risk could be to a particular type of man—a man looking for excitement, something to put an edge on the routine that became a gentleman's life. He'd been such a gentleman once. He knew the risk gentlemen sought came from simply belonging to such clubs as much as it came from participating in the clubs' activities.

There'd been legendary secret clubs in the past. The Hellfire clubs, the Order of the Second Circle, Wharton's Club, the Order of the Friars of St Francis of Wycombe, the list went on; all of them with two particular characteristics: they performed vulgar, oftentimes dangerous, rituals that were nothing more than dares they posited for one another in the form of ceremony, and their roll lists were secret. Even after more than a hundred years, no one was quite sure who had been a member of Wharton's Club beyond a few of Wharton's close friends. He and Adolphus, like other schoolboys who were gentlemen in training, had been raised on stories in the dark about the infamous Wharton Club, stories told by the older boys at school. It was one of the tamer rites of passage at school.

After a hundred years, did anyone care who those members had been? What was the expiration date on secrets before they stopped their haunting? Did anyone really care that Wharton's Club had eaten 'holy ghost pie,' named the devil president and admitted both men and women? Of course, in the short run, the club had cost Wharton his political career. The Dashwood Club had been more dangerous, though. Those members had all taken on aliases, he recalled. Biblical names all written in a book. Perhaps that was where Adolphus's club had got the idea for their literary names. Aliases certainly wouldn't have been Adolphus's idea. He wasn't much of a reader.

Aliases might not have been Adolphus's idea, but Adolphus had come to hold the power, come to see the possibilities for the journal. That was more concerning to Logan than his cousin's membership in a secret club. If Adolphus had the book, it stood to reason that Adolphus was a leader of some sort in the group, perhaps a recording secretary or perhaps even the current president. He who held the book held all proof of secrets. He could expose anyone at any time.

But not without exposing himself.

Still, Logan did wonder if Adolphus had thought to blackmail someone. Blackmail had a way of bringing out drastic behaviour. If so, that person would be desperate to recover the journal. Desperate enough to shoot a duke over it? Perhaps, if he was also a peer. He might think the secrecy of the club would keep him safe, and if not, his title would. If that was the case, he didn't want Olivia anywhere near a desperate peer with a gun who had already fired it once.

'Darlington House, Your Grace,' the coachman called down and Logan steadied himself before exiting the coach. It took some getting used to, realising he was Darlington, just as it had taken some time getting used to being Hailsham all those years ago. He would get used to this role, too.

Logan stepped down and straightened his coat, running through his list of objectives. He wanted to search his cousin's rooms and he wanted to interview the staff, particularly the valet who'd been given the bequest. He approached the steps leading up to the door with a certain reverence reserved for the dead. After all, this was the last place his cousin had been seen alive by anyone connected to the family.

Did he think he could hide her away and then carry on? Did he really think she would allow it? Olivia fumed as she unpacked her trunk. The maid had offered to help but Olivia had needed something to do, some way to vent her anger. He'd dismissed her! Handed her off to the housekeeper and simply walked out the door to take care of business that couldn't wait. She knew very well what that business was. He was off looking for clues about the potential of a secret society, for clues about Adolphus's last days.

She shoved a stack of undergarments into a bureau drawer. Did he think this was what kisses bought him? The right to decide for her? The right to exclude her? Only he wouldn't call it exclusion, would he? He'd call it protection. But she knew better. At the bottom of her trunk she came across the journal. She hated the sight of it, of all it might represent and all the worry it already represented. She looked about the room, finding no decent spot to stash it. She and Logan could discuss where to hide it later. For now, the bureau drawer beneath her nightgowns would have to do. And it would do. There was no reason to think it wouldn't be safe there. The staff was unaware of the situation, no one knew she was in Town and Logan had made it clear they would receive no callers.

'Your Grace.' The maid entered the room, looking unsure of herself. 'There's a caller.'

'His Grace made it clear we are not receiving,' Olivia reminded the girl politely. She must be new to the staff. 'Send whoever it is away.' Sweet heavens, they'd been here barely two hours.

The girl swallowed, clearly debating her options. 'Begging your pardon, Your Grace, it's that the caller is His Grace's brother and he says he'll wait.'

A finger of fear curled in her gut as her original suspicions rose once again. This was what it meant to live with secrets—always worrying, always wondering who was hunting them. Even now her mind was a riot of questions: How did Rahnald know they were in Town? What did he want? Was he indeed after the journal and that was why he'd come to try again? 'I'll be right down. He didn't bring any luggage with him, did he?' It occurred to her that it might not be as nefarious as she was making it out. Rahnald might be just as surprised to find them in residence as she was to find him calling. Perhaps he'd thought to stay here and then shown up to find that his brother was already in residence? Would he ask to stay anyway given the recent bad blood between them? She hoped not. She'd rather not have Rahnald staying under her roof and having another chance to get into her drawers again.

'Shall I have tea sent up?' the maid asked.

'No.' She did not want to encourage Rahnald to stay.

Downstairs she found Rahnald in a small parlour at the front of the house, probably a room used by the countess to receive personal callers. It was a cosy room and an informal one. He was fingering a shepherdess statue on the mantel. 'I'm not sure those will fetch very much,' she said coolly. She remained standing, not wanting to give Rahnald the impression that she had time to waste on a visit.

Rahnald turned with an easy laugh as if she'd not insulted him. 'They're Meissen. German. They're valuable if one's a collector. My father would get my mother a new figurine for her birthday every year.' He seemed very familiar with the inventory of the house. He gave her a winsome grin. 'You're shutting me out, Olivia, and rightly so. I've behaved beastly and I've come to apologise.'

'Your brother went down to the inn to see you the next morning but you were gone. He is not currently at home. You'll have to come back at another time.' She gestured toward the door but Rahnald gave no indication he'd understood the dismissal.

'That's all right. I've come to see you. It's you I wanted to apologise to, and I thought we might talk a little? We had such interesting conversations at Darlington.' He made it sound like more than two days had passed since she'd caught him in her bedroom.

'I am not receiving. I am seeing you now to tell you that in person since you did not respect the staff when they told you the same.' She refused to let Rahnald see how nervous he made her. If he *was* here for the journal, her nerves would confirm his own suspicions that she knew of it or even worse, that she had it in her possession. He would not stop stalking her, then.

'Will you not let me explain? Or has my

brother already poisoned you against me? I thought you were a free thinker, someone who thought for themselves. I made a mistake, Olivia. I wanted something of Adolphus's and I should have just asked for it instead of thinking to take it. I was hurt that he'd not left me anything.' Rahnald did contrition very well. No wonder the countess forgave him repeatedly. 'Perhaps I was jealous, too. Logan has everything, even you.' He gave a little smile. 'I was just striking out against him, and you, perhaps. It was foolish and immature. Grief can make fools of us all.' She did not like what he was insinuating beneath his handsome smile. Those insinuations struck too close to home to her own thoughts when it came to the feelings Logan raised in her.

'I hope Logan is not abusing your, um, hospitality?' He had gone back to fingering the Meissen. 'He will abuse it, though. Give him time. He can't help himself. He doesn't know how to love, not really.' Rahnald slid her a sly look from beneath his curls. 'He knows how to protect, how to be responsible, how to clean up messes, but he doesn't know how to love, not for the long-term. All his mistresses say the same thing. He burns, hot and intense, and such flame is not sustainable. It simply burns itself out. It saves him from developing real feelings he has to be accountable for.' He put the shepherdess down. 'If you're determined to be in bed with him, you should know.'

'I do not care for your crass allusion and I would like you to leave.' She would call for Ayles if Rahnald didn't acquiesce and hope that Ayles wouldn't have a conflict of loyalties over throwing Rahnald out.

'Perhaps I will come back at a better time.' Rahnald made her a small bow and to her relief showed himself out in a small display of temper, meant to demonstrate he was aware he'd been ejected from his own family home. Her former suspicion rose. Was he hunting the journal? Had he been looking for it? Was that why he'd come to Darlington Hall in the first place? Or was all this merely coincidence and her paranoid mind was connecting the two? On the other hand, if he *was* hunting the journal, it was proof that the journal did indeed mean something, that others might hunt it, too. It might be proof, as well, that something nefarious had happened at the men's weekend, and that Logan's fears about the debauchery associated with a secret society weren't unfounded.

It also sparked other worries—Logan was out and about in London alone. What if someone knew he was looking, knew he was here, and didn't want him to find answers? That was too much. She tried to rein her thoughts in; there was no basis for those conclusions. Certainly it was possible, as Logan would point out. But then again, it was *possible* to walk to Scotland; it didn't mean it was probable.

Chapter Sixteen

Such logic and a bottle of decent red wine kept her company for dinner, but only the wine seemed to be capable of offering any comfort. Whenever she reasoned away one fear, another took its place. Olivia pushed her plate away, the rabbit pie half-eaten, and poured another glass of wine. It wasn't on par with Darlington's red, but it would do. With luck it might drown the latest fear that sprang full blown throughout her lonely meal: that Logan was out in London alone, asking questions that might get him noticed by the wrong people. If there really was something insidious going on, whoever may have shot Adolphus might try and shoot Logan.

She took a healthy swallow of the red to drown the notion that he would die before they… Well, just before. She looked at the clock in the dining room. It was nearly nine. She'd held dinner and sat down late, hoping Logan would make it in time to join her. Where was he? He'd been gone for over five hours. Damn him for leaving her here to deal with Rahnald, and for not sending word about where he was. Perhaps he didn't want her to know.

Perhaps he's with his latest mistress? Perhaps all this worrying is for nought, and he's tucked up with a woman off Piccadilly in a modest apartment.

No. She would not countenance such thoughts. They were what Rahnald wanted her to believe. He'd been cruel to suggest it. If he'd been with Adolphus in Town for any length of time over the years, he'd known exactly how that would play with her mind; how she doubted herself; how she'd already failed to hold one husband's attentions.

Damn Rahnald, too, she thought uncharitably. If it hadn't been for his interruption a couple nights ago, the evening would have carried on to the logical conclusion begun on the daybed in the pavilion at Darlington. Had that only been two days ago? The world had been a slightly safer place then, and far less complicated. Rahnald had only been a tease. Logan had not known about the journal. There'd been no letter from the Hampstead coroner with its conjecture about a second shooter and an American gun, implying that Adolphus had not shot himself accidently or otherwise.

There'd only been a bubbling attraction between her and Logan, the delicious, teasing kisses on the daybed, and the rather explosive invitation of more up against the dining room wall; an invitation she'd accepted only to have it torn away from her. A footman stepped forward to clear her plate. 'I think I'll just take my wine and go up,' she replied when he asked if there was anything else she'd like. She took the glass and the bottle; neither had much left in them. Had she really drunk that much wine? Maybe. She had been at the table for almost two hours.

She tripped once going up the stairs and said an unladylike word. She was not feeling very ladylike at the moment. She was worried for Logan out alone and regretting the interruption two nights ago mightily against those worries. What if something happened to him? What if they'd missed their chance? She'd missed so many chances already: a chance at love; a chance at a family of her own. She'd played the good girl, married where her father wanted and look where it had got her. Now all she wanted was… Logan, even if just for a short time. Last night lying in his arms had been exquisite. She had felt safe, cared for.

In her room she let the maid brush out her hair and help her into a nightgown, her ears straining for the sound of Logan's boots in the hall. She was not going to bed, she vowed, not until she knew Logan was home safe. She thanked the maid and dismissed her. She reached for the bottle but it was empty. Damn. But there was a decanter in Logan's room just across the hall and that would be the first place Logan would go when he returned home, her wine-soaked brain reasoned. That made sense. She would go to his room and wait for him there.

There was an angel sleeping in his bed. A slow smile curled across his mouth as Logan stepped inside his room. She'd waited for him. It was late, though, much later than he had thought he'd be, and they'd had a long day. It was no surprise she'd fallen asleep. He spied the brandy snifter next to the bed, still moderately full. Perhaps the lateness of the hour had been helped along by the brandy as well.

He sat down gently on the side of the bed, watching her sleep. Her peace brought him peace. The evening had revealed some disturbing news, especially if those rumours at the club turned out to be true. There were things they must discuss and yet he would set those things aside until morning in order to preserve her peace a while longer, and perhaps his. Nothing would be real until he told her. The night could be theirs, needed to be theirs.

Logan leaned forward, pushing back a strand of burnished gold hair from her face as he placed a gentle kiss on her lips. 'I'm home,' he whispered softly against her mouth.

Her eyes flickered open, displaying a curious show of relief and desire. 'Thank goodness. I was so worried.' She struggled up. 'Logan, there are things we need…'

He pressed a finger to her lips. 'There are things we need, and none of them are words right now, my dear. Words will keep until morning.' In the morning they would share their news; he would tell her what he'd learned, they would go to the bank and see what was in the vault and everything would change. The world would get more dangerous tomorrow, would demand difficult decisions from them. But before then there was tonight. Tonight he could show her the pleasure she deserved, the pleasure he'd promised her. 'Tonight is for us.'

'And you are overdressed for the occasion.' She smiled wickedly, tugging at his neckcloth until it came loose.

'I'm glad we're in agreement on that.' His body came alive at her merest touch, his weariness and his worry evaporating. He kissed her mouth and tasted wine. Perhaps it hadn't been the brandy that had put her to sleep at all. 'How much wine have you had?' he murmured against her mouth, aware of her hands working the buttons of his waistcoat, of his shirt.

'Enough to know that I want this, Logan.' They had his shirt off now, his clothes a heap on the floor. 'When you were so late tonight, I imagined the worst, that you'd been set upon.'

'Shh, none of that now.' He kissed her one last time and broke from her long enough to tug off his boots; long enough to strip out of his trousers as desire thundered in his veins. He kicked aside his trousers and made to return to the bed.

'Wait. Stay right there.' She licked her lips,

her eyes lighting on him with appreciation. 'Let me look. I want to see you.' She was in earnest and it gave him pause, a reminder that this was not only about them slaking the desire that had been held at bay for weeks, but this was also an exorcism of the past, a chance to settle the ghosts of her marriage, to show her what pleasure could truly be. But in order to do that, he needed to let her set the pace. It would take all of his willpower but for her, he would manage it.

'I will expect you to reciprocate,' Logan growled as her gaze roamed his nakedness appreciatively.

'You are exquisite, like a Michelangelo sculpture, all muscle and marble.' She reached out a hand and traced the musculature of his arm. 'You're smooth and sinuous, fluid. I thought muscle was only heavy and bulky, but this is…you are…beautiful.' Logan tried to ignore the reminder of his cousin. She'd not meant to compare, she'd only meant to compliment, and yet how could she not be thinking of the comparison? He could hardly blame her for it. The intimacies of marriage had not served her well.

He felt the moment her eyes landed on his

phallus, saw the intimidation in her eyes and he moved to allay the concern. If it was more than concern, more than a history of intimate disappointment, if it was *fear* that put intimidation in her gaze, he *would* find a way to pummel his cousin from beyond the grave. He sat on the side of the bed, taking her hand and leading it to his cock. 'This is an instrument of pleasure. It is not a weapon,' he said softly, cupping her hand over its tender head. 'Do you feel that? The wetness? It weeps for you. Will you stroke me? Will you learn me?'

'Do you like that?' Her hand slid about him and he groaned.

'Yes,' he assured her. He liked it a bit too much. He needed to be careful or he wouldn't last and there was much to show her. He stretched out beside her on the bed. 'You'll like it, too. Let me show you.'

This was extraordinary, this idea of playing, of learning one another, of paying attention to what the other needed. Olivia gasped as Logan's hand slipped beneath her nightgown and sought the juncture between her thighs. She bent her knees, and her legs parted without thought, her body yearning toward his touch, curious to see what might happen next, what she might feel next. He slipped a finger along the length of her slit, finding the slick nub within, and her breath caught at the sensation of being stroked. He was right. She did like it. 'Is this what it feels like for you when I touch you?'

'What does it feel like to you?' Logan had stretched out alongside her, his green eyes glittering with want.

'I don't know. I don't have the words.' It was becoming hard to think of any words at all at the moment. 'It's like I want to explode, like I might let go of myself and I can't stop the letting go from happening.' A mewl purled up from her throat. 'Good heavens, Logan. Do that again.' She pressed herself against the palm of his hand, her body begging as wildness crept up on her, the sense of letting go stalking her with urgency now. He stroked her again and she bucked, biting her lip in a battle to keep it all in.

'Don't try, Olivia. Let it happen. This is for you, all for you. I *want* you to let go, to know what this feels like,' he coaxed, his voice a hoarse rasp as his glittering gaze held hers. She saw in that gaze that this was pleasure for him as well, that pleasuring her pleasured him; that they were in this moment, in this desire, together. She bucked hard once more and shattered, swamped by the realisation of that pleasure. She allowed the letting go to overwhelm her, to carry her away, but there was more to be had, and this pleasure had only whet her for greater pleasure, a pleasure that might be more intimately shared between them both. She was acutely aware that while Logan may have enjoyed this pleasure on her behalf, but his body needed, and deserved, satisfaction. She reached for him, drawing him up over her and he came easily.

'Are you ready for more, you greedy minx?' He laughed down at her.

She looked up at him, meeting his eyes with open honesty. 'I am ready for more.' This next layer of intimacy could be just for them; there was no need to lay any more ghosts. She wrapped her arms about his neck, pulling him to her and kissing him hard, feeling his body move to match hers, his phallus hard at her entrance, but this was no battering ram. His hand slipped between them, his fingers easing the way.

'You are indeed ready,' he murmured against

her neck, reaching for a sheathe from the trifle box beside the bed. In a quick motion he fitted it over himself and then he was there inside her, learning her and letting her body learn him in return until at last he was fully within. He was beautiful to watch in the throes of lovemaking: the way the muscles in his neck corded with passion's paradox of want and restraint; the sounds of desire that eddied up from his throat; the way his body tightened as release drew closer for them both.

'Hold on to me.' He bit hard at her throat, his words raw. She wrapped her legs about his waist, trapping him hard inside her, holding him close until their bodies were no longer separate but a single entity joined and whole as they soared together, exploding together like fireworks in the night sky, brilliant and vibrant and sudden.

Logan collapsed at her side, breathing hard to match her own racing pulse. Even in the throes of his own pleasure, he'd offered her consideration. He'd not collapsed atop her, had not put his comfort above hers even after seeing to her pleasure and perhaps at some expense to himself. Against her own volition, a tear trickled onto the pillow.

Logan's finger trapped it against her cheek. 'Did I hurt you? You should have said something.' Anger rumbled beneath his words.

'No, it's not that at all.' She found the strength to turn on her side so she could see his face. 'It's that it was so exhilarating, so astonishing, and I didn't know. I didn't know it could be like that.'

'That it *should* be like that. Lovemaking is an act of physical reverence as much as it is physical release.' He reached for her and drew her close; she could smell the faint tang of sweat on his skin; could feel the strong beat of his heart as it calmed. 'Now you know. I am glad,' he murmured drowsily against her hair.

'Me, too,' she whispered but Logan was already asleep. She'd forgive him for that. He'd earned it, and in truth, she wasn't far behind. Sleep was already tugging at her as well. It was all right; they had all night.

They made good use of the night, waking to make love twice more before dawn until Olivia was boneless. How would she ever manage to climb out of bed when morning came? And why would she want to? But like with so many things in her life, she simply had no choice. This was a night out of time. When morning came time would start again. Much to her regret. She thought she understood Icarus a bit better now as she drifted back toward sleep shortly before sunrise. Why would anyone ever want to come back to earth once they had flown so close to the heavens?

Damn it all to perdition and back. Rahnald swore to no one in particular in his bachelor accommodations off Golden Square. He thought he'd have more time. He'd thought he'd have better rooms, too. He'd been surprised to arrive at Hailsham House yesterday and find the knocker on the door and a wreath. He'd been counting on staying there while he was in Town. His brother had Darlington House for a residence now. Logan could damn well give him free run of the Hailsham town house. Instead, he was cooped up in his tiny rooms in Soho, a noisy, vibrant bohemian part of the west end, but not genteel, *and* he had to pay for these rooms.

He poured himself a drink, a tolerable whiskey at best. There were going to be a lot of such economies in his near future until he could smooth things over. Finding people in residence at Hailsham House hadn't been the only part of the visit that had not worked out as planned. He'd hoped by coming to London, he could avoid Logan long enough to get into Darlington House and look around. But if he couldn't avoid Logan, he'd hoped contrition would go far enough to perhaps get Logan to do it without asking too many questions. But Logan had come much sooner than he'd anticipated and he'd brought the duchess with him.

Rahnald knew exactly why Logan had chosen Hailsham House over Darlington. His brother wanted no reminders of his cousin around while he seduced her. Damn, but his brother had all the luck: a dukedom falling into his lap; a widow falling into his bed. Whatever luck Rahnald had managed to cobble together had disappeared when Adolphus died. He'd not expected that. He'd actually expected Adolphus's death to make him luckier, wealthier, and to solve problems instead of cause them. But it hadn't worked out that way. Yet, he amended.

He would get on the right side of this eventually. He would find that journal and all would be right again, he promised himself. He'd worked too hard for it all to come to naught. He would find the journal and eliminate anything or anyone who stood in his way. He'd already done it once. He would do it again. And again if need be because no one looked out for you except yourself.

Chapter Seventeen

This was what it felt like to wake up beside someone after a night of lovemaking: replete, refreshed, even revealed, deliciously exposed and exquisitely understood as a result. Logan lay still, refusing to open his eyes, letting his other senses reach out to the morning instead: the soft sound of her breathing; the vanilla-lavender scent of her hair on the pillow; the warmth of her body tucked against his. It was a perfect warmth that lulled him into a wondrous space between sleep and wakefulness. He wanted to stay in that space forever. There was comfort here, peace here, where the burdens of the world seemed far away and irrelevant. In this quiet world there was no one to worry over, no one to save, no one to lose. He was safe and the people he cared for were safe. Olivia was safe and perhaps that mattered more than anything. He ought to find that frightening, an indicator of how close he'd allowed her come, and oddly did not. What a strange little world this was.

The revelations filtered through his mind in a gentle parade of consciousness. Last night had been full of firsts for him. Never had he permitted himself to be so lost in passion; never had he ever not wanted to crawl out of bed after a performance and seek his own solitude. Yes, he supposed he did think of sex as a performance. His mistresses expected pleasure; he expected himself to provide it for both of them. And in truth his mistresses gave performances as well, also for their mutual benefits. They all had certain reputations to uphold. But last night had not been about performances. There had been a shocking amount of honesty that came with making love to Olivia and making love *with* Olivia. She had no finesse, no coyness. She held nothing back once it had been coaxed from her, once he'd shown her the way.

Such a response had both pleased him in the extreme and also surprised him. After her experience with Adolphus he'd not been entirely sure she would allow herself to give over to passion, to trust it and to trust him. He hoped when she woke that she would still feel it had been the right decision. He hoped she would not regret it and blame the wine. He wanted her to own that passion, and her right to claim it. She deserved to know that.

Is that why you did it? Was last night just for her? Just a very pleasurable pity party for a lonely widow?

His inner voice was starting to wake up, to challenge the soft revelations that had marched across his mind.

No, he answered it, swiftly, viciously, tamping down on supposition. *You know it wasn't.*

But that was a well-laid trap that merely served to spring the next question.

Then what was it? Is this the beginning of an affair? Is she to be styled your mistress living in the dower house while you search for a wife in Town? You can't bring her to Town for the Season. She's in mourning.

No, not his mistress. He would not demean her with the suggestion and she would never consent to such a position. She deserved far more.

If not that, then what? The urge to classify

her rose once again along with the need to understand what her place was in his life. But just as before, she fit into none of his precon-structed boxes. What did it mean? Did he need a new box for her? Would it even be worth it to construct one? She was to be his for a short time only and then he'd have to give her up. Except now he didn't want to. That was quite a new feeling indeed, and a worrisome one. The opposite of keeping was losing. One could lose what one had, what one kept. It was why he didn't keep mistresses longer than a year. Everything began with an end clearly in mind. Olivia was testing that rule.

She stirred in his arms, starting to wake and bringing a bittersweet realisation. When she woke the night would be officially gone. He kissed the curve of her neck, his phallus nudg-ing her buttocks. 'Logan,' she sighed his name and the morning was held at bay a little longer.

He delayed reality as long as he could. He made slow, lingering love to her, lay with her in his arms afterward, combing his fingers through her hair. They played maid and valet to one another. He did up her laces, and she tied his neckcloth, a secret smile in her eyes as her fingers worked. Whenever she touched him from hereafter, that touch would be a reminder of other more intimate touches. Those touches would be between them now forever.

By tacit agreement they walked in silence to the breakfast room, exchanging only smiles. No words. Not yet. There would be too many words necessary today and words changed things. Neither of them was in the mood for change at the moment. How wondrous it would be if things didn't have to change; if he might have Olivia by his side always; if he didn't have to marry his future duchess; if he didn't have to be who he was; if he could love her. But people didn't change by their own choice. He did not think he was an exception to his own rule, his own understanding of humanity.

They allowed themselves the normalcy of breakfast: a cup of coffee first; a few bites of eggs and crunchy toast with soft butter and orange marmalade. 'I went to Darlington House when I left here,' Logan began as if they were discussing an evening's entertainment. 'There was nothing. Not even the valet for whom the bequest was left. He has gone to the Americas. We shall not find him or hear from him again. The staff say he left within the hour of the solicitor bringing the money by.'

Olivia held his gaze over the rim of her coffee mug. 'You think that is telling. That he knew something and he was in expectation of something he was owed.'

'Yes, he was waiting and he had plans to leave that were premeditated if he was able to pack and go within such a short time.' The valet had left because he had the funds to do so, funds he'd earned doing something of significant risk, no doubt. The sum named in the bequest would not seem small to a servant. That sum had bought a man's risk and a man's silence at a great distance. The valet had not wanted to stay in England. 'Sometimes absence tells us as much as presence.'

'Speaking of presence...' Olivia buttered a second piece of toast as carefully as she chose her words. 'Your brother was here last night. He didn't say so, but I think he was surprised to see us in residence. He may have had hopes of lodging here himself, although he didn't have any luggage with him.'

'He has his own rooms in Soho,' Logan said grimly. 'Although he has to pay for them out of his allowance. What did he want?' He mentally added calling on Rahnald to his list of things to do. He'd promised his mother he would mend that particular fence once again.

He is the only family you have besides me and I won't be here forever.

'He wanted to apologise.' She was suddenly very busy with her buttering. Something else had happened.

'He's very good at that.' Lots of practice, Logan thought. 'Did he seem sincere?'

'No. Although I have no grounds for it, not in words anyway. He said he was just hoping to find a memento of his cousin and feeling jealous. It matches with your comments earlier.' Her eyes searched his face and he saw distress in that beautiful blue gaze. He ached to take her back to bed and ease those cares from her.

'And yet?' he prompted gently. If Rahnald had harmed her, said something to bring her pain, he would answer for it.

She shook her head. 'Logan, I don't want to speak ill of your brother. I don't know him well, and I don't want to come between the two of you.' She set down her butter-saturated toast, courage gathering in her gaze. 'I wonder if he's looking for the journal.'

Logan felt his stomach clench. His coffee

tasted like acid on his tongue. 'What makes you think that?' he asked, his tone casual but he knew how she thought that: the sudden, self-appointed visit to Darlington to 'help.' Logan remembered quite clearly now Rahnald's offer to sort through Adolphus's things. His mind coupled that with Rahnald's question, *Did he leave anything for me?* The long rambles Rahnald had taken about the house while it had rained. Unescorted rambles, he reminded himself. He'd thought nothing of it at the time. He'd not known about the journal then, and Rahnald was always restless, he could never sit still.

'I think he meant to ask me under the cover of a flirtation but when it became obvious he was gaining no traction there, he opted instead to try a quick rummage through my things and Adolphus's,' Olivia concluded.

'And having not found it, perhaps he concluded it was still in London at Darlington House, or perhaps elsewhere.' He would put men on guard at Darlington House and make sure the servants were aware his brother did not need to be accommodated there. He'd not found anything at Darlington House, but that didn't mean his brother was to be given free run of the ducal town house. It was the else-where that concerned Logan. Assuming Olivia was right, Rahnald would know where that *elsewhere* might be while they did not. It also meant Rahnald knew what the journal con-tained and quite possibly who was involved.

'Why didn't you say anything sooner?' He automatically took a swallow of coffee and then wished he hadn't. He had no stomach for food at the moment. This was worse than Rahnald's being involved in a 'little light lar-ceny.'

'Because I wasn't sure. Because I could have just been seeing connections where there were none. I didn't want more trouble between the two of you, especially when there was no proof. I didn't want you to have to choose who to believe.' Even now he could see that the idea distressed her out of concern for him. 'It would not be an enviable position to be in, Logan, and I would spare you that.'

That was usually his line. He did much to spare others difficulty. Her confession touched him not only because she cared for him, but also because she'd trusted him. It was ob-viously not easy for her to have shared her supposition with him. At last, he had the one thing he'd wanted from her—trust—a chance to show her that some men could be trusted. Last night she'd trusted him with her body; this morning she'd entrusted him with her thoughts. Even as he quietly celebrated that victory, he was aware that the hard part came next. Once he had her trust, he had to make good on it. He could not disappoint her. To paraphrase Voltaire, with great trust came great responsibility.

'It may be nothing,' she said again but Logan was not willing to dismiss it as much as he'd like to.

'Rahnald saw Adolphus in town. They went shooting right before the house party. It makes me wonder if they were closer than I guessed.' Perhaps they'd been friends. Logan closed his eyes and allowed himself a moment to send up a fervent prayer.

Whatever Adolphus is up to, please don't let Rahnald be involved.

Because all signs pointed to something deeper and darker than a few men playing around with guns in the countryside. This time he might not be able to save his brother from his own foolishness.

Logan steadied himself. One step at a time.

'I think we must consider the possibility. Thank you for telling me.' He might not have seen the connection otherwise until it was too late. 'We will go to the bank today and you can take care of the vault.' He paused, fingering his napkin. 'Do you think the vault is connected to the journal?' He was regretting they'd delayed in coming to London but she'd not been in a hurry at the time.

'Given what we think we know now, it seems likely.' She looked down at her hands, a sure sign that she was debating what to say, what to confess. 'I hope I have not made things worse by delaying our visit to the vault.' She looked up, abject apology in her blue eyes. 'I had hoped the vault would not matter, that it was full only of mundane materials of no real import, but that hope was rather naive. I should not have held on to it as long as I did. I didn't want to believe there were secrets, that I was complicit in keeping them. I feel like a child who hides under the covers so that the storm doesn't find her, but in the end the thunder still booms and the lightning still flashes, covers notwithstanding.'

Logan reached for her hand. 'It's not too late. We can still figure this out. We can still make things right. We'll go as soon as you're ready. I'll have the Town coach prepared and waiting.' He let his gaze hold hers for a long moment, letting her know that much more than the coach was at her disposal this morning; that he was at her disposal—his name, his title and all the power and protection that went with them. This next step in the puzzle Adolphus had left them had been placed squarely and unfairly on her shoulders but he would help her if she needed it; if she *allowed* it. They were alike in that way. They'd both spent their lives taking care of others, protecting others, shouldering others' burdens, cleaning up others' messes. It did put them a bit at cross purposes at the moment, he thought as he waited for her in the hall. He was eager to protect her and she was eager to spare him the trouble at a time when they could not afford to hold back, or to shield each other.

Coutts stretched impressively and imposingly along the Strand, white columns, arched windows and its two tall, white, rounded towers with matching cupolas rising into the grey sky of a London February. Olivia gripped Logan's gloved hand and stepped down from the coach. She fingered the key about her neck one more time in reassurance that it was there, although she'd touched it a thousand times since the solicitor had given it to her.

Remember, you are a duchess. Don't let them condescend to you.

In the coach they'd decided to let her handle everything. Logan would remain at her side as silent support unless he was needed. She appreciated that, especially knowing how tempted he must be to smooth the way for her, to sweep any obstacle out of her path.

But there were no obstacles to remove. The dark-coated clerk was deferential and helpful, offering his condolences as he led her directly to the Darlington vault and assured her she would not be disturbed. He helped her fit the key to the lock and then discreetly departed, leaving her to study the contents of the vault.

The vault was not large, merely the size of an overlarge broom closet, but jewels didn't take up much space. The walls were lined with shelves, mostly empty. Once Adolphus's mother had passed there was little need to keep family jewels in Town and they'd been moved to Darlington, although a couple cases remained here. She opened them, but these were pieces she did not recognise. They were exquisite and expensive; an emerald necklace, and a diamond parure. There were provenances with them, testifying to their authenticity. She would read those later. For now, it was enough to know they were not part of the family collection. If they had been, they could not have been given to her; they would have been entailed with the estate. Her stomach clenched; the beautiful pieces were already tainted with the knowledge that they were part of Adolphus's secrets.

Olivia trailed a hand along vacant shelves, the emptiness bringing with it sadness as if the empty shelves were testimony to a dying family. The extended family lived on in Logan, of course, but Adolphus's family was gone, all of them. The main line of Darlington, gone. She had not known it well. She took care of the dukedom, but she'd not probed its history, did not feel part of that centuries-old legacy. She'd taken care of its people, of its tenants, those who were part of the here and now, because they'd needed her. They'd been abandoned by those who were supposed to see to their welfare. But this was not her family, not her history.

There were three shoe-size boxes on the shelves in addition to the jewel cases. She drew a breath. Best to get to it, then. Those boxes needed to be sorted and apparently, she was the one meant to do it. She steeled herself and removed the lid on the first box, her breath catching at the sight: pound notes. A lot of them, banded together. Not just pound notes, but *one hundred pound notes*.

She sorted through the bricks of bound paper money in the box, the amount staggering. There must be ten thousand pounds here and this money was meant exclusively for her; it was not meant to be part of the entailment. Ten thousand pounds. This kind of money could change everything for her. It would keep her in style far beyond what the official thousand pound per annum allowance permitted. Why hadn't Adolphus simply included this money with that? She searched the box for a note, but there was nothing, no final word from Adolphus. But it was unnecessary. The intent and purpose of the money was clear.

To keep my secrets.

A chill stole over her. She replaced the lid as if she could keep the words trapped inside the box along with the money. This was hush money. A quiet blackmail beyond the grave; a final temptation. Some might call it a reward for her silence. To take this money would be a final commitment to whatever secrets his journal held. Where had the money come from? Had it come from the aliases in the book?

Her fingers trembled as she opened the other two boxes, one containing packets of deeds, and the other containing shares in investments: trading companies, ships, cargoes. She turned over the packets, studying them. Perhaps these were the official deeds to the properties attached to the estate? But no, if that were the case those deeds could not legally be left in her care or be kept from Logan, and the will had been clear: the contents of the vault belonged to her alone.

Had their marriage been more wholesome, she might have believed her husband had simply invested on her behalf. But their marriage had not been wholesome. It had been corrupt from the start, founded on deceitful principles, and the content of the boxes was excessive. There must be twenty deeds between the two boxes. More than enough property to provide a widow with a reliable income. Too much property, some would say. How was a widow to take care of all of it? Unless she was meant to sell some of it for additional funds?

He has made you independently wealthy, a little voice whispered. *He's taken care of your sisters and your father through the will. You need not worry again about finances for yourself or for them. All you have to do is take the deeds, the shares, the money, and walk away. Leave the dukedom to his cousin; don't worry about where it came from. Burn the book. Stop the questions. Stop asking why. Stop asking what. Walk away. Walk into the future you deserve, the future that you've earned. You've suffered enough, haven't you?*

Like the valet, who'd simply disappeared with a thousand pounds in his pocket.

It was tempting except for two things: the reward was too much. If her marriage had taught her anything it was that when something sounded too good to be true, it probably was. If he'd been willing to leave all this in exchange for her silence, the things he was hiding must be dark indeed. And there was Logan now. To walk away from Darlington meant to walk away from him. It would be necessary, though, in order to keep him from sharing in her culpability.

Or you can share all this with him. It was given into your care. It's yours now. You can choose to share it with whomever you wish; Adolphus cannot control that although he's definitely trying to influence that decision beyond the grave. Or you can say nothing.

She drew a breath and pressed a hand to her fluttering stomach. She called for the clerk. 'Could you bring a box please? I'll be taking these items with me.'

Chapter Eighteen

'This is worth a fortune,' Logan said sombrely after they conducted a thorough inventory of the boxes' contents, which were now spread out and organised on the long study table running down the centre of the library. A half-empty tea tray sat on a low table beside the fire in testimony to their hard work and long hours. They'd come home from Coutts and gone straight to their task, hoping that the deeds and shares would shed some light on how and why they'd been acquired.

'I know.' She sighed. 'It's too much, Logan, and that scares me. I don't know what Adolphus did, but it must be terrible.'

He nodded absently. 'It worries me, too.' His concern-filled eyes met hers. 'I don't want Rahnald caught up in this, whatever it is.'

She touched his hand in commiseration. After all Rahnald had done, Logan's first concern was still for his brother. 'I hope so, too. I hope I'm wrong. I don't want you to have to choose between your family and the dukedom.' Or between her and his brother. She wanted them to all be on the same side. She let out a breath. 'What do you make of all this, other than there is a lot of it?'

'There's shares in mines, in cargoes from the Far East. It's a very diversified portfolio.' He thumbed a stack of papers. 'The money in the box has likely come from these investments. I wish I could leave it at that but the money and the deeds had to come from somewhere. I'd like to know where.'

She would, too. 'It's been kept apart from the estate books. There's no record of any of this in the ledgers.' Which only furthered the concern that this was another secret to keep, or perhaps it was attached to one big secret. It was also perhaps another proof of the private, secretive life her husband had led apart from her, a life she'd known nothing about until it was too late.

'If it were payments for gambling debts, it wouldn't be recorded.' Logan was taking a second look through a stack of deeds. 'These must have been from some high-stakes games that he was part of. I might be a nobleman myself and prone in earlier days to wildness, but I've never understood how a man could so easily wager a home on a turn of a card or the speed of a horse, or when someone will marry.'

'You are more responsible than most.' She smiled. 'I suppose it's the thrill that attracts them, something to set their blood pumping for a short time.'

'Well, whatever it was, plenty of peers lost property to my cousin. Look at this. The Marquess of Lockdale, the Earl of Ayrshire, Viscount Durham. There's more and it all seems to have happened in the last seven years.' Logan furrowed his brow, reaching back, perhaps, into his memory. 'Although I don't recall anyone talking about it. One would think there would have been talk in the clubs if Adolphus was on a winning streak of such note, or if men were losing a lot. People might callously wager an estate but that doesn't mean they can afford to lose it. There should have been talk especially with all the losses occurring so close together and at the same person's hand.

I was about Town. I would have heard. The clubs would have been full of it.'

'Unless they weren't gambling debts? Perhaps they were legitimate sales? Perhaps nothing was lost? Perhaps they received cash from Adolphus.' She looked up hopefully from her stack of investment contracts. Perhaps they were making too much of this.

'Then why keep it separate from the estate? Why not include it as part of building the estate's assets? Why leave it just to you? And so secretly? If he intended it for you, why not just include it in your settlement from the will instead of making a big deal out of the vault?' Logan grimaced. 'I'm sorry. I don't mean to be deflating. Your scenario would be nice. But do you think it's likely that these are harmless investments, acquired through sales?'

'No,' she said with soft disappointment. 'Why would he be interested in building assets when he had no interest in developing the estate? Besides, as you said, if it was all aboveboard there would have been talk at the clubs. Neither party, it seems, wanted these transactions to be public.'

Logan started, something moving in his eyes. 'Say that again.'

'No one wanted the transactions to be public?'

'Another set of secrets. Do you think they could be attached to the journal? That maybe they are all part of the same secret? Hand me the journal.'

'We don't know what the names in the journal stand for.' She handed him the journal and watched his eyes move over the lists, his finger running down the pages.

He looked up, his green eyes lively. 'Maybe we do. Maybe we can use the deeds and contracts as a cipher. Come look at this.'

She came around the table and stood beside him, catching the coiled energy that radiated from him. He was close to something and that excitement was contagious.

'Do you see these dates? Look at this date when Newberry Cottage was turned over to Adolphus. It was four days past this date here.' He pointed with his finger. 'Newberry Cottage belonged to the Earl of Swithin, according to this deed. Legal documents require the use of real names. But here in the book Oberon is listed four days earlier as having lost to Odysseus.' He flipped the page. 'Look, there's another win for Odysseus on the fifth of June,

1839. Look through the deeds and see if there's one that Adolphus took over a few days later.'

It took a little while to sort through the pile. She found it at the bottom of a packet. Her breath caught. 'Here it is. There's a deed for a place in Hampstead Heath called the Grange. That's the name of the place where the party was. It's on the death certificate.' She had to calm herself. After weeks of getting nowhere, they were getting somewhere. 'Do you think Odysseus is Adolphus?'

Logan nodded. 'It seems probable. I think what we should do next is make a list of properties, who owned them and the dates acquired. Then we can cross reference the list to the ledger.'

'From there we can decode the journal.' She finished his thought and he nodded again. 'I'll read if you want to write.' They made a good team. She liked working with him, thinking with him. This was not a new realisation. She'd recognised this when they'd worked on the estate books and when they'd visited the village and the farms. At the time, she'd wondered if he was merely pandering to her, trying to appease her to smooth his own way. She no longer doubted how genuine his efforts were, how much he respected her opinions and knowledge. He could have shut her down earlier, dismissed her concerns about Rahnald, but he hadn't, even though it made things more difficult.

'You're staring.' Logan glanced up from the list.

'Just thinking.' But she smiled and she might have blushed.

'About me, I hope?'

'Yes, but not what you might think.' She couldn't resist teasing him a bit. Women probably fantasised about him all the time, about kissing him, touching him, seducing him. He was likely expecting her to say something about wanting to kiss him. 'I was thinking about how well you treat me and how appreciative I am of that. You see me, Logan.' She would remember it always, even when this was over and they had gone their separate ways.

He lifted her hand to his lips and kissed her knuckles. 'Everyone deserves to be seen and I definitely see you, Olivia.' Then he winked. 'Now, keep reading. Back to work, minx. You won't distract me that easily.'

The task went quickly and a list took shape. Within the hour they had what they hoped would be the cipher. 'Well, shall we test it?' Logan set aside his pen and blew on the list. 'I'll read a date from the ledger and you tell me if there's a corresponding date that happens shortly afterwards and I'll add their alias to our list.'

'Oberon is the Earl of Swithin. His name comes up again. Poor fellow, he's unlucky,' Logan read. 'Lockdale is Robin of Locksley. That's not very original.' He glanced up with a laugh. 'Viscount Matlon is Don Quixote,' then added, 'if we're right.' But it seemed that they were. 'Unfortunately, we don't know what was wagered or lost in the other contests. It looks like Matlon wagered something with Oberon on April nineteenth 1840 and Matlon won.'

'I wonder what the wager was about? That's the next question, isn't it? What were they wagering on? Each question seems scarier than the last. After all, what's worth betting a house or stocks on? High stakes require high risks, usually.' She tentatively floated the question.

His hand closed over hers. 'Yes, but I am not sure the ledger can tell us any more. It's told us quite a lot. We have a partial cipher that I think translates into a potential guest list for the house party. These people were likely at the party. I wonder if one of them was upset about a wager? Or perhaps they challenged Adolphus to a wager and something went sour with it? Perhaps Adolphus lost and refused to pay?' Or perhaps he'd cheated. When a man was on a winning tear, people became suspicious of such good luck.

Her mind was starting to race with ideas. 'Did Odysseus lose any wagers?'

'Yes, look, here's one. And here's a few more. I wish we knew what he lost, hmm? He wins more than he loses, though. But we don't know who he lost to, because we don't have a deed to track through.'

'Rahnald's name hasn't come up,' Olivia offered. That should ease Logan's mind a little.

'There are still names we can't decode from the ledger. His name could be among those, and if he never wagered against Adolphus and lost, we can't figure out who he is.' Logan was still worried; she could see it in his face.

'Do you think he'd talk to you if you asked him? Maybe he's in trouble and he's scared?' Perhaps it would make Logan feel better if the brothers could talk.

Logan shook his head. 'If he's involved, I am hesitant to show our hand or let him know that we have the journal, that we have the list and that we have a partial understanding of who is on the list. I would not want him to tell anyone else.' He gave a grimace. Rahnald was not known for his discretion. 'I would doubt Rahnald is the only one looking for the book, especially now that we know what it is. A record of secret wagers and secret transactions. Whoever possesses this book *and* knows what the wagers are about has enormous opportunities for blackmail. If people didn't want the loss of property to be known then, they probably wouldn't want it exposed now.'

'Do you think that's why Rahnald wants the journal? To blackmail people?' Olivia began to put the packets back into their boxes.

'It's a possibility.' Logan leaned back in his chair. Evening was falling outside. They'd worked the afternoon away. 'It would certainly explain why he hasn't asked for money recently. Now, without the book, he hasn't the authority for blackmail.' He slid her a glance. 'I wonder, too, if Adolphus wasn't engaging in a little blackmail as well as winning wagers. If the book was in his possession, he knew everything about everyone—their names, their wagers, who won, who lost and what exchanged hands.'

Olivia set the box aside and went to the long window that looked out over the lawn. It was a lot to take in, in part because it was so overwhelmingly tragic and so far-reaching. They'd made headway today but she knew it was still just the very tip. There was more to uncover. She felt Logan come up behind her. He wrapped his arms about her and she leaned into his strength.

'You are not in this alone, Olivia,' he murmured at her ear.

'Why do you suppose he did it? A secret society of wagers, taking property from his friends, from other peers. He had enough land, enough money and he cared very little for what he had. Why would he want more? Why would he seek to ruin others? To collect leverage against his so-called friends? He had no reason for it; no need for coin; no need for revenge. He had a perfect life, a life others would be jealous of.' Others like Rahnald.

'Some men are never satisfied. Give them comfort and they want adventure. Give them ease and they want hardship. Not everyone is cut out for the life they have.'

She could see his reflection in the window-pane and smiled. 'Are you, Logan Maddox? Are you cut out for your life? You weren't born to be a peer and now you're a duke.'

'I am content enough. Sometimes we have to adapt if we are to survive.' His voice was warm and intimate and she felt herself start to relax after a tense day. 'Have you read any of the work from Charles Darwin? He published *The Voyage of the Beagle* a few years back. He has ideas about natural selection, that only the fittest prevail, and that fitness is determined by adaptability and the ability to reproduce.'

'So you survive? Because you can adapt?'

'Because I choose to adapt,' he corrected.

'And you'll reproduce.' She gave a sad laugh. 'What does that mean for me? Does your Mr Darwin suggest I will fade away if I cannot have children?' How that saddened her; what damage his cousin had done her.

His breath feathered at her ear. 'From what you've shared, the problem was Adolphus.'

'You are generous, Logan.' She sighed. 'No one believes it, though. You know what he looked like, big, bold, healthy, virile in the extreme. He was the perfect man in body and form.'

'Still, that's no guarantee of reproductive success.' He pressed the argument, she knew, on principle only. He would not bet the dukedom on it. He was the duke now; the line was in his hands. She could not let him squander his prospects on a potentially infertile duchess, even if he could wait two years for her to finish mourning. Not that it mattered. He would not marry her. He'd been very clear on that and it was for the best. Those were just the issues on his side of the equation. There was also the reality that she was not free to marry. She had her family to think about. They would lose their funds from Adolphus if she broke the contract. Of course, if she took the money in the vault, they wouldn't need those funds. She could help them herself.

But that would require you to keep the secrets anyway. If you exposed the secrets you would not be able to collect rents or dividends from deeds that were perhaps wrongly or illicitly taken from others.

'I can't keep any of it, can I?' This had lived at the back of her mind all afternoon as they'd made their lists and cracked their code. If she had that money, the income from the properties, she could support her family on her own and the conditions of the will could go hang. But Adolphus had caught her neatly. If she wanted to circumvent the provisions of his will, she had to take the money. Either way, the money or the will, both ensured she kept his secrets.

Logan's arms tightened about her. 'You could. We could stop looking. We could destroy the book and pretend it never existed, that we never heard about the bullet in his thigh, or that we ever questioned the nature of his wound. You're not the only one who's thought of it. The money would free you and me.' It would free him from fear of discovering his brother's involvement as well. They both stood looking out the window in silence. 'Could you live with that, Olivia?' he asked at last. It was tempting.

The question was pregnant with implications. If she said yes, he would make it happen. He would bring all his power to bear to make the journal disappear. There would be no proof of wrongdoing or of scandal. The deeds were legal. They could not be contested even if the losing party chose to complain, which they could not do without exposing themselves. Whatever rumours might attempt to float through Society would lack substance and soon disappear. It could be done.

'No, I could not,' she answered firmly. 'I could not take that fortune and know that my securities were acquired through ill means.' Everything pointed in that direction. 'Perhaps that might change if we knew what the wagers were. If they were just men consensually gambling and losing, then I'd feel less guilty. But if Adolphus was blackmailing anyone, or if this was more than wagers, I would not want it.' The secrecy still bothered her. Something had been hushed up and Adolphus was dead. They did not have all the answers she needed. 'What's the next step?'

'I think tomorrow we go to the Grange,' Logan offered quietly. 'There may be some clues there.'

She turned in his arms, wrapping her arms about his neck. 'And between then and now? What's *our* next step?' She wanted to chase away the revelations of the day and recapture the more pleasant revelations of the night. Was it possible to duplicate such pleasure? How long did such pleasure last? But even as she asked the question she knew the answer didn't matter.

They had tonight; that was all they were guaranteed. Tomorrow they might learn things that would require her to walk away from him in order to protect him and the dukedom from scandal. Even if they did not, she still had to let him go. The Season would be starting in two months and he had a wife to find. He could be hers only for a little while. That would have to be enough. It was what she'd promised herself. She could not break that promise even though she'd changed her mind.

Chapter Nineteen

She could only be his for a short while. One night. Two nights. One month. Two months. Logan was not sure it would ever be enough. As they climbed the stairs, he was only sure that one more night would *not* be and that they could not last. He could not allow it.

If today had shown him anything it was that Adolphus had left him with a mess, that if not handled correctly, would result in a scandal that would follow the Maddox family through history for generations to come. He may not be able to separate himself from the scandal as the duke, but he could separate Olivia from it.

She was only a Maddox by marriage and that marriage was gone now. He could ensure she was jettisoned from any ensuing mess and the DeLacey name would rise above scandal.

It was the best he could do for her and it was what he knew how to do. Never mind that his often-silenced heart was asking him to do something different, to consider something different regardless of what they found at the Grange.

He held out little hope that the visit to the Grange would exonerate Adolphus. More likely, it would condemn his cousin; fill in the missing pieces of what they didn't already know. It might even condemn his own brother. This little pocket of peace he and Olivia had created would crash tomorrow. There would be pieces to pick up, repairs to be made. He would save her first. Hers would be the first pieces he picked up.

Will she allow it? Would she understand that it is all you can offer?

That was his conscience talking. His heart was waking up, though, most inconveniently, and had something else to say about it.

You can choose to offer her more. You can choose to do more than save her.

For the first time in a long time, he didn't dismiss the idea out of hand. Instead, he thought, *I could. Maybe I could. But oh, the cost. Am I up to it?*

To lose her would destroy him.

Inside his chambers the fire burned in the grate and a lamp had been left on the table beside his bed where covers were invitingly turned back. 'Let me undress you tonight,' he whispered, his voice already thick with desire. He wanted his hands on her; wanted to imprint the feel of her, the sight of her, on every part of his memory. 'I did not see nearly enough of you last night.' He kissed the back of her neck, where fabric and hair had left a bare spot of skin exposed. His hands worked her laces loose, loose enough to push her black gown from white shoulders, to let it fall to the floor while his fingers moved on to petticoat tapes and corset stays. 'Turn around.' He murmured the instruction, low and fierce with need, when she was at last left only in the thin linen of her chemise. 'Will you take it off for me?' A delightful flush took her skin at the suggestion.

She was nervous and he would not have that from her. Last night he'd pushed back the folds of her nightgown and she'd felt protected from his gaze perhaps, or perhaps she'd felt protected from fully acknowledging the source of her own pleasure even as she claimed it. But not tonight. Tonight he wanted her naked beside him, nothing separating them. 'Do not worry, Olivia. You will be beautiful to me.'

'It's not that.' She was suddenly shy, this woman who'd strode into Coutts this morning with the confidence of a general; this woman who'd turned down enormous temptation today in order to do the right thing. She was strong. He was not used to seeing her shy, uncertain. 'It's only that I've not been naked with a man before.'

What a boor his cousin had been. He'd leave it at that. Adolphus's failure would be his victory. 'Then I shall have the privilege of being the first.' He stepped toward her, eyes locked on hers, his fingers gently untying the pink ribbon of her chemise. 'Raise your arms. Pull it over your head. Yes, just like that. I think the gesture is sexy,' he whispered, watching. 'It thrusts your breasts into relief, exposes them, makes them vulnerable for just the briefest moment while your arms are above your head, and in that time a million fantasies run through mine.' He bent his head, kissing first one breast and then the other, a warm hand kneading gently, a thumb running over the tips until he felt them turn hard with want of their own, a shudder rippling through her. He guided her to the bed. 'You must sit for me, so that I can worship you as you deserve.'

Ah, this was so much better. He knelt before her between her thighs, able now to take her breasts into his mouth, to lick at them until a moan escaped her, to trail kisses to her navel and below, to watch her fall back on the bed as he put his mouth to her curls, to tease out with his tongue that hard nub that lived within. He closed his eyes and lost himself in her, feeling each tremor that shook her, hearing each delicious cry. She was shy no more as she sought her release, arching up against him until she had it. Her release was his pleasure. It was a most intimate pleasure to watch her claim her passion's due, to watch the slim column of her neck arch, to hear her cry out and to know he was the only man in the world who'd seen her like this. The first. This was his gift to her and a gift to himself. But in those moments a new, greedy hunger stirred deep inside him. He didn't merely want to be the first. He wanted to be the last, the only. These were not comfortable thoughts for a man who'd sworn himself off love. Instead, they were very much the thoughts of a man in the throes of that emotion.

'Come inside me,' she begged. 'You need

pleasure, too. I want to feel you inside me.'
What had begun as slow and wicked play, had
suddenly turned fierce, desperate and fast. He
fumbled for a sheathe and quickly slid it on, his
response to her tacit and swift, perhaps even
rough. There was nothing he wanted more than
to be inside her, riding the waves of her recent
pleasure, rousing her to more.

He thrust into her hard, his body unyield-
ing in its desire and hers answered. Mouths
nipped, hoarse cries ripped from throats, bodies bucked. There was no nuance, no art to this,
just a rabid seeking of pleasure that culminated
quickly, explosively, leaving them breathless
and sweating, hearts pounding. This was what
desperation felt like. In those moments he was
certain she knew it, too, that they were fated
to be apart, that for the sake of one another,
they had to give each other up. There was absolutely nothing that could come of this. How
was it that he could pick up the pieces for everyone else but himself? There was no future
for them. Logan thought there'd never been
anything he'd wanted less than a future without Olivia. Could he give her the future she
deserved?

You can choose to change. You can de-

cide to trust in love again. If you think the only reason people don't change is because they choose not to, then you can choose everything—choose your own destiny. Choose to love again; choose to ignore social protocol; choose to ignore scandal. Choose yourself for once.

It's not that easy, he argued with himself.

But his inner voice had a simple epiphany for him as he drifted off to sleep. *Yes, it is.*

And with that epiphany came a plan: he would put the question to her in the morning before they went to the Grange so that she knew and he knew in his heart that this was without conditions; that he would marry her no matter what because there was the world they were required to move in, and then there was the world they inhabited together where things like scandal couldn't reach. His mind was made up.

Her mind was made up when she awoke. She would go to the Grange with him and when that visit revealed whatever secrets it held, she would return to Surrey and move into the dower house immediately because *this*: nights like last night and the one before it and the one before *it*, simply could not keep happening. She would never want them to end and the longer they went on, the harder it would be to put a stop to them.

It was already hard enough. Her mind might be made up but that resolve was not enough to get her out of bed. That seemed unfair. Mental resolve *should* be enough. But it wasn't. She wanted only to lie there beside him, watching him sleeping, studying the dark sweep of his lashes against his cheek; the unfettered expression of peace on his face that was often hidden during the day; the rise and fall of his sculpted chest.

She resisted the urge to trace the musculature of that chest with a finger. It would wake him and she really ought to rise before he woke. If he woke, he'd make love to her and seduce every last ounce of reason from her. She'd forget her resolve and the reasons for it. They were good reasons: she had a family to protect, scandal to avoid, her own reputation to consider and always, secrets to keep. There were other reasons, too, mainly that she didn't trust herself *or* Logan. She'd chosen so poorly with Adolphus. What made this decision any different? What happened when Logan tired of her? He was notorious for running through women, and her husband had tired of her early in their marriage. That seemed a foreboding combination. And that was just the physical consideration of their being together. Was she really willing to invest all she had in a man who saw people only as problems to be solved? Once she was *solved* would that, too, contribute to his interest waning when she was no longer intriguing to him? She'd not always been a smart woman when it came to men; she hadn't had the skills, the insights that came with experience, but she was a smart woman now and she needed to consider the situation from all angles besides passion; besides how she felt when she was with him: on fire with life, burning with it, brimming with it, appreciated. *Seen. Understood.*

Do you truly want to give those things up? her heart prompted. *Those are no mean qualities; they are rare and hard to come by; will you not fight for them?*

It would be a short-term victory only. Even if she could miraculously hold his attention, miraculously sustain that passion within their relationship and overcome his penchant for problem solving, the external world would intrude too much. She would overcome those obstacles only to be faced with other insurmountable walls of scandal that would ruin them from the outside as surely as those other issues could ruin them from the inside.

There was simply too much to combat. Two fronted wars never ended well. It would be best to leave with the memories of these three fleeting nights intact and untarnished. She quietly threw back the covers and slipped out of bed. She would dress in her room and begin packing. She would absolutely stop second-guessing herself and wishing for what couldn't be. This was what must be done no matter that her heart wished it could be otherwise. She merely had to get through today, get through the visit to the Grange, and then she could start to put these days with Logan behind her.

'Olivia, are you in here?' His voice was behind her, calling her name in soft morning tones reminiscent of seduction the night before as she turned from the window. The door to her room opened and Logan stepped in, draped in his blue banyan, the robe left unbelted and hanging open to reveal peek-a-boo glimpses of man and muscle beneath the silk; entirely naked man.

'Logan, you're up.' She felt self-conscious and overdressed in a travelling costume. His gaze was critical as his eyes roved over her, taking in her clothing.

'I am up. As are you. Up, dressed and packing.' His gaze drifted to the clothes on the bed, the bureau drawers left open; her trunk at the foot of the bed, items already inside. He slanted her a look. 'Did we decide we'd leave today, and I've forgotten?'

Her hands clenched in the folds of the gown she held. '*I* have decided to leave today when we return from the Grange. I will go back to Darlington Hall tonight. But you are welcome to stay in London. I can make the trip on my own.' She attempted to end on a cheery note, trying to assert her independence, a subtle reminder that they need not live in each other's pockets once their last task was completed. What more would there be left for them to uncover after the Grange today?

'The hell you will leave on your own.' Logan was all indignant disbelief. 'If you want to return today, then we will. Together. You are not travelling alone. However, may I ask what prompted this decision?'

She busied herself with her trunk, folding in gowns, anything to avoid looking at him. 'I need to oversee the renovations to the dower house. It's time to settle there. I've overstayed my welcome at the Hall and you've been most generous. But we both have lives to get on with and that will best be done under separate roofs.'

He seemed to consider this for a moment, or perhaps he was considering whether or not he believed it; whether or not she was lying to him. 'I'm supposed to believe that after last night? You will have to do better than that, Liv. Perhaps a few weeks ago that would have been true. But no longer. I have a better idea.' Logan moved toward her, reaching for her hands. 'Let's get on with our life together and forget about separate roofs.'

Olivia's hands froze inside his grip. 'What are you talking about, Logan?' She very much feared she knew.

'I know this must seem like an unorthodox proposal, but I am talking about marriage. Marry me, Liv.' His eyes glittered and he offered her a seductive smile that turned her insides to a soft boil of intimate heat.

'Marry you?' she repeated, stalling in order to get her wits under control. These were the words her heart had longed to hear, and her mind had feared. Hadn't she just held this debate with herself as she'd lain in bed considering her options? Hadn't she just made up her own mind? Hadn't she just won that debate with her reasons? How was it that two words from Logan could make such a dent in those defences so that she could barely remember what those reasons were, let alone why she'd found them valid?

'We can't. There are a million reasons why.' She tugged her hands away and he let her go.

'Name them, the reasons, Olivia.' He challenged her, taking a seat on the edge of her bed, demonstrating his deadly patience. This was how he solved problems; he waited them out, took them on one by one and dismantled them. She didn't want to be dismantled.

'Don't do that, Logan,' she fired back, taking refuge in anger. 'I am not a problem to be solved. I don't want to be solved. Is that what this offer of marriage is? A solution to *me*? To the problem of what to do about me?' She waved a hand between them. 'A solution to *this*? This affair, or whatever it is we've embarked on? I can't be your mistress so I am to be your wife?' She put her hands on her hips and gave a shake of her head. 'You needn't marry me, Logan. I didn't expect it. This *thing* between us wasn't supposed to lead to marriage.'

'You were just using me for sex?' Logan had the audacity to laugh.

'You know I did not make that decision lightly.'

'I *am* serious, Olivia. You are right. We did not start this with an intent to marry, but intents change. Mine have.' Something deep moved in his green eyes that stunned her, that pushed hard against the walls of her doubts about herself, about him. What did she have left if she didn't have that with which to defend herself? She'd be an exposed warrior, entirely naked.

But naked with Logan was nice, good. Safe.

No, that was not the image she'd meant to invoke. Damn her untrustworthy heart. But it was hard not to think about nakedness with Logan sitting there, his banyan gaping open, reminding her of exactly what he was promising her.

'Logan, think about the dukedom. Think about how a marriage would look between us. Even without Adolphus's secrets, we would be a scandalous pairing. You marrying your cousin's widow within weeks of your cousin's death? Even if we waited until spring, it would still be entirely too soon.' Surely, that argument would carry weight with a man of responsibility.

But he was all rake today, searing her with his eyes, incinerating her arguments with his words. 'I am sure I can make an argument about the need for an heir in the cradle that supersedes any need to continue mourning for two years, and there is no law preventing you from marrying when you like.' No, just social preference. Just the possibility for scandal.

'No law perhaps, but my sisters will lose their funding from Adolphus's trusts,' Olivia reminded him. 'This is not just about our decision. What we decide affects others.' But Logan was unconcerned and the next obstacle fell too easily.

'There is more than enough money in the Darlington coffers to see to your sisters' Seasons and dowries. Let the trusts go. I will take care of your family.' How easily he overrode all the conditions Adolphus had put in place; all the controls designed to ensure she kept his secrets. And Logan didn't stop there. 'I can get a special license on the grounds that the dukedom demands it. That to wait puts the line in jeopardy.'

'But the Crown also hates impropriety. To marry the new duke within two months of my husband's death? There *will* be talk, Logan. You will be saddled with a scandal. Two of them, really. People will say you had no business marrying a woman who'd not managed a child in four years of marriage.'

'You and I know better, though, and time will tell.' He grinned wickedly. 'When we have our own children, we'll have the last word. I simply do not care if there is one scandal or two. Do you? We can wed and still do our familial duty. We'll honour mourning for Adolphus together in the countryside. We needn't flaunt ourselves about London. We'll have a small, private service at the Darlington chapel. No one can be offended by that or the idea of doing one's duty.' Logan shrugged, a mischievous grin on his lips. 'Who knows? Our scandal might come in handy and distract people from the circumstances of Adolphus's death. Or vice versa. Perhaps his death will distract people from us.'

She did not like where this argument was going, mainly because she was losing and because it was bringing to light other issues, less practical issues. He was doing a great job of solving problems but that wasn't love. It was, however, what worried her most about a relationship with Logan. Could there even be a relationship? Or would it always be problems and solutions? Was that all he was capable of giving? 'Is that what we'll tell people? That we married for duty? Responsibility? Is that the truth? Is there nothing more?' For her the truth was something more—that she was in love with a man who might not be capable of loving her in return.

'Can you not say the word, Logan? You want me in your life, in your bed. What about in your heart?' The one place she wanted to be the most. 'You've been very open about not being a proponent of love. It was for fools, was it not? While I am cognizant of the honour you do me, Logan, and I do recognise all that you offer me, a true partnership, for instance—' *and pleasure beyond compare*, she added mentally '—I will require more than that. I cannot marry a man who sees me as nothing more than a problem to solve. I will require his heart.' She was being hard on him but sometimes honesty demanded it. She went to him and knelt before him, softening. 'I know you've been hurt before. I know love has not been kind to you. You loved your father, your older brother, Rahnald, and all of them have broken your trust in love. But I would need you to love again. I have to protect myself, Logan. I've been hurt, too. I cannot go through such betrayal, such disappointment, again.'

He was quiet for a long while, his eyes holding hers. 'Me neither, and yet here I am, naked before you in all ways.' Simple words. Powerful words.

Her heart spoke: *He is willing to open himself up to love, for you. All for you. He is offering you all you've asked of him.*

'I will love you whether you marry me or not, Olivia. I don't think I can escape it now.' He reached for her hand and lifted it to his lips. 'Can I take this as a yes, then?'

She shook her head, and his eyes went a thunderous grey-green at the gesture. 'Words are easy, Logan. We owe it to ourselves to wait. We should decide nothing until we know what really happened with Adolphus.' She was stalling, unwilling to believe in herself and in him completely.

When things were too good to be true...

'No.' He swept the argument away with a wave of his hand. 'Adolphus has decided enough for you already, hasn't he? Last night I thought as you did, that we should wait until we knew more about what we might be facing. But then, as you lay in my arms, it occurred to me that it didn't matter what we discovered today. I would still want you, in my life, in my bed. Whatever Adolphus was part of won't change that. What I feel for you is not conditional. This is our choice. No one else's.'

It took all her willpower to say, 'Then it's my choice. I want to wait. We should decide nothing until we've been to the Grange and know exactly what we're up against.'

Chapter Twenty

The house known simply as the Grange was off the main road through a quiet village, and it gave one the impression of being out in the middle of nowhere. The road leading to the stone house was rutted and ill kept, not a road that saw regular use. The house itself didn't look much better on the outside. Logan reached beneath the seat and removed a case. His pistols. He was prepared for trouble, a reminder that they were not sure what awaited them: Would they find an empty house with nothing but ghosts or something more dangerous?

The coach stopped and Logan helped her down, giving the coachman instructions to drive the team around. 'Hopefully, this will not take more than an hour. Feel free to go back to the village and warm up. It's bitter out today.' Logan gave the coachman a coin for a hot drink at the inn.'

'The house doesn't look as if it's been lived in for a while. I can't imagine Adolphus wanting to come here.' Logan went first, knocking at the front door and scrubbing at a window to peer in when no one answered. 'Looks better inside.' He flashed her a grin, trying to put her at ease.

The door took a bit of work to get open, the hinges stiff from the cold, but it was not locked. Perhaps in the chaos that had likely ensued with Adolphus's death, no one had thought to lock the door, too worried about their own hides to care, or perhaps there was simply no need to lock doors this far from anything. Once inside, the Grange surprised with its comforts. It bore the stamps of a men's hunting lodge, all the things Adolphus found comfort in. Sturdy oak chairs and tables were gathered in clusters in the main hall where people might congregate around an enormous brick fireplace that had probably warmed the house for centuries. A short hallway led to the kitchen and a small room that appeared to be acting as an office or study. A staircase led to bedrooms above.

'Let's start in here.' Logan gestured to the little office but Olivia paused, overwhelmed with the import of being in this place. Adolphus had been here. Had met his end here. 'Are you all right? If it's too much…' Logan was being kind, too kind, after she'd refused him this morning.

She shook her head. 'No, it's fine.' She gathered her strength. She would not falter here at the end. She would see this through, whatever lay in wait for her.

The office contained a desk and chairs set by the window looking out over the drive. The wall of the small room was lined with bookshelves populated with books. Olivia studied the spines, reading titles. 'They're mostly treatises about firearms and guns.' She wrinkled her nose. 'I had no idea so much had been written about the topic.'

Logan had taken to walking the floor, listening for loose floorboards. 'Whatever we need to find, it won't be in plain sight.' He smiled when she threw him a questioning look. 'They didn't go to the great lengths of that journal just to leave other papers out in the open.' But the floorboards gave up nothing. Logan sat behind the desk and tried the drawers. 'Aha, this one is locked.' He grinned at her but the grin turned to a grimace as he struggled with the lock, resorting finally to prying it open with the poker from the fireplace, breaking the drawer irreparably. There would be no disguising that someone had been here and that the drawer had given up its secrets. Perhaps it didn't matter. This was her property now anyway. It wasn't as if someone could accuse her of trespassing.

He pulled out a box and set it on top of the desk. She stopped searching the bookcase and watched his face change as he scanned the papers. 'Olivia, come look at this. It's their club charter, for lack of a better term.'

She took the paper from him, looking up to meet his gaze, seeing in it the horror that was likely in her own. 'My word, Logan, it's a duelling club.' She sat down hard on a nearby chair, letting her mind wrap itself around what that meant. 'They came out here to shoot things.' Not things. It was not so tame as that. To shoot each other. Her eyes could not leave the words on the page of the charter.

On this day, the fifteenth of June 1835, the club heretofore known as The Pistols

*Club is formed with the purpose of hon-
ing a gentleman's duelling skills in the
conduct of real duels...*

The document went on to describe the rules
and regulations. She read them out loud as if
hearing the words would banish her sense of
disbelief. "Members may challenge one another to duels. Those duels will take place as
part of club business during its quarterly meet-
ings. Members may wager on duels. Members
who choose not to duel must appoint a duel-
list to take their place such as a servant." She
stopped reading, horrified. 'Logan, they shot
at each other, for entertainment, for the thrill
of it.'

'And more.' He frowned, holding aloft a bat-
tered leather book. 'I've found their by-laws.
They had other gun-based rituals besides the
duels. For initiation one must stand with a
card in their hand and allow a member of their
choosing to shoot the card. A demonstration of
great trust, I assume.' But his distaste for such
behaviour was evident.

'I don't want to hear any more.' Olivia
pressed a hand to her stomach. The realisa-
tions were coming fast now. 'Those duels are

the contests and wagers listed in the journal. Adolphus shot people for those properties. It really, truly is blood money, isn't it?' She gave a harsh laugh. 'All I want to do is burn the book, to make it all go away, to pretend I'd never seen it, and it's the one thing I can't do. I can't let Adolphus get away with this.'

'It's not just him, though, Olivia. It's everyone involved. They consented. The club *is* voluntary. They knew what they were getting into,' Logan reminded her. 'I know you'd like this to be black and white, with good and bad clearly delineated, but it's not going to be like that.'

'Not all of them consented. I can't imagine servants consenting, but I can imagine them not having a choice, not being *given* a choice. We can't simply do nothing. This club is wicked, evil. It condones murder or at least its attempt. How do we figure out who was perhaps forced to stand in for a master who didn't wish to fight his own duel?' Olivia said fiercely.

'I don't know that we do.' Logan's brow furrowed. 'I suppose, though, that the valet might have been such a person. But he was paid substantially, so I'm not sure how 'forced' he felt. We may never know.'

He was right and yet that answer wasn't good enough. 'I can't let this go, Logan. Adolphus asked me to keep this secret and I can't. I can't take the money. I can't take the deeds, not knowing how they were acquired. I want to return them. We can give the deeds back.' But even as she said it, Olivia understood the flaw in her logic. It could not undo what had been done, and in its own way it validated the wickedness. Logan was right; the men who had wagered had done so voluntarily. Giving back the properties and stocks didn't right a wrong. Their families might not even be aware of how the property had been lost. Giving things back might bring on more trouble by exposing what neither party wanted brought to light.

Logan came around the desk and took her hands, his touch a steadying influence amid her shock. 'We will think of something, together, but not right now. Right now we just need to sit with it, accustom ourselves to it. We'll think better then.'

'I don't know that I will ever accustom myself to it.' She drew a deep breath. 'I was prepared for gambling debts, for blackmail even, but not for this.' She met his gaze, the silent message between them.

This was so much worse than she'd imagined.

Duelling was illegal, of course. If anyone knew the Duke of Darlington had been engaged in such a practice for the deliberate accumulation of a fortune, it would taint the dukedom for generations, and other families, too. Was it right for her to decide for all of them?

At the moment, however, she was more concerned with Logan. She could not let Logan bear that burden because of *her* choice. If she did something about this great wrong, there would be scandal. Could she simply let it lie for him? To save him from a scandal of this magnitude would require she'd have to live with that lie forever. But if she didn't, another kind of forever would slip away; the forever he'd offered her this morning; the forever she'd turned down for the same reasons she was contemplating walking away from exposing the secrets: to save him. Why did love require such sacrifice?

She was slipping a little further away from him; he could see it in her eyes. He was desperate to hold on to her. He could not lose her so soon after finding her; so soon after opening himself to love. This morning had not been the conclusion he'd hoped for. He still hoped she might rethink her position. She hadn't said no; she'd merely said they needed to wait. It was practical and he understood that even as he'd tried to sweep those considerations away. At least, he'd hoped she'd rethink it up until now. The revelations of the duelling club were making it harder to hold on to her. If he truly loved her, wouldn't he set her away from the scandal? Spare her the difficulties that would come? Bear the scandal on his own as the duke? He could weather it in ways she could not. He could spare her. Wasn't that what love was supposed to be about? Love was selfless not selfish.

It was selfish to keep her in scandal's orbit, just as it was selfish to ask her to keep the secret and allow it to fall out of history unaddressed when he knew how much the truth bothered her. It was foolish, too. He knew too well that neither of them could be satisfied for long knowing that such a depraved wrong existed because they had allowed it. Still, he had to find a way. He gave her what hope he had, wanting it to be enough for now. 'We'll figure it out, Olivia. Don't give up.'

Don't give up on a solution; don't give up on us.

He bent his head to her forehead, his hands wrapped about hers, giving her his strength even if he couldn't give her answers.

Had he not been so concerned for Olivia, he might have heard the boots in the hall sooner. As it was, he was taken entirely by surprise. 'Ah, brother, I see you've found our clubhouse, or is it that you've come to join? You always were the better shot, but I've been practising.'

'Rahnald!' Logan leapt to his feet, his instincts wanting to draw Rahnald's attention from Olivia. If Olivia was right, Rahnald was dangerous. He stepped toward his brother. 'What are you doing here?'

'Same as you, I suspect. I am looking for something our cousin left behind. I stopped by Hailsham House and they told me where you'd gone. I thought I might join you. Two heads are better than one and all that.'

'Your club?' Logan stepped toward the bookcase, keeping Rahnald's attention. 'You're a member as well?' How dangerous was Rahnald? If his brother thought he knew very little, would Rahnald leave them alone?

Rahnald's eyes darted to the box on the desk and the papers strewn on top. So much for being able to play ignorant. 'Yes, I am. Hadn't you figured that out yet along with everything else? I see you've read our charter.'

'What is happening out here is despicable,' Logan growled.

'No one gets hurt, not really. It's very safe,' Rahnald said casually. 'Most of the gents put their servants up for the fights, so we aren't maiming each other. Adolphus's valet was brilliant. Of course, Adolphus trained him himself. Certainly, there's the occasional wound. Maldon got nicked in the arm once.'

'And your cousin *died*,' Logan replied tersely, aghast at Rahnald's callousness. What Rahnald described was little different than human cockfighting, only with guns.

'Because he didn't keep his word,' Rahnald said coolly. 'Not because of the duels, although the duel became a good tool for disposing of him.' Rahnald drew back his jacket and took out a slim, elegant-looking pistol with practised nonchalance. This was not one of the Bond weapons he'd had at the house when they had shot at targets. 'Adolphus and I had an arrangement. We were to split the proceeds from the wagers and when he didn't hold up his end, I had to take action.

'Why would he agree to share? Why not win your own wagers?' Logan asked, anxious about the gun in his brother's hand and the smallness of the room.

'Because I threatened to expose him and the club.'

'You were blackmailing him?'

Rahnald looked up from polishing the barrel of the gun with his handkerchief. 'Yes. I didn't want to do it, but when we met in December and he didn't pay as I'd asked, I had to do something. A man isn't respected if he doesn't enforce what he is owed. You know that, Logan. You taught me that, to stand up for myself.' Where had he gone wrong with his brother?

'I did not teach you to blackmail people.' He'd taught his brother kindness, and respect and the obligations that came with having wealth; at least he'd tried to. Tried and apparently failed.

Rahnald gave the gun a dangerous wave in his irritation, the light catching the maker's mark along the barrel. 'Stop quibbling, Logan. You want to hear how this ends, don't you? That's why you're here, isn't it?'

'New gun? I don't recall seeing it before.'

'It is new. From America, a Colt-Paterson.' He smiled broadly. 'It's a revolver, it can fire more than one shot before reloading. Convenient.' The warning froze Logan's blood. Should Rahnald want to, he could shoot them both without pause. Any sacrifice Logan made would not stop him, would not save Olivia. That was all that mattered in these moments.

Protect Olivia; save Olivia. Because, by God, he could not lose any more people he loved.

The words pounded through his head, a litany of survival. Nothing else would matter if he failed at the one task.

'Now, may I go on?' Rahnald pouted. 'Adolphus welshed on his word and I was intent on keeping mine. So at the January meeting, I challenged him to a duel. I don't think he was surprised. He knew I'd be coming for him. Our last meeting in December didn't end as congenially as I'd hoped it would.'

'You shot him.' It was not a gigantic leap of logic given that the bullet had come from a

Colt-Paterson and Rahnald stood there waving what was likely the only one in England. 'In the thigh.' So much for Rahnald's reference to how safe the club was.

Rahnald's gaze drifted to Olivia. 'I did you a favour. I freed you from that marriage, and even if he'd lived he could not have bothered you with intimate attentions.'

Olivia was white-faced. 'I never asked to be freed.'

Rahnald gave a shrug as if to say *suit yourself.* 'I did you a favour, too, brother. I got you the dukedom. Although I regret it. You've not been very grateful. But there's still time for that. Now you know what happened. We need to work together to make sure no one gets their hands on a journal that was kept listing all the wagers, and we need to divide up the proceeds of Adolphus's winnings. I'll take over the club now that Adolphus is gone.'

'And find someone else to blackmail?' Logan surmised.

'Probably. Gentlemen aren't terribly good at keeping their words. They're easy targets.' Rahnald gave a smile. 'So where's the journal?'

'It's not here. We've looked,' Logan said,

careful not to give anything away, not the least being any indicator that they had the journal. He was reeling from his brother's revelations. It was worse than he'd thought. It worried him that Rahnald had told him everything. Did Rahnald mean for him to not leave this place, too? One usually only told one's secrets when there was no harm in those secrets being repeated. Right now his biggest concern was getting Olivia away from here.

'Well, that's all right because I've changed my mind. I don't just want the journal. I want the dukedom, and you're the only one standing in my way. It's always been you in my way, Logan. Now it's time to get out of my way.'

'Rahnald, that's madness.'

'Let's settle this in the manner of the club. A duel. I win, I get the dukedom. You win, and you can explain to Mother how you shot her baby. She'll hate you for it, Logan.'

'I will not duel you, Rahnald. I certainly won't shoot you.' Logan tried to reason with him. Had he failed his brother so badly that his brother had no compunction about taking a life? About shooting his own sibling?

Rahnald gave him a wicked grin and levelled the revolver at Olivia. Her eyes went wide and a gasp escaped her lips as her hands gripped the desk. 'Yes, I rather think you will. If not, I'll shoot her. First.' Logan felt a wave of nausea sweep over him seeing her at the mercy of Rahnald's gun. 'And then I'll shoot you where you stand. I have lots of bullets.' He spun the chamber to illustrate the point. Logan cared only for that first bullet, the one that could steal his world. 'I'm in charge, now, Logan. Not you, and you can't stand it, can you?'

The only thing he couldn't stand was losing Olivia. He would not lose her. He could *not* lose her. He would grovel, he would beg, he would crawl on his belly, whatever it took. He didn't think, didn't hesitate. 'Put the gun down, Rahnald. I'll duel.'

'No! Stop it, both of you,' Olivia cried, her outrage overriding her fear. 'This is ridiculous. You are brothers.'

'What is ridiculous, Your Grace—' Rahnald fixed her with a chillingly obsequious stare '—is that my brother has had his perfect life handed to him on a platter while I scrape by. What is ridiculous is that you, too, have been given a fortune to ignore a gentleman's peccadilloes and yet you insisted on unearthing secrets that don't concern you. Yes, I know about the deeds, about the money. Half of that is mine. It is what Adolphus promised me. He broke his word. *That* is how we got to this.' He waved his gun for emphasis. 'You both have forced this by butting your noses into where they don't belong. Now, if you please, Your Grace, accompany us to the duelling ground. You can count off the twenty paces and play second to us both. Bring the case. I see my brother was expecting trouble. I'm glad in that at least I have not disappointed him this once.'

Chapter Twenty-One

One. Two. Three. Olivia counted off twenty paces with slow, even steps, trying to control the surreal horror rippling through her. If she let it have its way, it would obliterate all thought. She would be of no help to Logan. He needed her to have her wits. She needed them, too.

Four. Five. Six. She did not think she was safe from Rahnald. There was nothing to stop him from shooting her as well if Logan was dead. Seven. Eight. Nine. Ten. Except maybe an admission that she had the journal and a promise to turn the journal over to him. She could bribe him with some of the proceeds from the vault, too. It would open herself up to a lifetime of extortion, or it might just delay his desire to dispose of her once she had nothing more to give. She pushed the thoughts away and finished counting. She had to focus on Logan now. That was the first priority.

Logan stood at the centre of the duelling field, his face stone-set. Watching him check the weapons brought it all home to her in horrid clarity. He was laying down his life for her with no guarantee that he would be able to pick it up again, even though she'd refused him this morning.

She let that one thought roll through her mind: *she'd turned down his proposal and yet he was still willing to die for her.*

That was the action not of a man who merely protected, but the action of a man who *loved*; who was selfless to the end for those he cared about; the action of a man who loved *her*; loved her enough to protect her, to die for her even if she didn't love him back.

That last wasn't true. She *did* love him. Did he know? Did he guess? She did love him. *You've made a terrible mistake in refusing him.* And now it was too late. He could die without knowing, without hearing the words from her lips. He deserved to know. She'd accused him of being unable to truly love this morning, of not knowing what love was. She'd been utterly wrong. Perhaps it was because he'd always known that he'd shielded himself from it so thoroughly, and now he'd laid down that shield for her and what had she done? What had she said? And now he was about to die. Maybe. She could not give up hope.

She returned from counting out the steps and Logan solemnly offered first choice of pistols to Rahnald. Rahnald had not expected that. He reluctantly surrendered his revolver to her, as he exchanged it for one of the duelling pistols. Olivia breathed a little easier. At least now he wouldn't have the luxury of a rapid second shot. She could hear the countess's voice, *Logan will always be the better shot*. She hoped the countess was right.

The two men made a final check of their weapons and turned their backs to one another. 'Count us off, my dear,' Rahnald drawled. She swallowed hard. She would not look at Logan; she would not let anything he might see in her face distract him. There was so much she wanted to tell him, to say, starting with 'I love you,' followed by 'I was wrong. Ask me your question again,' but he didn't need emotion right now; he needed concentration. And yet, it was killing her to let him go like this, without a moment, without a chance to tell him she loved him, to tell him how sorry she was.

This was all her fault. If she'd told him about the journal sooner, if they'd come to London earlier... What-ifs spun around her head. Those were no guarantees this wouldn't have happened. She was just torturing herself now. She'd dragged him into this and now he might die. He *would* die if Rahnald had his way. Did Logan understand that? That Rahnald was not looking to delope, to satisfy honour? This wasn't about honour to Rahnald; it was about survival, about opportunity. He could not allow the club's covenant of secrecy to be broken. He would be drummed out of Society if that occurred. He had to protect himself and there was a dukedom waiting for him, one shot, one heartbeat, away.

She began to count again. What would Logan do? Would *he* delope and hope for the best from his brother? Or would he recognise that he *had* to shoot, had to choose? This was not what she wanted to happen. She did not want Logan choosing between his family and her. She did not want him facing his brother at twenty paces with no choice but to shoot for his own preservation and for hers. Rahnald would not hesitate. Did he realise that? Hopeless causes, he'd said, were those whose outcomes we knew before we even tried to save them but cleaned up after them anyway.

You say your brother doesn't surprise you anymore. Then you know what he's about today. Don't give in to him, she prayed. *Come back to me whole and safe so we can have that life together you promised me this morning.*

'Sixteen. Seventeen.'

Rahnald's step stopped. His body began to pivot. Her mind registered the intent in rapid motion. Dear God, he was going to turn early and fire! Her grip clenched around the revolver still in her hand. She'd not given it a second thought, so intent had she been on Logan and counting off the steps. Her only thought was to prevent Rahnald from firing early. Logan wouldn't stand a chance if he did. In her haste, her thumb fumbled with the safety, she cocked it, aimed and fired with a yell. Rahnald was not going to kill Logan, not when she needed to tell him how much she loved him, how much she needed him, how wrong she'd been and how much she wanted the life he offered her.

* * *

Olivia! Logan turned at the sound of gun-fire mingled with Olivia's scream. His mind registered events, a split second of fear taking him with the expectation that he'd been hit. Rahnald had fired early, the dirty bastard; he'd heard the shot. But where was the bullet? He wasn't hit, praise God, but Rahnald was down, clutching his hand. And Olivia... oh, God, Olivia. She was pale and bent over. If she'd been hit by mistake...he covered the distance between them at a run.

'The bitch shot me!' Rahnald howled, rolling on the ground, gripping his hand.

'I didn't mean to. I had to do something.' Olivia was wide-eyed and shaking when he reached her. He had her in his arms.

'Are you hurt? Are you all right?' His own fear was threatening to choke him. 'What happened?' He reached for the gun at her side. 'You fired this? Or did it go off by accident?' She could have shot herself in the foot or the leg.

'No accident. She did it on purpose!' Rahnald cried.

He met Olivia's gaze with his own, calming her. 'I did. I shot at him on purpose,' Olivia managed. 'He turned early, Logan. He was going to fire on seventeen. I had to stop him. I couldn't let him.'

Everything he'd dreamed of seeing was in her eyes: *I could not let him take you from me; could not let you go without telling you I love you.*

The last three words mattered most.

'You did well.' Logan's voice was hoarse with relief, not just over being alive, but the relief that comes from knowing that one's love has not been given in vain. His heart was full and there was much to say, but not here, not in this place, not now. She nodded, in tune with his thoughts. 'Will you wait for me at the house?' he asked quietly.

A soft smile took her face. He could live on that smile. He *would* live on that smile. 'I'll be waiting for you. Don't be long. We have a life to live, together, and it will require...some work.' She made a silent promise to him with her eyes and it strengthened him for the tasks to come. Whatever happened from here on out, they were in it together. Forever.

Logan studied his brother on the ground. This had to end here. His brother was a menace to the family and to himself. Coddling him, cleaning up his messes, had not helped him develop good judgement or an appreciation for honest behaviour. Perhaps Logan was to blame for some of that. And yet, he could not turn his back entirely on his brother. What Rahnald needed was a strong dose of reality and penance. Logan hoped his mother would forgive him for what needed to be done next.

He approached Rahnald, kicking the dropped pistol beyond Rahnald's reach out of an abundance of caution. He was aware of Olivia retrieving it and putting it back in the case as he knelt beside his brother. 'Let me see your hand.' He unwound his neckcloth, prepared for the worst. Had Olivia shattered his hand? She would only have been at eight paces. He hoped not. It was hard for a man with a shattered hand to do an honest day's work.

He took Rahnald's hand and grimaced. How typical. 'It's a graze, nothing more.' He bandaged it for good measure, though, against the chance of infection. 'You know I can't let this pass, Rahnald.'

'I wasn't aiming to kill. You know that,' Rahnald pleaded. He suddenly seemed less like the conniving madman in the study and more like the boy Logan knew. Logan steeled himself. He could not give in. He could only save Rahnald now by giving him up; something he should have done long ago.

'No, I don't know that. You shot our cousin.' That was so surreal, he could not quite accept it. Rahnald had committed murder.

'By accident. I meant to wound him, not to kill him. How was I to know there's an artery in the thigh? Why are you taking his side? You didn't like him and he was a horrible fellow. I swear it was an accident.'

'That's not how it sounded inside a little while ago when you were threatening to shoot me for the dukedom,' Logan said quietly. 'You've made no secret of your jealousy, not just today. I am sorry for you, Rahnald. You don't appreciate what you have in front of you. You're always wanting more. It has to stop.'

Rahnald hung his head. 'I know. You're right. I'll try harder.'

'Yes, you will. I am putting you on a ship for Australia tonight. You can work for your passage and when you get there, you can find a profession that suits you. I am giving you a chance to make something of yourself. No one in Australia will care if you're the brother of a duke. In fact, it's probably best you don't tout that about. They'll like you better if you're just plain Rahnald. But you are never to show your face in England again.'

'You don't mean it,' Rahnald sputtered.

'I do mean it. I'd prefer not to send you to Australia with any other injuries. You will go acquiescently unless you'd prefer to stand trial for the murder of the Duke of Darlington and take your punishment that way? There's always a choice, Rahnald.' He glanced in Olivia's direction. Always a choice. He'd made his choice last night and again this morning; to love, and now that he'd decided, he was eager to get started. He would see Rahnald aboard a ship and then his future awaited.

She was waiting for him in his bedroom, dressed in a silky white robe, her hair down, a vision of hope, a vision of his future, *their* future, when he returned from the docks. A hot bath steamed before the fire and brandy stood at the ready. 'Time to wash your cares away.' She came to him, taking his coat, his waistcoat, his shirt; each layer removed brought him closer to her. How had she known what he needed? The day had been hard; putting Rahnald on that ship had been one of the most difficult things he'd ever done. Rahnald had pleaded and begged and promised the moon. But he was finished with that, for all their sakes.

'You did a brave thing today, in sending Rahnald away. Your father would be proud. You did what was needed, what was necessary, even though it was hard.' She helped him out of his trousers and into the tub.

He sank into the water and closed his eyes. 'I hope so.' He let out a sigh and reached for her hand. 'I was not the only one. You made a hard decision today, too. Don't think I don't know how difficult it was, or all the ghosts you faced to make it.' He opened his eyes. 'But I am glad you did. What changed your mind?'

She reached for the soap. 'You did.' She swallowed hard, her lip trembling. 'You were so obnoxious this morning, solving all the problems, all the reasons we couldn't be together and I refused you and then, *then*, even after I turned you down, you were willing to die for me, to face your *brother* at the end of a duelling pistol. For *me*. If that's not love, then I don't know what love is. That's when I knew it was real for you.' She shook her head and a tear fell. 'I don't ever want it to feel that real again, Logan. I thought I would lose you.'

He gave a laugh. 'I thought something similar in the study. Agreed, let's not do that again.'

'Agreed.' She reached for the soap. 'Let me wash you tonight,' she whispered at his ear, taking a warm cloth to his skin. It felt so good to have her hands on him, stroking him with the soap, her hands in his hair, and when she poured a warm pitcher of water over his head, he felt baptised, born anew into her love.

'The future starts tonight, Olivia.' He pulled her close for a kiss, never mind the splotches of water his touch left on her robe. 'I love you in white,' he murmured.

Epilogue

The next time he saw her in white was at their wedding, seven days later. He'd insisted on it. White for a new start, he'd told her. White for setting the past behind her. There was no one to see but them. There were few guests, only his mother and Carrick and his new wife were present to satisfy the need for witnesses. If anyone thought the bride should have worn black to her own wedding, they could take that up with him.

He did not regret it. When the doors to the little stone chapel at Darlington opened, framing his beautiful bride in the medieval archway, the morning rays of the sun of a very early spring limning her like an angel's aura, he knew the decision had been the right one. She'd found an unclaimed white gown in London, done in simple lace and silk. Delicate long sleeves of lace encased her arms and covered the scalloped neck of the bodice, tapering to an exquisitely tight waist and the soft folds of an unadorned white silk skirt. On her head she wore a wreath of white roses from the Darlington hothouses and there was a matching bouquet in her hand, tied with a blue ribbon. If he wasn't mistaken, she also carried his mother's white Bible.

'I've always wanted a daughter,' his mother had said tearily when they'd shared their news. His mother had thrown herself into wedding preparations despite the lack of guests and the short notice. Logan had allowed it as a means of taking her mind off Rahnald. She'd shed tears of a different sort over that part of their London adventure. Ultimately, however, she'd understood.

Olivia began the walk down the short aisle to the altar with its vases of flowers and greenery and candles. Each step was a beginning of healing for them. They would be a family again. He, and his mother, and Olivia, and whatever children they were blessed with. Those children would be loved. He would rebuild all that had been broken at Darlington.

Together, he and Olivia would make it a wholesome place again. They'd made other pledges, too, to spend whatever time it took to track down those who'd been abused in the duelling club and offer reparation in the form of cash, or land from the funds and deeds Adolphus had collected. Both he and Olivia agreed it would have to be done discreetly, perhaps in ways in which the recipient would never be quite aware of the source of their good fortune or the reason for it. But the two of them would know, and that would be enough.

Olivia reached him, and all thoughts of the future fled, his mind taken up entirely with the present, with her beaming smile and the love in her eyes. He took her hand and the vicar began the service. He barely heard a word of it. Carrick had warned him he wouldn't. Carrick was right. What he heard instead was love. It was there in the beating of his heart, in the small tremble of Olivia's voice as she said her vows, the little sigh she gave when he said his, and then it was time to kiss her; to claim her before the people who mattered the most to him; time to lead her down the aisle for the open-air carriage drive back to Darlington Hall where there would be a quiet celebration.

'What were you thinking back there?' Olivia laughed as she settled her skirts in the carriage. 'You seemed lost in thought during the service. Were you regretting your choice of honeymoon destinations already?' she teased. They'd decided to travel to her family's estate and introduce Logan to her father. Logan was determined to make it clear to the earl that he needed to stand on his own feet and manage his daughters and his own affairs without leaning on Olivia. It would be his wedding gift to her, one more chain removed; one more step toward true freedom for his beloved Olivia.

'If you must know, I was thinking of you.' He leaned forward and stole a kiss, to the cheers of the villagers who turned out to wish them well. 'I was thinking that of all that I've inherited, my duchess is by far my favourite,' he murmured against her mouth, and kissed her again.

* * * * *

COMING SOON!

MILLS & BOON ®

Coming next month

LORD LANCASTER COURTS A SCANDAL
Helen Dickson

His eyes continued to watch her as she walked along the deck to return to her cabin. Her step was one of confidence, as if she sensed hidden dangers ahead but determined nevertheless to enjoy them. She moved gracefully, with an added fluency that drew the eye to the elegance of her straight back and the proud tilt of her head. In that dazzling moment when she had turned her head and met his gaze, he had not been prepared for the impact. The attraction had been instantaneous. The unexpectedness of it astounded him, and Anna would have been surprised if she had known the depth of his feelings as she walked along the deck.

Continue reading
LORD LANCASTER COURTS A SCANDAL
Helen Dickson

Available next month
www.millsandboon.co.uk

MILLS & BOON

THE HEART OF ROMANCE

A ROMANCE FOR EVERY READER

MODERN

Prepare to be swept off your feet by sophisticated, sexy and seductive heroes, in some of the world's most glamourous and romantic locations, where power and passion collide.

HISTORICAL

Escape with historical heroes from time gone by. Whether your passion is for wicked Regency Rakes, muscled Vikings or rugged Highlanders, available the romance of the past.

MEDICAL

Set your pulse racing with dedicated, delectable doctors in the high-pressure world of medicine, where emotions run high and passion, comfort and love are the best medicine.

True Love

Celebrate true love with tender stories of heartfelt romance, from the rush of falling in love to the joy a new baby can bring, and a focus on the emotional heart of a relationship.

Desire

Indulge in secrets and scandal, intense drama and plenty of sizzling hot action with powerful and passionate heroes who have it all: wealth, status, good looks…everything but the right woman.

HEROES

Experience all the excitement of a gripping thriller, with an intense romance at its heart. Resourceful, true-to-life women and strong, fearless men face danger and desire - a killer combination!

To see which titles are coming soon, please visit

millsandboon.co.uk/nextmonth

JOIN US ON SOCIAL MEDIA!

Stay up to date with our latest releases, author news and gossip, special offers and discounts, and all the behind-the-scenes action from Mills & Boon...

 @millsandboon

 @millsandboonuk

 facebook.com/millsandboon

 @millsandboonuk

It might just be true love...